MODERN MONSTERS

MODERN MONSTERS

KELLEY YORK

Entangled Publishing, LLC
2614 South Timberline Road
Suite 109
Fort Collins, CO 80525

Entangled Teen is an imprint of Entangled Publishing, LLC.

Visit our website at www.entangledpublishing.com.

Edited by Stacy Abrams and Tara Quigley
Cover design by L.J. Anderson
Interior design by Jeremy Howland
Photography by Single girl (c) Kamira/Shutterstock
Couple (c) coka/Shutterstock
Two girls (c) asife/Dollarphotoclub
Cup (c) Brent Hofacker/Shutterstock
Face (c) Paul Matthew Photography/Shutterstock

Print ISBN 978-1-63375-002-9
Ebook ISBN 978-1-63375-004-3

Manufactured in the United States of America

First Edition June 2015

10 9 8 7 6 5 4 3 2 1

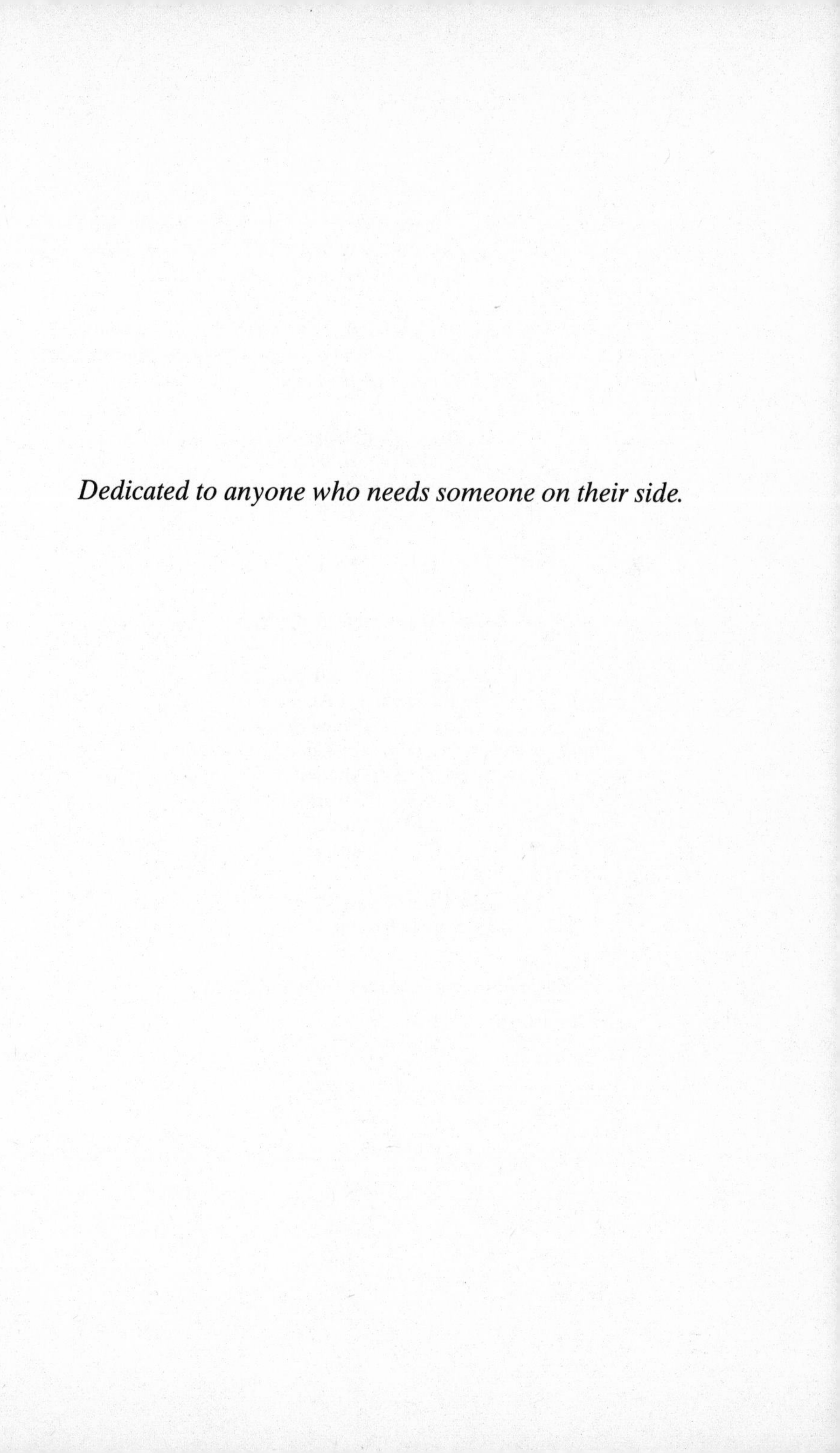

Dedicated to anyone who needs someone on their side.

Chapter One

Aaron Biggs leans over me to ask, "How's it going, Vic?"

His freckled face and dyed black hair obscure my light. I squint at the page of algebra equations on the cafeteria table, decide they aren't going to make any more sense to me whether or not I pause to see what Aaron wants, and look up at him. "Um. F-fine?"

"Super." He flashes me a grin. "My brother and his buddies rented out a cabin on the lake for a party this Friday. He said it would be cool if I invited a few people."

I'm used to playing receptionist. This invitation is not meant for me, but for my best friend, Brett. I am not important. I am tolerated by association. I am Vic Howard, Brett Mason's Best Friend, so while people don't always care to learn anything about me, they do recognize my face. Being cool to me, they seem to think, is a way to stay cool with Brett. At least Aaron knows my name instead of referring to me as "Hey, you." Of course, that's only because his mom and my mom are also best friends.

Aaron doesn't leave until I've written down his information: address of the party, phone number, and time. He stresses that there will be booze, food, and girls. Plenty of girls. College girls, even. The idea makes my throat dry. I can hardly talk to a girl my own age, let alone one older than me and with undoubtedly a great deal more life experience.

It's Wednesday, meaning I don't even see Brett until tennis practice after school. This also means I'm parking my butt on the bleachers outside the tennis courts and watching for the next two hours while Brett and a handful of others knock balls back and forth while wearing shorts that are way too short for my comfort.

When they're done, Brett slips through the gate, mopping sweat off his forehead and grinning my way. "Yo."

Sometimes when I look at Brett, I still see the chubby, pimple-faced kid with braces and glasses whom I befriended in third grade. Maybe that's why he doesn't impress or intimidate me the way he does everyone else. I knew him back when nobody else wanted to. "P-party invite," I say, short and to the point. Even though Brett has never made fun of my stutter, it's habit to keep sentences short. I hand him the information I took down.

Brett takes it and skims it over. "The lake, huh? Could be fun. Do you want to go?"

"The invite was f-for you."

"And you, by extension. I'm not going if you aren't going." He crams the paper into his duffel bag.

Parties aren't my thing. More often than not, I end up being the loser sitting on the couch and watching Brett mingle and make new friends. Not that I'd want him clinging to my side the whole time—that'd be even lamer—but still...knowing he likes me to tag along is what convinces me to go to his social outings. No one else may care that I'm around, but Brett does. "Maybe."

Brett plops himself down beside me. "Do you have other plans?"

He always gets me there. "I m-might..."

"You don't." He laughs. "Come on. It's something different, yeah? Not some lame kegger while so-and-so's parents are out of town where we'll get yelled at for breathing on anything."

It is something different...except I don't like different. Brett nudges me with an elbow—once, then again when I roll my eyes and don't answer right away, and a third time, until: "Fine, I'll go."

"That's my boy." He claps me on the back, shoulders his duffel bag, and jerks his chin toward the parking lot. "Now let's get out of here."

Friday after school, Brett and I head to his place so he can get showered and dressed, all while lecturing me about the importance of wearing something nice and "at least run a brush through your damned hair, Vic," because my dark curls look unruly no matter what I try. Then we swing by my house so I can drop off my stuff and get changed. We're planning on grabbing a bite to eat on our way to the lake. I'm thinking the combination of a bunch of drunk people and a large body of water is a really bad idea, but what do I know? *Don't be a buzzkill*, Brett would say.

Mom is in the kitchen nursing a cup of coffee. As I'm heading out the door, I stop to tell her, "Going to the movies, then I'm s-staying at Brett's tonight. Be home tomorrow." This is more of a formality than anything. Mom doesn't care where I am if I say I'm with Brett. She assumes anyone with a 4.0 grade point average must be a good kid. A good influence. *Ha.* Since it's just Mom and me and she doesn't really care what I do as long as she thinks I'm not getting into trouble, I pretty much have free rein to do whatever.

Mom halfway twists around to smile vacantly. "That's good. Tell him I said hello." No further questions. Not that I expected any. Brett is outside, honking, so I leave without a good-bye.

Not counting the hour-long stop for dinner at a restaurant, the trip only takes about forty minutes. There are something close to thirty cars crammed haphazardly together outside the lake house already, because Brett insisted on showing up fashionably late. Everyone else has probably been here a good hour or two. Brett parks close to the end where it isn't as crowded. Even from here, I can make out the sound of music blaring, along with the shouts and cheers of people splashing around in the lake on the far side of the house. I should not have eaten that greasy cheeseburger and fries at the diner, because my stomach is in knots.

The lake houses are two stories separated by a stretch of beach, so the noise from a party isn't likely to bother the neighbors. I looked this place up online last night (I like having a good idea of what I'm getting into before an outing) so I know they're pricy rentals. I know it has four guest rooms upstairs, two bathrooms, its own kitchen, and a hot tub out back. Shrubs line the walkway to the front door.

Brett leads me inside. It's one of the rare instances where I get to see him out of his element, because here he isn't Mr. Popular with everyone. (Yet. We'll see what happens by the end of the night.) Out of the sea of faces, I recognize maybe half. The rest must be friends of Aaron's big brother, students of the local colleges. The people who are familiar to me aren't people I've ever talked to much, anyway. Nearly everyone in the immediate vicinity is older than us, with the exception of Aaron, who just so happens to be making his way over from beside the patio doors with two plastic cups in hand.

"Glad you could make it!" He shoves a beer into Brett's hand and one into mine. "Got food in the kitchen with the keg. There's a chick in there mixing drinks, too."

Brett doesn't smile, but he looks around with an appraising nod that suggests he approves. He leaves my side and drapes his free arm around Aaron's shoulders despite being a good three inches shorter, and casts a look my way as though to ask if I'm coming. I don't particularly care for Aaron, nor do I want to trail on Brett's heels all night, so I shake my head mutely. Brett shrugs and they drift away from me. Brett is saying, "Why don't you introduce me to a few people?"

I give it twenty minutes before he's either making out with someone or getting into deep conversations about the merits of whatever college these people go to versus some of the colleges on his (or rather, his dad's) wish list.

Where does that leave me? Standing just inside the front door with a beer in my hand. I hate beer. It tastes like battery acid. Not that I've ever tasted battery acid, but it's what I suspect battery acid would taste like. I try a sip anyway, like maybe I've forgotten and tricked myself into thinking it tastes horrible.

Nope. Still battery acid.

I don't want to abandon my cup just yet, so I wander through the house, observing the various clusters of people talking, dancing, shoving their tongues in each other's mouths, mingling, having fun—everything I am not a part of. I'm in my own little bubble, unacknowledged by everyone.

In the kitchen, I discreetly dump my beer out in the sink and toss the cup into the trash. Before I can get far, someone spots me drink-less and shoves another red plastic cup into my hand. At least this one doesn't smell like piss in plastic. I'm pretty sure this drink consists of orange juice and vodka, with a little umbrella poking out to make it look fancier than it is.

The throng of people and the steady rumble of various conversations going on at once is making me claustrophobic. I make my way out back, which is much better. The air is cool and sharp and smells of water and sand. Paper lanterns hang from the trees, providing a dim but helpful glow to the stretch of rocky beach the house rests on.

There is no sign of Brett, which means he's still inside somewhere. I don't really care about finding him just yet. As long as he's having fun, then whatever. I'm not going to be the dude who puppies around after his best friend because he can't function socially on his own. If that means sitting here until he comes looking for me? Cool. That's sort of how these things go. Brett wants me to come with him, even in groups, but I never know how to interact. We've gone to the movies, bowling alleys, laser tag, arcades, and just hanging out at Brett's place with his friends from school or his tennis group. Some of them are nice enough guys; I just prefer to keep to the sidelines, out of the way.

My drink stays in hand while I people-watch. I spot Aaron's brother stripped down to his boxers, conversing loudly with a handful of people with lake water lapping at their legs. One guy I remember seeing at school floats around on a pink raft, tethered to the shore so he doesn't drunkenly drift away. A couple near the back door are arguing. By some miracle, despite their slurred speech, they're being quiet enough not to attract too much attention. A girl behind me is throwing up in the bushes.

My stomach rolls in sympathetic nausea at the sound

of her heaving. A quick look around tells me that either none of her friends are here, or they don't care that she's spewing her guts all by herself. I weigh my options: go inside and pretend I didn't see anything, or help her before she falls over and passes out. Possibly in the same bushes she's getting sick on.

In the end, it isn't really a question. Maybe I'd like to turn my head the other way, but I'm already setting my drink down and coming up behind where the girl is bent over, hands on her knees, long blond hair a tangled mess around her face. She's taking small breaths, shallow and quick, and whimpering. I squint. Now that I'm getting a better look, I recognize her from school.

"C-Callie?"

Callie Wheeler moved to town in the middle of last year. I knew her only because Brett and I have both shared classes with her at some point or another. She jerks her head around in my direction so fast she nearly falls over, and I catch her by the elbows. Her gaze floats across my face. She's probably trying to place my name. Most people don't pay enough attention to know it. Just as she opens her mouth to say something, I see the color drain from her face. I help turn her back around just in time for her to throw up again, and I rub awkward circles across her back, unsure what else to do. Only when she's done does she straighten up and slump against me. I hold on to her arm and place the other hand on her hip to turn her around to head for the house. Such is the joy of getting here late; everyone else is already plastered.

Callie wobbles on her feet, eyes closed to slits so small

I doubt she can see where we're going. "Who're you 'gain?" she mumbles.

I have to hold on to her waist to make sure she doesn't stumble coming over the threshold of the back door. "Uh. V-Vic. Vic Howard?" Why do I feel the need to make it a question? As though I'm asking, *I'm Vic, is that okay*? "I'm a f-friend of Brett Mason's. We've had classes together."

"Oh," says Callie, and her eyelids droop and then close as we reach the steps that lead to the second floor. I'm left to haul her up them one at a time because she isn't lifting her feet much.

Given we aren't in someone's permanent home, I'm not worried about which room I take her to. I figure the first bedroom I come to on the left will do fine. Callie groans as I lay her down on the bed—on her side, in case she throws up again—and tug over a small wastebasket in hopes that she'll use it instead of, say, the floor. I lift her legs up onto the mattress.

When I straighten up to pull away, she paws at my arm. "Don't...don't call my dad..."

"I won't, I promise. But I'm g-going to leave you here, okay? Try to sleep."

Callie rolls her red and blurry eyes up to look at me. She manages a smile before shifting further onto her stomach, flopping her head against the pillow, and passing out almost instantly. She's going to be in for it with her parents if she stays here all night, I'll bet, but that isn't my problem. She's safe and she's comfortable. I've done my part.

Heading back to the party, I stop halfway down the stairs where I have a better view of the people lingering in the living room and near the back door. Callie isn't the only one passed out: the couch is occupied by a couple pawing at each other and a guy slouched back against the cushions, surrounded in plastic cups like he came here for no purpose other than to get as drunk as he could as fast as he could.

I'm searching for anyone who might go to my school and who might be a friend of Callie's so I can let them know to check on her. I see plenty of people I know, but I don't remember seeing Callie ever hanging out with any of them. Hell, even if I did spot one of her friends, I probably wouldn't know it. I see Chris Christopher (yeah, that's really his name) passing a joint around to Helen Barkley and Robbie Kurtis. Patrick Maloney, one of Aaron's best friends, bumps into me as I come down the stairs while he's going up, along with Eric and Jacob. Probably in search of a free bathroom or something, or to scope out the rooms to bring girls to later. Nobody looks twice at me.

The smell of weed is so strong at the bottom of the stairs that it almost makes me gag. I don't feel much like going out back again, so I wade through the crowd to the front door and squeeze outside.

It's amazing how much quieter it is from the front porch. The party is a world away, nothing but distant sounds of splashing and shouting, and I try to decide if there's something wrong with me that I'm incapable of mingling and having a good time like everyone else here. Like Brett. I've never "lived it up" at a party. I've never hooked up with a girl. I've never gotten so drunk that I threw up in the bushes. Given how much fun everyone seems to be having…am I missing out?

We got here two hours ago. Brett could be out in ten minutes or five hours. There's never any telling with him. It depends entirely on if he found something to entertain him: a conversation he enjoys or a girl he can flirt with. I have little else to do but utilize the abundance of games on my phone to entertain myself.

It's another two hours before Brett texts me:

you ok? where are you?

I respond, and in a few moments he emerges from the house with a smile. He's been drinking, but Brett never gets sloppy drunk, just happy drunk. Kudos to him.

He tosses me his car keys. "Ready to get going?"

They hit my knuckles and then the ground when I attempt to catch them. "Yeah. Meet anyone?"

"Nobody worth calling later." Brett crams his hands into his pockets and heads for the car. I grab the keys from the dirt and follow. Driving is always exciting. I've had my license for a year, but Mom doesn't have money to help me buy a car, and even after saving all summer I'd only ended up with enough cash for something I'd be humiliated to be seen in. Getting behind the wheel of Brett's semi-new hybrid is always awesome. Although I had planned to stay at his place, he informs me that he has things to do bright and early in the morning so we might as well drop me off at my house.

While Brett dozes in the passenger's seat, I focus on getting us home in one piece, letting my mind wander. This is my car. I'm driving home from a party I was invited to, not because of who my best friend is but because people wanted me there. I have the windows down and my sunglasses on, smiling at anyone we meet because I'm not self-conscious that my hair is a mess or I'm too tall, too skinny, too dorky, or too not worth looking twice at. When I get home, I'll have a bunch of texts waiting for me:

> ***thanks for coming tonight, man! and it was great meeting you, let's hang out next weekend.***

It's a common daydream of mine. One that ends when I pull up outside my house and Brett opens the door and circles around to the driver's side as I'm stepping out. My fingers curl around the keys. "You, uh, s-sure you should be driving yet?"

"Dude, give me my keys. I'm good. I'll text when I get home to let you know I made it in one piece, yeah?" He pries them out of my hand, claps me on the back, and gets into the car. "I'll see you Monday."

Then he's driving away, and I'm left feeling—not for the first time—that this is what the world has in store for me. Being someone's stupid, stuttering shadow. The designated driver. All of this is someone else's life. I'm just along for the ride.

Callie is a nagging concern in the back of my brain all weekend. Did she get home okay? Was she in trouble with her parents? How hungover was she the next morning? Does she even remember that someone helped her up to a room? I have no idea where she lives, so riding my bike past her house isn't an option. Instead, I have to wait for Monday. Second period, I work as an assistant in the front office. It isn't hard to take a quick peek at the locker assignments to tell me where I'm likely to find her between classes.

Brett meets me in the hall and on our way to the cafeteria for lunch, I tell him I want to take a detour. He gives me a quizzical look but goes along without question. My eyes scan the crowded hall for locker numbers and when I come across Callie's, I slow down but don't stop. There's no sign of her. Maybe she doesn't go to her locker between classes; some people keep all their books with them.

As we walk away, I notice someone who isn't Callie approach Callie's locker. She's about Callie's height, but with longer, darker hair. She messes with Callie's combination lock, pops it open, and begins clearing things out. Not just books but clothing, makeup, and miscellaneous junk.

I stop in my tracks, frowning. Why would she do that?

Brett shoves a finger into my ribs. "Hello? Earth to Victor, are we going to get lunch or what?"

Lunch. Right. I turn my gaze ahead and force my feet to move. Worst-case scenarios are running through my head. Did something happen to her? Alcohol poisoning? Choked on her own vomit? Her parents were so mad they cut her up and stuck her in the freezer? Guilt is gnawing its way up my insides; if something happened to her, will it be my fault?

"What was that about?" Brett asks.

"N-nothing. Just looking f-for someone."

What happened to Callie?

Chapter Two

Brett drops me off at home right after school, citing some college applications to fill out and email. Fair enough. I have a test to study for, and my studying time takes about five hours longer than the average person. If I'm lucky, I'll retain a quarter of the information I'm trying to cram into my tiny brain.

Times like this—when I'm on my bed hunched over books, index cards, and notes—make me wonder what it's like to be in Brett's head. He's always been a brain, and his parents have pushed and pushed him to be brilliant.

But…I've worked hard for it, too, and I have always come up short.

I don't know what it is. I've tried different methods of

studying, but staying focused is impossible. By the time I finish reading chapters six and seven in my history book, I've forgotten most of it and have to go back and reread them a second, third, and sometimes even a fourth time. Writing notes helps, but only a little. The sound of the television in the living room is distracting, echoing down the hall. For that matter, so is the knocking.

Knocking?

Oh. The front door.

I pause, listening. Mom's footsteps. Answering the door and saying worriedly, "Hello? Is everything okay?"

There's an undercurrent to her voice that draws me from bed to poke my head into the hall. Beyond Mom stand two police officers, a man and a woman, and their eyes immediately move from her to me.

"We're looking for Victor Howard. Is he home?" the lady asks.

"Victor is…" Mom turns, eyes wide and worried as she looks at me. "He's right there. What's going on? What is this about?"

The male responds, "Just have a few questions for him, is all."

It takes effort to force myself slowly out of my room and down the hall. My chest is tight. "U-um, I'm V-Vic." Stupidly, I offer my hand out to them, unsure what else to do. They glance at each other. Neither of them takes my hand.

"I'm Detective Sherrigan and this is Detective Carter, Waverly Police Department," the man says. "We came to ask you about a party you were seen at Friday night."

My insides are mush and my legs are jelly. I slowly lower my hand, watching Mom from my peripheral. As she steps aside to let the officers in and shut the door, her eyes are so wide that I'm expecting them to fall out of her head. Oh. The explaining I'm going to have to do after this will be amazing.

"Okay," I say, wringing my hands together. "I-I was th-there."

Sherrigan writes this down in his notepad. Carter remains poised, hands folded in front of her and expression grim. "Do you know a Callie Wheeler?"

My spine stiffens. "Is she okay?"

"Is that a yes?"

"Y-yes. I know her. S-sort of."

While Sherrigan is portly and looks like he'd be a nice guy any other day of the week, Carter is the sort of cop you don't want to mess with. Short. Hair pulled back into a serious bun, ruby-red lipstick that makes her look like she just tore out the throat of her enemies with her teeth. She doesn't look impressed by me in the least. "Care to tell us what happened with Callie at the party that night?"

"I was at the p-party and she was, was, um, th-throwing up outside." The words are coming harder, catching in my throat, tripping over my tongue. My hands are cold, clammy, made worse by my inability to get the words out as quickly as I want to. I can picture them in my head, but they're getting lost somewhere in translation. "S-s-so, I…I…"

"Spit it out, son," Carter says.

I breathe deeply. Try to start over. One sentence at a

time. "I…took her upstairs. B-because, um, she was…drunk. Put h-her to bed and…and…that w-was it." I look between the two of them, increasingly unsure if honesty is the best response right now. "Is she okay?"

"No, Victor, she's not okay." Carter dips her chin and peers over the top of her sunglasses. "She was raped."

"Raped," I repeat, because the word doesn't have any meaning right away. It takes a second to process it, to digest it, comprehend its meaning. *Rape.* Any act of sexual intercourse that is forced upon a person.

The word flow stops all together. I stare dumbly at the detectives.

I should have stayed with her. I should have—I don't know. I should have done something more than what I did. I had just thought…she would be safe there in that room.

"I'm afraid I don't follow." Mom's voice is a few octaves higher than usual. It happens when she's anxious. "Is that all you came to ask him? Obviously he doesn't know anything about this."

Sherrigan turns to her, but I don't think his eyes ever really leave me. "Ma'am, your son is being accused of raping Callie Wheeler."

Gravity has suddenly gotten a very strong hold on me. I don't move for fear that it's going to yank me right to the floor and swallow me whole. Maybe that wouldn't be a bad thing. I could do with disappearing right about now.

There are three sets of eyes on me. All questioning. All waiting for me to say something. I wait. Wait for Mom to come to my defense. *Victor? No, he'd never do anything like that.* Instead she's staring at me with an expression I don't think I've ever seen on her face before. Some concoction of disgust, confusion, and horror.

This is a dream. A nightmare.

It's so stupid that I have to force myself to say, "I d-didn't do anything..."

Carter asks, "Would you be willing to come down to the station to give a statement and submit to an exam?"

My insides are twisting, melting, knotting into an incomprehensible mess. "I j-just told you what I know." Which was, effectively, nothing. Callie was fine when I left her.

And then she wasn't.

Sherrigan and Carter continue to stare at me, not saying a word but clearly unwilling to take no for an answer. I look at Mom helplessly and she keeps her eyes averted, mouth screwed into a firm look of disgust. I just want her to reassure them that I wouldn't do this. That I'm her son and I'm not perfect but I'm an okay kid and she knows me better than that, and yet...nothing. The vision of her standing there not helping me begins to blur as my eyes water.

If being questioned clears my name, then why not? I don't know exactly what more I can say to them, but if it helps, if maybe something I say can lead them to who really hurt Callie... "I'll go."

The next hour slithers by in a blur. I'm a minor, which means Mom has to come with me—and yet I find myself being placed in the back of Carter's car while Mom follows behind us in her car. Why, to keep me from talking to her? I'm too afraid to ask questions. What if it makes me look guilty?

I have a right to an attorney, Sherrigan tells me when we arrive at a small clinic twenty minutes from home. I nod at this because I'm supposed to acknowledge it, but it still doesn't feel real. Mom lingers by her car. I see Carter approach her and speak, to which Mom shakes her head and murmurs something urgently to her while the look on her face makes my heart sink. Carter walks away, leaving Mom to get back into her car. She isn't coming in. Maybe it's stupid for me to be surprised. Mom hasn't been there for me in years, so like many other things, I'm going into this blind and alone.

Nothing comes back into focus until I'm seated on an exam room table in my boxers and a flimsy hospital gown and left by myself for a few minutes.

Deep breaths. I wish Mom would have come with me. I wish my dad were a presence in my life instead of a one-night stand of Mom's seventeen years ago. I wish I could call Brett. I wish I had left Callie to throw up in the bushes by herself. No…better yet, I wish I had never gone to that stupid party to begin with. I should have told Aaron to go screw himself.

I hear Sherrigan's voice outside my room speaking to someone else. No matter how hard I strain, I catch only glimpses of the conversation.

"…never saw his face…"

"…more than seventy-two hours…"

"…victim said she recognized…"

They're talking about Callie and me. I squeeze my eyes shut. I don't want to hear any more.

When Sherrigan finally comes back into my room, it's with a female nurse at his side. She's almost as tall as he is and her smile is guarded but not unfriendly.

"Hello, Victor. I'm Rosie."

She already knows my name and I'm not sure my tongue is going to cooperate with me, so I just wring my hands between my knees and nod.

Rosie asks, "Do you know where you are?"

There's a lump in my throat. I swallow it. "A d-doctor's office?"

"Well, yes." She pulls over her spinny stool and has a seat. "To be specific, this is the Sacramento RTC. We deal specifically with rape victims and, occasionally, suspects."

Is this where they brought Callie, then? Did they shove her into one of these uncomfortable gowns and subject her to being prodded at? My chest constricts at the thought. How does someone even begin to process being violated and then having to spread her legs to let a doctor poke around?

"What's going to happen," Rosie explains, "is Detective Sherrigan will remain present while I collect some samples. Swabs, blood, hair, fingernail scrapings."

God, my mouth is so dry. "Okay."

"Did they have you sign the consent paperwork out front?"

I nod. Rosie flips through a file—my file—and frowns, glancing at the detective. "His mother can be present."

Sherrigan clears his throat. "She, uh, opted not to."

I can tell even he's thrown off by that. What mother

wouldn't want to be by her kid's side when she knows he hasn't done anything wrong?

"Okay. Well..." Rosie shakes her head, closes my file, and sets it on the counter. "Victor, just to reiterate, you've consented to this examination willingly. You are not under arrest and you are free to end the exam and leave any time you want. Do you understand?"

Somehow I feel like this is just a formality. If I were to say screw this and walk out, would they just arrest me for not cooperating? Would Mom refuse to take me home until I did? Still, I manage a nod. "U-understood."

Nobody I've ever talked to enjoys a normal physical exam, and this is even worse. Rosie has me stand. She tells me each thing she's going to do before she does it and yet there is nothing I have ever experienced in my life like this. She takes a swab from inside my mouth. Scrapes beneath my nails. Takes samples of my hair—from more places than one. Her hands are gloved but icy. She asks me questions about my medical history, if I have any illnesses, and what I've been doing the last week or so that can explain any lacerations or bruises on my body. That part is tricky. I'm gangly and awkward and prone to running into things and tripping. Half the time, I don't remember where my bruises came from.

Sherrigan's phone rings and he hesitates but ultimately says, "I need to take this. Excuse me," and steps into the hall. Which I'm fairly certain he's not supposed to do. He's shadowed me every step of the way since we got here and that tells me it must be protocol.

Now that we're alone, I ask, "Did you d-do the exam on Callie? The…the girl they said I…"

I look down at Rosie, who is crouched in front of me, taking a photograph of a cut on my left knee. I don't remember how it got there. She doesn't look up. "You're smart enough to know that I can't answer that."

Yeah, I guess so, but… "I just w-wanted to know if sh-she was okay."

That makes her lift her chin to stare up at me almost thoughtfully. "Well, she was raped, so I imagine she isn't feeling very okay right now."

Guilty heat immediately floods to my face, and since she's down there, in order to not look at her I have to turn my gaze to the ceiling. I wonder how often she has to do this and if she gets suspects in here who are guilty and know their DNA is going to give them away. What must that be like? I'm not sure I could personally stomach dealing with those kinds of people. "Your job sucks."

Rosie pauses, rocks back on her heels, and laughs. "Yeah, it kind of does, doesn't it?" She motions for me to turn around and I do, trying to hold the back of my gown shut. By now she's seen me all kinds of naked but it hasn't gotten any less embarrassing. "It isn't all bad, though. I've helped a lot of victims find peace of mind and justice, so it's worth it in the end. I just wish there wasn't a need for my profession to begin with."

It's such an honest outpouring that it catches me off guard. "What about…" I gesture helplessly at myself. "Like me?"

"Suspects, you mean?" Another picture, this time of a bruise on the back of my thigh. Think I might have backed up into someone's desk or something for that one. "You're just another patient, Victor. I've had plenty of suspects come through here who were later proven innocent, so I try not to be judgmental right from the start."

"Oh." I fall silent while Rosie finishes with her photos, and when she stands up I turn to face her. "Do y-you think I did it?"

"I can't say that I know." She leans over my file, scribbling notes in typical doctor's chicken scratch I can't begin to decipher from here. Then she turns her attention back to me and her expression softens. "But I will say that if you did do it, then you're a good actor."

Rosie takes the collected samples and file and leaves me alone to get dressed again. Clothes have never felt so good. Sherrigan and Carter return for me before long. Rather than put me back into the car to go home, though, they lead me to some kind of break room where I'm instructed to sit at a table while they take seats across from me.

Carter says, "Rather than lug you down to the station, we figured we'd take your statement here. If that's all right with you."

I nod because I don't want to be stuck with these two any longer than I have to. "I already t-told you wh-what—"

"Hold on a sec." Sherrigan places a tape recorder on the table between us, opens his notepad with pen at the ready, and then looks at me. "The time is eleven thirty-five p.m., date is April fifteenth. Sherrigan and Carter, taking statement for the Callie Wheeler case…" He rattles off a case number and then looks at me. "Please state your name."

For some reason, being recorded makes me break out into a cold sweat. These two really believe I hurt Callie, don't they? I fold my hands in my lap and slouch back, unable to get comfortable in the plastic chair. "Uh…V-Victor Howard."

"All right, Vic. Please begin."

"What…what am I supposed to say?"

"Start from the beginning of your night." Carter isn't writing anything down, but she's watching me with such intensity that I want to climb under the table and hide. "Be as specific as possible. Times, names, places. Anything that will help paint us a clear picture."

A clear picture. Okay. I wet my lips nervously and start with Brett and me leaving school. I recall us eating at the diner, the time we arrived at the party. Every detail I can remember, I reiterate, from the couple I saw arguing to the purple flowers on the bushes Callie threw up on.

When I arrive at the part about putting Callie to bed, Sherrigan stops writing notes and leans forward. He speaks almost amiably, like I'm his son or nephew. "Callie's a good-looking girl, isn't she, Vic?"

I pause. "Uh. Sure? Sh-she's pretty." When she was busy throwing up everywhere, I can't say I was paying much attention.

"Good-looking girl like that, especially when she's been drinking… Sometimes they forget themselves and start hanging all over guys." He shakes his head. "It'd make sense, you know. She was drunk, you thought she wanted it..."

Deflection: a police technique of providing moral justification for the suspect to have committed a crime.

He's empathizing with me, as though he would have done exactly what they're accusing me of doing. All he wants is to get me to admit to having sex with Callie and everything would fall into place for them from there.

I wring my hands together tightly in my lap. These people are not my friends. These people think I'm guilty... or maybe they don't even care if I'm really guilty and they just want someone to pin this on. All of my anxiety, all of my upset, has shaped itself into anger. I don't want to talk to Sherrigan and Carter anymore.

The detectives keep me for two hours total, asking the same questions over and over, making me repeat parts of my story to throw me off. I can't imagine what's going through their heads right now, but I'm envisioning a flashing neon GUILTY sign. I don't even know what's going through my head right now or how to process all this. Am I going to jail? Can they prosecute me without physical evidence? I should have watched more *Law & Order*.

It's nearly 2:00 a.m. by the time I'm given permission to leave. In retrospect, I think I could have ended the interview at any time, but I kept hoping...I don't know. That I would say something that would magically get them to believe me.

In the end, I guess it doesn't matter.

Mom doesn't ask how it went. She remains silent and expressionless the entire drive home. I'm desperate to ask her what I should do, how I should handle this, but Mom has never been the best at advice.

When we get home, I trail behind her with my shoulders hunched forward and a need to say something. I can't just go to bed and act like this never happened. Mom shuts and locks the front door behind us. I take a deep breath as she turns to walk away. It takes everything I have to make my voice work. "I'm s-sorry, Mom. About the party. I p-promise I wasn't drinking."

She goes still, turns, and slaps me across the face.

Hard.

The sting radiates down into my jaw. I recoil, hand to my cheek. What just happened?

"How dare you," Mom whispers, her voice trembling with rage she's obviously been biting back all night. "How dare you. That poor girl..."

My mouth opens. The words won't come out. "I...I..."

But it's no use. My normally mousy, quiet mother isn't interested in whatever I have to say. "*GO!* Go on! I can't look at you, you're disgusting!" And it's all I can do to scurry out of the entryway and retreat to my room.

I don't understand. I don't. I... What did I do? *Why*? I've never been in serious trouble. I've never hurt anyone. I know I'm not the world's best son, but what have I ever done to make my own mother think I would lay my hands on another person against her will? I wanted to protect Callie. I certainly never meant to leave her open for someone else to hurt her.

I sink to the edge of my bed, breathing fast, clutching my knees. Thoughts running a mile a minute. Even from across the house, Mom's sobs reach my ears from the kitchen.

I need to leave.

The only place I can think to go is Brett's. Of course, I have to wait for Mom to head up to her room so I can sneak out the back door, grab my bike from the side of the house, and get out of here before she notices. Will she be angry that I took off? Undoubtedly. But at this point I don't care. I don't think it matters.

Brett's place is two miles away. Even though it's cooled down in the late (early?) hour, I'm dripping sweat by the time I roll my bike into his driveway. I breathlessly make my way around to the side of his house, phone to my ear to call him. It takes a few rings but his irritated, sleepy voice finally answers. "What the hell?"

"Let me in."

Brett pauses. Sighs. He hangs up but a moment later, the back door is unlocking and sliding open and he's poking his head out with a frown. "Jesus Christ, man—"

"The p-police were… They…" There it goes again. My ability to speak.

He rubs at his eyes, still trying to wake up. "The *what*? Dude, calm down. Get in here."

I slip inside and follow Brett up to his room. Brett's house has always felt more like home to me than my own. His parents are good people, and his mother in particular has always treated me like an affectionate mother would. Maybe that's part of the reason my mom hates her.

In his room, Brett flicks on the bedside lamp while I shut the door and stand there helplessly, not even sure where to begin. In typical concerned Brett fashion, he sits me on the edge of his bed, hands on my shoulders, and stares at me intently. "Deep breaths, Vic. Take your time."

Sometimes that's all I need: a reminder that the world isn't going to implode if I take a few extra moments to formulate each word as I speak. I close my eyes and take the instructed deep breaths…

I tell Brett about the police. About Callie. I tell him about Mom, too, because I don't know if maybe I'm the one overreacting and her response was legitimate. Brett listens and nods, his frown deepening as I speak. When I'm done relaying this information, I'm sapped of all my energy. I don't know if I want to laugh or cry. Frankly, I'm still waiting to wake up.

Brett sinks into his desk chair and leans back. He slides off his glasses and rubs at his eyes with a sigh, like the story took a lot out of him, too. There's something nostalgic about seeing him in his glasses; he only ever wears contacts to school anymore. "Damn…"

"N-no kidding."

"Man, look… Whatever happened, we'll work it out, okay? You know Dad and I will have your back."

Brett's dad is a defense attorney, but I don't want things to go that far where his services are needed. The idea of getting up in front of a courtroom… For that matter, the idea of poor Callie having to get up there and explain what happened to her…I can't imagine it. I don't know her well, but what little I do know made me think of her as a pretty, nice, smart girl.

I lean forward, elbows on my knees, head in my hands. I hurt all over.

"I'm sure the cops will be questioning everyone," Brett says gently. "I won't tell them anything if they come here."

I stop breathing for a moment. "There's nothing to tell."

"Well, yeah, I know. I just meant— "

"Meant what?" I raise my head to stare at him. "D-don't you believe me?"

Brett holds up his hands. "Dude. Yes. Of course I do." He laughs. "I don't think you'd know what to do with a girl."

There have been many times during our friendship where I've wanted to punch Brett. This is one of those times. He must be able to tell by the scowl on my face because he's quick to backpedal.

"Sorry. I don't really know what to say to all this, but I believe you. Just last year I watched you crying over a dead cat on the side of the road. You wouldn't hurt a fly, Vic, and anyone with any brains is going to tell the cops that."

I relax. If there's anyone I want to believe me, it's my best friend. Brett may have changed a lot over the years, but in times where I've needed him—*really* needed him—he's never let me down. Not once. He was there at the hospital when I had my appendix removed two years ago. He was there on my sixteenth birthday when Mom had to work and I would have otherwise been home alone with the flu. He was there to defend me when kids made fun of my stutter. He was even the one who got me started on word definitions; he noticed I had a knack for memorizing the words I was helping him study, so he bought me a dictionary and ever since I periodically teach myself a random new word.

Even now, when he's got plenty of friends and acquaintances and doesn't need me around, he's kept me by his side. I'm still the guy he sits with at lunch and calls with news and questions before anyone else.

Brett pats my back. "Why don't you stay here tonight? Stay for a few nights, if you need to. At least until your mom chills out. Maybe my mom can talk to her."

"I d-don't think that'll help." I sigh heavily. Mom thinks Mrs. Mason is a lazy good-for-nothing (her words, not mine) because she's a stay-at-home mother, and she assumes all of Mr. Mason's clients are serial killers and rapists. Although given how she reacted to these accusations, maybe she thinks I *need* a defense lawyer.

God, the look on her face keeps popping back into my head and making my chest hurt. Maybe running away from my problems for tonight will be okay.

Chapter Three

The guest bed in Brett's house is more comfortable than my own bed. Too bad it doesn't really help me fall asleep. My brain is moving too fast, still running over the same questions again and again. Wondering. Worrying. Mom doesn't call. I text to let her know that I'm at Brett's, but she doesn't write back.

Brett must have told his parents what's going on, because the next morning they're both extremely quiet. They probably don't know what to say. Before we leave, Mrs. Mason gives me a five-dollar bill for lunch and pecks me on the cheek, telling me to try to have a good day.

These are things my mom hasn't done for me in years. When I was little, she was better about it. She'd pick me up and hug me, kiss me, tell me how everyone said I looked just like her, with her same big blue eyes and long lashes. She'd tell me she loved me. I don't really know when that changed. Sometime around middle school, I guess.

Brett fills the car with his usual banter and easy conversation on our way to school. I wish I could feel any level of comfort, and I know he's trying to keep things on a light note for my sake. It's appreciated, but it isn't helpful.

We part ways for the first half of the day and I try not to think that every time someone looks at me, they're aware of what's going on. That the cops visited the house of every student and told them what happened to Callie, and that I'm responsible for it. *Paranoia*: a mental condition characterized by delusions of persecution. That's all it is. People aren't talking about Callie or me. Nobody knows.

Except—

I remember the girl getting stuff out of Callie's locker. One of her friends, obviously, so maybe she knows something. If I could get a message back to Callie through her friend, maybe…

I ditch Brett at lunch in favor of going to Callie's locker. I don't know the girl I saw, and asking around seems like looking for trouble. So I wait. Hoping I'll at least spot her coming down the hall when lunch ends. The first bell goes off. The hallway fills with students as they head to class. I stay where I am.

Second bell.

And there she is.

I push away from Callie's locker as I spot the girl weaving through the crowd. I attempt a “Hey!” but, given the number of people, I don’t blame her for not turning around.

She rounds a corner. Instead of going into a classroom, she walks out the double doors leading to the quad, maybe heading for the library or the gym. I jog to catch up, reaching out to touch her shoulder. “Hey—”

The next thing I know, the sky is above me and I’m hitting the ground as my legs are knocked out from under me. I see stars. In broad daylight. *Concussion:* minor brain injury that may occur when one’s head strikes an object. Ow.

The girl’s face comes into view as I’m blinking the white from my vision. “You following me, jackass?” she snarls. “I know who you are. You’ve got some fucking nerve.”

I push myself up to sit, scooting back on the concrete to avoid getting struck again in the event she lashes out. “N-no—I mean, y-yes. I j-just wanted—”

“Wanted to what? I’ve got nothing to say to you.”

“I…I saw you at Callie’s l-locker…”

“If I had my way, they would have thrown your sorry ass in jail already. You realize they’re getting a restraining order against you.”

“I—”

“Better not let me see you in the parking lot, ’cause you’d better believe I’ll mow you down.”

“*I didn’t touch her!*”

The heat of my voice startles me. I’m not a yeller. I keep quiet, under the radar. But those words felt like they were going to burst out of my ribs if I didn’t say them. Callie’s friend is watching me with a smoldering glare.

"Right. She just made it up, then."

"N-no. I didn't say…say that." Once I'm sure she isn't going to use some weird karate move to put me on the ground again, I pick myself up. "I'm just saying it w-wasn't m-me."

She squints, looking me over. Studying me. I'd feel less exposed lying naked on a silver tray in biology being sliced open in the name of science. "Why were you following me?"

Why was I? What, exactly, did I want to ask? What did I want to say? I rub the back of my neck, ducking my head. "I wanted to s-see if you could deliver a m-message."

"Uh-huh. What kind of message?"

"T-tell her…I d-didn't do it. I swear on my life. And…" The guilt. It comes out of nowhere and slides its slivers into my lungs, making my chest tight. "Tell her I'm sorry."

She folds her arms, gaze steely. "Sorry for *what*?"

"For not keeping her safe." That's what it comes down to. No, I didn't rape Callie Wheeler, but I feel like it was my fault it happened. The number of things I could have—should have—done to prevent it seems staggering. The weight of my guilt makes it hard to breathe. Brett was right: I wouldn't hurt a fly. I've never made fun of anyone. I've never gotten into a fight. Even the idea of hitting someone makes me unhappy.

Callie's friend lets her arms drop to her sides. She huffs out a breath. Miraculously, she doesn't sound quite as furious as she did before. Just wary. "Yeah. Whatever." Then she's turning her back on me and storming off in the direction of the library. I watch her go. The sway of her hips is mesmerizing.

Or maybe that's the concussion talking.

Brett laughs his ass off when I tell him. "You got laid out by a girl? Nice."

I sink down in the passenger's seat of the car, trying not to mope. "D-don't be a dick."

"Sorry, sorry. What did she look like?"

"Uh... Dark brownish-reddish hair, I guess? Soft-looking..." I space out for a second. She had a really nice mouth. Like, ridiculously nice. It was probably her most defining feature.

"Nice hips? Curves in all the right places?"

My brows draw together. "Yeah. Now that you mention it..."

Brett nods. "That sounds like Autumn."

"Autumn?"

"Autumn Dixon, I think. She's Callie's best friend. I had a calculus class with her once. She's a firecracker, man, let me tell you."

"I noticed." It was...kind of hot. Nerve-racking, but hot. Probably not the sort of thing I should be thinking about given that Autumn threatened to run me over with her car and I've been accused of raping her best friend.

Brett glances at me once, twice, three times. "You don't have a thing for this girl, do you?"

I look out the window to avoid letting Brett see how my mouth twists funny and my face gets red. "I d-don't even know her."

"Doesn't mean you can't think she's hot."

"Sh-shut up."

"Hey, I'm just making an observation. If you want me to put in a good word for you…"

"Sure. That'll go over great," I mutter.

Brett laughs again. I let the conversation drop. He's done this any time I've shown interest in a girl…which I have. Plenty. Girls are these fascinating creatures. Beautiful in all shapes, sizes, colors. He teases me for not having a "type." How can I possibly have a type when they're all so intriguing? Girls who read. Girls who play sports. Girls who draw, paint, dance, cheerlead, wrestle, sing. I've yet to meet a female who wasn't good at something while I sit here uselessly and have an anxiety attack at the thought of trying to talk to them.

Well, at least I got through that awkward introduction phase with Autumn. Not so sure I left a good impression.

We don't drive directly to Brett's place. He pulls up outside my house because I've already worn the same clothes two days in a row and I'm too tall for any of his things to fit me. I brace myself before opening the car door with a sigh.

Brett, to my relief, gets out with me. At least I know Mom won't yell in front of him. I think. I hope. I let us in the front door and she appears in the living room, drying her hands on a dish towel and staring holes into the back of my head as I inch down the hall toward my room.

Brett says, "Hey, Ms. Howard!" and Mom grants him the ghost of a smile.

In my room, I grab a spare gym bag from the closet and begin shoving whatever I can fit inside. Clothes, hairbrush, toothbrush. Anything I think I'll need in the next week or two, because I don't plan on having to slink back into my own house like a fugitive every other day. Brett watches from the doorway. When I go to step past him, he puts a hand to my chest and raises his eyebrows.

"You should talk to your mom."

"And say what?"

"I don't know. Just talk to her. Maybe she panicked or something and she's calmed down now."

I wasn't getting that vibe from her. Sighing, I push the bag into Brett's arms and go off to find Mom in the kitchen where she's assembling something to bake. She bakes when she's anxious or stressed. I came home once after she'd gone in for a job interview to find three pies, a peach cobbler, and two dozen cookies. At least she's good at it.

"Mom?" I stop in the adjoined dining room, keeping the kitchen table between us.

Her back is to me and I see the stiffening of her shoulders. She slides a hand back through her messy curls before turning to face me. "What?"

I'm having a hard time even looking at her face. She slapped me the last time I saw her. My mother has never, ever believed in that sort of thing; she never spanked me growing up, never even laid a hand on me aggressively. "I d-didn't do it, you know. I promise I didn't."

Mom leans back against the counter and rolls her eyes to the ceiling.

"Why won't you b-believe me?"

"I don't know what to believe right now, Victor," Mom says tiredly.

"Okay." This is not the answer I wanted. My emotions are warring for dominance: confusion versus anger versus hurt. "I'm gonna s-stay with Brett until you figure it out."

Mom doesn't argue. No protests, no questions, no nothing. As usual. She only nods once and turns away, back to her baking, letting out a suffering sigh. I'm not a violent person, but I have the strongest urge to flip a chair just to disrupt the stagnant tension in the room. As frustrating as Mom can be, she's never acted like this before, and I'm at a loss for what to say, what to do. Normally, I would know how to appease her annoyance or her anger. This time…

All I can think is this: if my own mother doesn't believe me, what hope do I have that the police—and Callie—will?

Chapter Four

When I turned sixteen, my desperation to get out of the house and do something on my own led me to Rick's Convenience Store and gas station two blocks from home, where I asked for a job and got one. To this day I don't know why I was hired on. Me, who can hardly get out a sentence to strangers without stuttering…

But Rick's Convenience Store—which isn't even owned by any Rick, but rather by a guy named Amjad—has been my place of employment for more than a year now. Amjad moved to the States after his wife passed away, and he didn't have enough to pay someone full time, so…here I am. Minimum wage and all the slushies I can drink. Too bad I don't even like slushies, but Brett has taken advantage of the offer.

It's a much longer trip from Brett's place to work, but in the year I've been here, I've called in only twice. Both times when I was extremely sick and Brett insisted. Amjad is kind in all the ways most bosses wouldn't usually be, and I've never wanted to let him down.

He takes one look at my face when I come into work at the end of the week, and instantly he knows something is off. "What is wrong with you?"

"Long week," I say, but I try to give him a smile so he doesn't ask questions. He leaves me alone while I pry open boxes and stock the fridge shelves with soda and energy drinks. Given the rising heat outside and the lack of real air-conditioning in the store, being back by the fridges is welcome. Every time I slide open a door, the chilled air glides across my face and down the front of my shirt.

I've always liked hiding back here. The supply room is dark and cooler than the front of the store. From behind the fridge units, I can see through the cans and bottles into the shop aisles. Now and again, I catch glimpses of Amjad playing his sudoku games at the counter.

But mainly, I like when people come into the store. I like watching them. It's not like being stuck at a party where people can see me lingering alone in a corner with a drink I won't touch. Here, they won't notice me at all. Sometimes it's fun to watch people when they don't realize they're being watched. I don't do it long enough to be considered creepy or anything—just for a few seconds at a time. It isn't uncommon to see kids from school, either. Truthfully,

I probably learn more about them and their families here than I do from sharing classes with them.

I've learned bad-boy Tommy has a girlfriend from an all-girls Catholic school who calls him "teddy bear" and he goes to church with her every Sunday, after which they stop by the store to share a cherry slushie. I've learned Aaron Biggs and his brother live not just with their mom but also their grandmother, who is hard of hearing and always insists on coming inside with them to pay for their gas. Patrick Maloney, Aaron's best friend, has come in a few times, always with different girls hanging on his arm. Chris Christopher started coming in the day he turned eighteen and could legally buy cigarettes. Just like he did at the party, he always smells like pot.

People are different outside of school. But if they saw me, they would try to keep up appearances. Makes things awkward.

A couple of people come and go while I'm in back during the afternoon rush, when everyone is stopping to get gas on their way home from work. By the time I'm done stocking, things have slowed down and I feel safe emerging again to put product on the shelves.

Amjad eventually asks, "Is it a girl?"

I nearly drop a box of Lay's snack-sized chip bags all over my feet. "W-what?"

"Bothering you." He peers at me from behind the counter, pointing in my direction with his pen. He always insists real sudoku players use pens. "Some girl break your heart?"

A wry smile twists at my mouth. "No." Not exactly, but I don't want to explain the truth to him.

He huffs. "Girls! They're headaches. But wonderful. Whatever you did wrong, you go apologize. Make it right."

"It's n-not a girl," I say with amusement.

"Then what is it?"

Deep breath. I stick a few bags of Doritos in their designated place. "Have you ever...been accused of s-something you didn't do?"

Amjad opens his mouth to speak, pausing when the door chimes. He holds up a finger as though to say *hold that thought* while the boy who just entered goes immediately to the back of the store. I duck my head and focus on getting the chips put away. He walks past me with two six-packs in hand, which he places on the counter, and offers Amjad a twenty. Amjad looks at it, at the beer, then at him.

"ID, please?"

The blond guy grins, spreading his hands. He can't be any older than me. "C'mon, man. I left it at home."

Amjad smiles back at him. He taps the placard on the counter that states that ID is required for anyone who looks under forty. The guy's bright demeanor fades quickly, darkening to a scowl. He crams the twenty into his pocket and walks out, muttering about terrorists as the door swings shut.

Terrorist: a person who uses terrorism in the pursuit of political aims. That is, something Amjad definitely is not. The word makes my spine stiffen. It isn't the first time someone's thrown that insult around in this store, and Amjad always shrugs it off.

This time, though, he looks to me with his eyebrows raised. "I believe the answer to your question… Does that count?"

"It c-counts," I agree solemnly. "How do you not let it bother you?"

He shrugs and picks up the two six-packs. "I pity them."

"What? Why?"

"Ignorance is a great weakness. To not try to learn truths and allow judgmental stereotypes cloud your mind…" He opens the fridge, places the beer back in, and lets it swing shut while turning to me. "Why would you not pity someone so foolish?"

Never thought of it that way. But then again, does that advice really apply to me? I'm being accused of rape, something any guy at the party could have done. Not being a terrorist while I work at my small business that I built practically from the ground up all by myself.

On his way back up front, Amjad pats me on the back. "Whatever bothers you, Victor, let it roll off the shoulders. You're a good boy. No worries."

I smile at him while wondering why my own mother doesn't agree.

Chapter Five

The whispers about what happened to Callie have started.

I hear them only because I've been listening for them, and because Aaron stops by our table at lunch to lean over and talk about it with Brett as though I'm not there.

"Did you hear about Callie?"

Brett hesitates, glancing at me while I pick apart my bologna sandwich. "Yeah, I heard."

"The cops came to my house. My brother's in such deep shit for throwing that party and letting in underage drinkers."

I feel a frown pulling at my face. With what happened to Callie, being caught drinking at a dumb party would be the least of my concerns.

Brett scoots over, nudging me in the process, to make room for Aaron to sit beside him. "What did the police say? Like, do they have any leads or anything?"

Aaron sits with enough force to make the cafeteria bench rattle. "Yeah, but they wouldn't tell me who. It was a group of drunk people… Had to be from the college, though; none of the friends I invited would do something like that. Though, honestly, it isn't that big a surprise something like this happened."

"Not cool," Brett warns. Aaron holds up his hands.

"Just calling it like I see it, man." He leans forward to peer around Brett. "What about you, Vicky? They come to question you, too?"

An eerie, icy-veined stillness takes me over. I don't look at him. He said he didn't know who was under suspicion, but does he really? "Th-they came to talk to me," I mutter. "I d-didn't see anything." I think it's only a matter of time before word gets out that I'm the one suspected. I'm surprised Autumn hasn't told everyone yet.

From the corner of my eye, I see Aaron watching me with a look so intense it makes me want to slide under the table. "Well," he says, "it's pretty bizarre. If I find out who did it, I'm gonna cave his skull in."

Aaron then goes off on a tangent with Brett, talking about school and sports, so I tune them out. I scan the cafeteria for Autumn, wondering if she told Callie that I spoke to her. Probably not, and I don't really blame her. But…maybe I should find her again, just to ask how Callie is doing.

During my office assistant period the next day, I pull up Autumn's name in the computer to see her schedule.

Autumn Dixon
Semester 2 Class Schedule

Period 01 - Computers II (L. Smith)
Period 02 - German II (T. Ulrich)
Period 03 - American History (M. Schwartz)
Period 04 - Creative Writing (P. Zinfandel)

Mostly electives. She's a senior, like me, so she's already gotten her required classes for graduating out of the way. No wonder I've never had a class with her. She was probably in Calculus II while I was struggling my way through Pre-Algebra. She's in German right now in the east wing. I'll cut out of the office a few minutes early to get over there and wait for the lunch bell to ring; they never complain.

People begin flowing into the halls, but Autumn is easy to spot among the crowd. Her head is down as she's trying to cram things into her backpack. I take a breath. This could be a bad idea. No, it most definitely is. She isn't paying any attention to what's going on around her and will probably walk right past me if I don't say anything.

"Uh…Autumn?"

"Yeah?" she asks, turning toward me. It doesn't register whom she's speaking to until she looks up at my face, then her expression darkens significantly. "What the hell do you want?"

I have no real idea. Looking at her makes my mind draw

a blank. "I j-just wanted to ask how Callie was doing."

She narrows her eyes, yanks her backpack zipper shut with force, and slides the pack over her shoulder. "Wow, that is *so* none of your business."

I glance around anxiously, not wanting people to overhear. When I move closer, Autumn tenses like she's ready to put me on the ground, but she doesn't pull away. I just want to be able to speak quieter.

"Th-they took DNA, you know."

"I'm aware."

"So you'll find out it wasn't me."

She purses her lips, meeting my eyes easily. "We'll see about that."

My sigh is an exasperated one. "W-why does it s-sound like you *want* me to be guilty?"

Autumn doesn't miss a beat. "Because if it's not you, we have no other solid leads and Callie will come back to school always wondering who it was and if she's going to run into him on the street. I don't want that for her."

Her words strike a chord. I don't want that for Callie, either, and I'd never thought of it like that. Is the reason she hasn't come back to school because I'm here? Autumn mentioned a restraining order. I have no idea how that would work with school. "I'm sorry," I tell her, and I mean every word of it. "B-but it wasn't me."

For the first time, Autumn doesn't look angry. She just looks…sad. I almost wish I could be guilty if it would bring them some peace of mind.

"There were a ton of p-people at the party," I point

out, wanting to make her feel better. "Th-they don't have anyone else?"

Autumn hesitates, folding her arms across her chest and looking down at her feet. "I'm not talking about this with you," is all she says before brushing past me and heading down the hall.

I'll take that as a no. If Callie pointed me out specifically, then maybe they really have no idea. If there were thirty other guys at that party, where would they begin in picking one out? They'd have to go through every single person and get DNA samples. That's assuming they can figure out the party list in its entirety.

I meet up with Brett in the cafeteria. He already has his tray of food and I really don't have an appetite, so I just sit across from him empty-handed. He raises an eyebrow and slides a soda he grabbed for me across the table. "I was starting to think you got lost."

"T-talking to Autumn," I mutter, wrapping my long fingers around the can and thumbing away some of the condensation on the outside of it.

Brett shoves a few fries into his mouth, pauses midchew, and frowns. Swallows. "What? Why?"

"Wanted to know how Callie was."

"I'm sure that went over great. Aaron probably told his friends the police questioned him and his brother, and now everyone knows what happened."

A headache is threatening to encroach. I pinch the bridge of my nose. "That's not fair to her."

Brett frowns. "No offense to Callie Wheeler, but I'm

more worried about *you*. If word gets out you're, like, their prime suspect, you're never going to hear the end of it."

I pluck at the metal tab on the top of the can, every obnoxious twang enunciating Brett's concern. "Yeah, well. I don't know what to do about it. Any of it."

That night, Mr. Mason sits me down in his office to better explain some of the police procedures to me. He's gotten more information out of the detectives than I could. Then again, he's the lawyer. Of course they'd tell him more.

"Before we really get into all this," he says, folding his hands atop his desk and looking over the top of his glasses, "I need you to be one hundred percent honest with me, Vic. Whatever you say won't leave this room."

I feel small in the leather chair in this big office surrounded by degrees on the wall and books whose words are beyond my level of intelligence. "O-okay."

Mr. Mason asks, "Did you rape Callie?"

He has to ask me this. I know he does. Despite his being a defense attorney, I know him well enough that— "N-no. And y-you wouldn't be doing this for me if you thought I had."

A smile crosses his normally serious face. "Touché. Well, let me tell you a few things from the police side of things. First of all, Callie didn't submit for a rape kit until right at the seventy-two-hour mark, so—"

"W-what does that mean?"

He pauses, slides off his glasses. "Sorry. Basically, a rape kit is collected for minors within seventy-two hours of the rape taking place. I don't know all the details yet, but I have a feeling they won't find much in it."

"Why?"

"She didn't report anything right away. One of her friends had to convince her to tell her parents, who then reported it to the police."

One of her friends… Does he mean Autumn?

He continues. "Added to the fact that they were trying so hard to get a confession out of you, it sounds to me like Callie probably washed away most of the evidence, or the attacker was likely wearing a condom, so the rape kit isn't going to give them much."

"Then what's the point of doing one?"

"Procedure." Mr. Mason shrugs. "Perhaps the off chance some evidence was spared. Without it, it's just your word against hers, and then it comes down to a matter of which of you can make yourselves more credible to a jury."

I close my eyes and remember what Autumn said. If my name is cleared, they have no idea who to look for next. I'm the only one she could pinpoint. How would that make her feel, when they don't find anything physical linking me to this and the only evidence is Callie's word?

At the same time, my insides twist at the idea of her actual rapist being out there somewhere, wandering the halls of one of the local colleges or even our school itself. Patrick, James, Devon, Eli…all the faces I can recall seeing at the party. I could have walked right by Callie's attacker and not known it.

"Right now, the police have several people who saw you go upstairs with Callie." Mr. Mason shakes his head. "But a few others saw you come back down, and when asked about the times, there are a few who can verify you simply weren't up there long enough to have done something to her."

"What about others?" I ask. "Other p-people who went upstairs…" I passed by three guys—one of them from my school—even just coming back down after leaving Callie in that room.

"It was a party, Vic. A lot of people went up there at some point to pass out or use the bathroom. I promise you aren't the only one being questioned—several boys from your school are—but you are their primary suspect because you were the guy everyone saw with her and the only one she could name. Besides that, you're the easiest one to pin the blame on. She named you, people saw you going upstairs… Some of the other witnesses have said you're kind of a loner, too. I hate to say it, but this precinct is known for being lazy on the evidence-gathering end of their rape investigations."

I have a lot of questions that I can't stomach actually asking. Like, what does Callie remember? How did she not see the person's face? Was she just that out of it? These are details Mr. Mason might know, but the words won't make it past my awkward tongue. I just say, "Okay," and listen in silence while he directs me. Don't speak to the police without him present. Don't try to contact Callie to clear the air. I'll be going to court in a few weeks, since they're serving me with a restraining order and I need to follow it to a T. Don't discuss the case with others. I'm guessing Brett is exempt from that rule, all things considered.

When I finally leave his office, I'm drained. It's barely been a week since the party. Every day, it gets a little worse. Like bags of sand are steadily being added to my joints, making every limb heavy and hard to move. Someday I'm going to wake up and not be able to get out of bed from the pressure pinning me down.

Brett is waiting for me when I come upstairs to his room. He sets his tablet aside and looks at me over the top of his glasses. "Everything okay?"

"Everything's perfect," I mumble, sinking to his floor and sprawling out. It's almost painful to will my muscles to relax. "I hate this."

"I don't blame you."

"G-guess at least no one at school knows I'm the suspect."

Brett averts his gaze in a way that makes me uncomfortable. "Mm."

"What?"

"Nothing," he says.

"You're lying."

He heaves a sigh and slides off his glasses to clean them. "No, it's just…I mean, Aaron knows. And some other people." There goes any hope I had of getting my body to relax. I stare at Brett but don't say anything, waiting for him to continue on his own. He adds helplessly, "The cops questioned everyone they could who went to the party, Vic. They asked about you specifically since Callie pointed you out, so…it's not hard for them to put two and two together."

I slowly turn my eyes to the ceiling and pick out the pattern of a kangaroo and a cat in the stucco. "So when he talked to us at lunch…"

"He knew."

"And you th-thought it was smart not to tell me? Thanks."

Brett points at me with his glasses and frowns. "Don't do that, man. I was trying to protect you. You've got enough on your plate to have to worry about dealing with whatever people like Aaron might be saying."

What would Aaron be saying, I wonder? He looked at and spoke to me so casually the other day. What was he really thinking?

Then I remember that Aaron was at the party, and if he saw me take Callie Wheeler upstairs, that makes him a suspect, too.

Chapter Six

By Monday morning, everyone knows.

And I say "everyone" because if *I've* noticed people are talking about something, then enough people know that it might as well be everyone.

When we get to school, I ask Brett, "Should I try talking to Autumn again?" He laughs and punches my arm.

"You've so got a thing for that girl, don't you?"

I slide open my combo lock to my locker, frowning around the heat rushing to my face. "I d-don't know what you mean."

"You've already talked to her a couple of times and she hasn't had anything nice to say. So either you're a glutton for punishment or you're just infatuated with her. Which I would totally understand; she's hot."

Infatuation: foolish or all-absorbing passion.

I wouldn't go that far. Sure, I think Autumn is gorgeous and I like that fierce loyalty of hers, but that doesn't mean I'm *infatuated* with her. Besides, she hates my guts and I can't formulate a coherent sentence to her that doesn't involve Callie, so— "Just meant to s-see how Callie's doing."

Brett shrugs. "Frankly, I doubt she'll say anything to you one way or the other. Didn't my dad tell you to avoid talking to anyone about the case?"

"Yeah," I agree sullenly, shutting the locker door and slouching against it. Brett pats my shoulder with a sympathetic smile before turning to head to class. I wish I could handle things the way Brett always does, with this effortless sort of confidence that everything is going to be all right. Me? I lose sleep and can't focus on tying my own shoes, let alone struggling to make sure I don't have a nervous breakdown between now and graduation.

While I head to class, I open my ears to the people around me instead of trying to tune them out like usual. In particular, I pay attention to Aaron's group near the bathroom, which consists of five other guys who all know Brett but probably couldn't tell you my name.

Yet the moment I come within hearing range, Aaron stops in midsentence and makes no move to hide that he's staring at me. His friends turn to do the same and I keep my gaze on the floor, mesmerized by the way my shoelaces hit the linoleum with each step. I don't get far when Aaron calls out, "Hey, Vic."

My shoes squeak to a halt. I feel like my body has shrunken in on itself, like my shoulders could collapse forward and fold into my rib cage and I could sink into the floor, because when I turn around, all six of them are looking right at me. Aaron smiles. "C'mere a sec, would you?" he asks, inclining his head toward the bathroom.

This is a bad idea. I shove my hands as deep into my pockets as I can, taking a step away. "I've g-got to get to c-class…"

Patrick Maloney, who I last saw at the party heading upstairs with Jacob and Eric, moves toward me and swings an arm around my shoulders. "It'll only take a minute. Aaron wanted to let you in on something the police told him."

I know the cops have been speaking to anyone who was at the lake house, so it's plausible Aaron knows something that I don't—especially since his brother was the one who threw the event. Still, there's a heavy ball of dread rolling around in my stomach as Patrick ushers me into the bathroom, and that feeling does not lessen when I'm standing there against the wall with all of them around me and Aaron is a foot or so in front of me, no longer smiling.

"I heard the cops brought you in for some kind of test."

Where did he hear that from? Only Brett knew, and there's no way he would've said anything. Unless—no… Mom wouldn't have said anything to Ruthie Biggs, would she? They're friends, but no way. What's more, Ruthie wouldn't have told her son when she has to know he's got a big mouth and wouldn't keep it to himself. Right? I have to swallow hard to make my dry mouth cooperate. "Uh, y-yeah."

He crosses his arms, legs posed slightly apart like he's trying to make himself look casual and instead comes across as intimidating. "Huh. What'd they have you do, jerk off into a plastic cup?"

"N-no," I mutter, looking down at the floor. "It's r-really none of your b-business. I've got to go to class."

Trying to move past them is a bold move and it backfires. Patrick slams the palm of his hand into my chest, shoving me effortlessly back to the wall where a light switch jabs uncomfortably into my shoulder blade. "You screw a girl while she's unconscious and that's all you've got to say for yourself?" He pushes me again.

My vision is blurring. I can't seem to get a proper breath in. I am teetering on the verge of an anxiety attack and no longer am I stuttering…I simply can't speak.

"Easy, Patrick. Come on now, Vic," Aaron chides, "let's hear it. Tell us what happened. Make it a good enough story and maybe we won't tell the cops. Honestly, I didn't think you had it in you, but I guess if it's the only way you were ever gonna get laid…"

My fingers bend, curling into tight fists just itching to hit him. Six against one aren't great odds, though, and I'm already shaking. I just want to get away. Patrick pushes me again, and again I hit the light switch, but this time, I slide down a fraction of an inch until the switch clicks off… and thanks to the lack of windows in the bathroom, we're plummeted into darkness. I take the chance while they're startled and cursing and searching for the switch to duck beneath Patrick's reaching arms and dart out the door.

I don't wait to see if they'll follow. I run down the hall, around the corner, and into the adjoining halls where Callie's locker is because I'm hoping they won't think to look for me here. In retrospect, once I reach the courtyard near the library and I'm trying to catch my breath as I drop to a bench, I realize I could have gone to class. I would've been plenty safe there.

No, I don't want to face anyone in class. I want to know how Aaron found out about the police taking me to the clinic. I want to know why my mother would tell anyone that kind of information…even her best friend. She had to have known what a terrible idea it would be. Because now if Aaron and his friends know, the information is fair game. Anyone can know that the police think I raped Callie Wheeler.

It takes me thirty minutes to sneak off campus past the guy who monitors the parking lot and get home. If I were eighteen I could sign myself out of school for the day, but I'm not there quite yet. Mom is at work still and will be for another two hours, and I'm cool with that. I'm exhausted and I haven't been sleeping well over at Brett's, despite the comfortable bed. The couch is familiar and with the TV on low and my bare feet kicked up onto the coffee table, it doesn't take me long to doze off.

The sound of Mom's keys in the door jolts me from a dream I can only vaguely remember, wherein I was back at the party, trying to will myself to go upstairs to check on Callie again…like doing so could prevent all of this from happening.

I sit up and shake off the sight of those stairs in my brain, twisting to look as Mom comes in through the front door. She pauses when she sees me, and then sighs and slips off her shoes by the door and hangs up her keys. "You didn't tell me you were going to be home."

"I live here." Meaning I shouldn't have to give her warning.

She gives me a sour look, stepping into the living room. "Why weren't you in school?"

Yeah, I sort of figured she'd know. They would have called to report my absence. "Bad day."

"That's not a reason future employers are going to accept, Victor." Mom stops at the end of the couch, crossing her arms with a frown.

I look down at my hands. "Um. D-did you tell Ruthie Biggs wh-what was going on?"

Mom is silent long enough that I immediately know the answer. "Why?"

Knowing she totally spread my business around makes me want to crawl under the couch and not ask anything further. "B-because Aaron and all of his friends know. They were asking about it."

"I really don't think Ruthie would have told her son anything I said to her in confidence," Mom scoffs.

"No one else *knew*, Mom."

"Well, it wasn't her. Now drop it." She turns to walk into the kitchen.

I should drop it, but I don't want to. Normally when Mom gets mad, I'm quick to back down and change the subject, but now I'm being attacked from almost every other aspect of my life. The least my mother could do is be on my side. That being said, I get up to follow after her. "Wh-what exactly did you tell her?"

Mom keeps her back to me, setting her purse on the island counter and opening the fridge to find herself something for dinner. "I don't see why that matters or why it's any of your business. Remember, you got yourself into this mess. You have no idea what it's like to have everyone looking at me like they have."

Mom and I have fought plenty before. Or rather, her passive-aggressive tendencies have tripped even my temper and I've snapped at her until she was reduced to tears, and by some turn of events, I was always the one in the wrong who ended up apologizing whether it was actually my fault or not. I'm not sure Mom has ever said sorry to me. For anything. Yet I've been apologizing all my life.

I'm not feeling in a very apologetic mood at the moment. "What *you're* going through? Are you kidding?"

She turns to me finally, a package of defrosted chicken and a bag of salad in her hand. Her expression is neutral but the typical sheen of tears in her eyes is present, telling me she's about to let loose the waterworks. "I could lose my job over this, Victor. What were you thinking? Haven't I raised you better than that?"

My jaw falls open but the words won't come beyond, "Wh-what?"

"I taught you to be a gentleman. I told you *never* to touch anyone unless she asked you to, didn't I?" The first few tears begin to slip down her cheeks and my gut twists. Yeah. I have been raised like that. It's always been common sense, to be gentle, to be patient and kind, and although I'm not perfect, I like to think I try my best. I've never hit anyone. I'm not intentionally mean.

"Mom," I start, taking a step closer. Maybe I *am* being selfish. I've been so wrapped up in what this meant for me that I didn't stop to think what people will do or say to *her*. Because if kids from school who were questioned know I'm a suspect, then their parents know, and our town is not all that big.

Like I've done a hundred times before, I try to reach out to hug her, never knowing the response I'm going to get. Will she bury her teary face against my shoulder and sob, or will she turn away? It's always a guessing game. Sometimes my apologies aren't enough to make her happy.

She steps back. "Don't touch me."

That's a new one. I go still, letting my arms fall to my sides. Mom hiccups and wipes at her eyes, trying to look stern and only succeeding in looking more of a mess than she is.

"Go to your room, Victor. I don't want to look at you right now."

Ah. That part isn't new. Not really, anyway. *I don't want to look at you.* That started around my early teens and the first time the words left my mother's mouth, my heart about shattered. There is nothing anyone has ever said to me in all my life that aches quite like that.

Which is why I say nothing. I retreat to my room as instructed and sit on my bed, fingers in my hair, eyes closed, trying to pinpoint the exact moment when my mom stopped loving me.

Chapter Seven

Tuesday morning, I call Sherrigan and he tells me, "The process takes several days, Victor. That's assuming they don't have a backlog at the lab. And let me tell you, they *always* have a backlog."

Come Friday, I've still heard nothing. With my restraining order hearing approaching, I had been hoping I'd have some good news by now. I try calling Sherrigan again as Brett and I get to school, but no one answers. I close my eyes and drop my head back against the passenger's seat of Brett's car. He's parked outside of school but hasn't abandoned me to go inside. I can sense his eyes locked onto me worriedly while I hang up with a defeated sigh.

Any moment, the lab could be sending my DNA results

to the detectives, and they're sure to hear before even Mr. Mason does. Amjad told me when I went in to work last night that he's never seen me look at my phone so much in all the time he's known me. I still can't bring myself to tell him what's actually going on. If he wants to believe I'm having girl problems, I'm okay with that. Work is the one place I can go where I get to pretend to be normal.

"Nothing?" Brett asks when I lower my phone.

I shake my head and get out of the car. Brett follows, but thankfully doesn't press me for info. I can still sense his concerned gaze on me, though. That's just Brett for you. Maybe he isn't the greatest at verbally expressing that he cares, but he has his ways of showing it. The only fights he's ever been in growing up were ones where he was defending me, and the last few days, when we walk down the halls, I feel like he's tense and ready to snap at anyone who says anything to me.

We don't speak as we head inside. Brett goes his way and I go mine, though he does fist-bump my shoulder gently before he goes. He prefers to keep his books on him at all times, and I prefer to cram whatever I can into my locker and get it as needed. There are usually people getting into their lockers all around me at any given time, so I don't notice her at first. Not until I realize she's leaning her shoulder against my locker and staring right at me when I lift my eyes.

"Uh, h-hey Autumn."

Autumn has her hair twisted up into a messy bun today. Her leggings are slashed at the knees, probably violating dress code, and her thigh-length tank top has a skull and crossbones on it with the disclaimer underneath: *this is not gang-related*. Cute.

She doesn't smile. "I want to talk to you."

Great start to my morning. Somehow I doubt she's here to apologize for treating me like a leper. "O-okay. Here?"

"Outside." She inclines her chin in the direction of the nearest double doors leading outside to a section of picnic tables where some students eat lunch. I follow her to a table where I remain standing, afraid any sudden movements will provoke her. She sits on the table itself, feet planted on the bench, elbows on her knees, and stares at me. "So."

"S-so?"

"You probably haven't heard yet, since Callie just found out less than an hour ago…but the DNA results came back."

My heart leaps into my throat. "Okay."

"They didn't find any of you in, like—" She gestures awkwardly. "I mean, nothing in her rape kit matched up with you."

I feel like someone has pricked my side and let all the tense air out of me. My eyes close while I take a deep breath to reflate, feeling lighter and more confident this time. "That's g-good, right? If they have s-someone else's DNA—"

"They don't," she cuts in. "When Callie came back from the party, she scrubbed herself down more than once. By the time I talked her into going to the cops, there wasn't really anything left." Her eyes narrow. "So, you know, it's not like you're off the hook."

My shoulders begin to sink as I remember Mr. Mason

telling me that a lack of physical evidence just means it could be Callie's word against mine in front of a jury. "Oh. Then…why are you telling me this?"

"Because I wanted to see your reaction." She examines her polished nails and I get the feeling she's purposely avoiding looking at me now. That's a first. "You didn't seem surprised."

"That's b-because I told you, I didn't do it." The first bell rings for class. Autumn doesn't seem in a hurry to move. If I play hooky a second day, Mom is going to murder me. "I really need to go…"

Autumn heaves a sigh and waves dismissively. There is no anger in her this time. No sense that she's going to lash out and grind my face into the concrete. Instead she seems almost…defeated? Sad? I wonder how Callie felt when she got the news. If she still fully believes it was me or if the lack of evidence has left some doubt in her mind. I wish I could talk to her, but the restraining order kind of prevents that. Hell, Mr. Mason wouldn't even want me talking to Autumn, but I can't help it.

I should be going to class; I have less than a minute to be in my chair. And yet…instead I'm slowly letting my backpack slide to the ground and I'm sitting next to Autumn on the table so that we're hip to hip. Neither of us says anything because it's a bit awkward and I don't know what to say that would be comforting. I don't even know that my presence will do anything more than irritate her, but I have this gnawing need to make her feel better, and if this is all I can do…

"It's only been a week, but everyone's talking about her like she's some kind of ghost," Autumn eventually says. "At first, our creative writing teacher asked every day if I would bring Callie her homework, and now he doesn't ask about her at all. Sometimes he just looks at her empty seat like... like she's dead or something. People talk about her in past tense and I hate it."

I scuff my heel against the bench. "Will she come b-back to school now?"

She shrugs. "At some point, she's gonna have to. I mean, for finals if nothing else, or she isn't going to walk with the rest of the seniors. But every time she thinks about it, it just...freaks her out, you know?"

Can't blame her, but I also don't know what to say.

Autumn sits with me until long after the last bell has rung. When she gets up, it's all at once; still one moment and then sweeping up her backpack and sliding off the table to begin walking away without a word to me. No "thank you," but no "piss off," either. Maybe this is an improvement.

I don't know why, but I don't tell Brett about my conversation with Autumn. It seems like something personal meant just for the two of us, and I don't feel the need to spread Callie's—or Autumn's—business with anyone. For that matter, I didn't tell him about the incident with Aaron and his friends in the bathroom, either. This is my problem, and Brett has enough on his mind with finals and college applications to have to worry about me…again, like he always has.

But news apparently travels fast even when I keep tight-lipped, because at lunch he stares at me, avoiding looking at Aaron when he passes by, and asks, "When were you going to tell me?"

"About what?"

"You know what." He glances askance at Aaron's table. "I heard what happened and I was going to wait for you to say something, but…"

I refuse to lift my head. "N-nothing to tell. I just, you know, he w-wanted to talk to me."

"With a group of his friends?"

A frown pulls at my features. "H-how did you even find out?"

Brett gives me a long look. Ah. Right. Someone probably saw them drag me into the bathroom, or maybe Aaron himself said something. "Tell your mom, man. She can talk to Aaron's mom so he stops being a dick."

"Mom doesn't care."

"She's your *mother*. Of course she cares."

I pick at the crust on my sandwich. No response for that. On a basic level, yes, I know my mother loves me because she's my mother. We used to be close. She would read me bedtime stories and tell me how much she loved me, and that I was her reason for getting out of bed in the morning. She went on my field trips with my classes. Packed my lunches with extra treats. Got up early on Sundays to make me blueberry French toast before church.

To this day, I'm still trying to figure out what it is I did to make her distant. If there was some defining moment that changed our relationship. Now, as always, I draw a complete blank. It's not like she woke up one day and started ignoring my existence; it didn't happen all at once. It was a gradual process, until I finally realized that things had drastically changed.

Brett nudges my foot under the table. "What aren't you telling me?"

Lots of things. I'm not telling him how I'm hardly sleeping at night and how, despite that Mr. and Mrs. Mason are great, I miss being at home in my own room. I'm not telling him how exhausted I feel after sitting down to conversations with Mr. Mason, or how the hardest part about all this isn't how everyone else has treated me, but just that Mom doesn't believe I'm innocent.

What I tell him instead is an attempt to focus on the positive so all the things I don't want to say can remain tucked safely in the recesses of my mind. "The DNA came back."

Brett's spine straightens. "Really? So you're cleared, right? What did they find?"

"N-nothing of mine," I say, forcing a weak smile, and purposely leaving out the fact that a lack of physical evidence doesn't necessarily mean I'm cleared.

He taps his plastic fork against his lunch tray. "Well, duh. Someone else's, then?"

"I d-don't think so." Not that Autumn told me, anyway. She said they didn't find anything because of Callie washing any viable evidence, but she could very well have made that up.

"Well…that's a weight off you, isn't it?" He grins. "No evidence means they can't really prosecute you for rape."

I try to smile in return, despite not being so sure. Like Autumn said, I'm not off the hook yet. Though some part of me does feel a little lighter, and that feeling lasts long after I've gone to work that night and returned to Brett's, where Mr. Mason is there to greet me with a smile as he pulls me into his office. Brett follows us and this time, Mr. Mason allows it.

"Good news," he says brightly, and proceeds to reiterate the information we already knew. Hearing it again, especially coming from him and not from Autumn, makes it sound better, more hopeful. He must be in a good mood, because he doesn't tell Brett to leave so we can talk in private like he usually does.

"It's great," I say when he's done, even though I don't entirely know what it means for me. Thankfully, Mr. Mason is good at explaining every step of this process so I haven't been left too in the dark.

He takes a seat and we sit in the stuffed chairs across from his desk as he explains. "First, they don't have much to convince a judge for a restraining order anymore. This temporary one will stay in effect until your hearing on the sixth, but they'll probably have to drop it."

Brett rolls his eyes. "It's not like Vic would've gone to talk to her anyway. They don't have any classes together."

"True. But when Callie was ready to return to school, if

they had gotten a permanent restraining order into effect, Vic would've been the one forced into switching schools."

Oh. I hadn't known that. Frankly, I'm not so sure I'd survive going to school without Brett. The idea in and of itself is terrifying.

Mr. Mason continues. "They obviously have no physical evidence to charge you on. A party full of drunk kids doesn't make for reliable eyewitnesses, and since there are so many varying stories about when you went upstairs and came back down again, they're struggling for a leg to stand on."

"Even w-with Callie identifying me?"

"The wording she used is pretty sketchy." He rummages through his papers to locate a stack in particular. "She told the detectives that she remembers you were present at some point when you took her to the bedroom, but that she couldn't say with undeniable certainty you were the one raping her. Your face is just the last one she saw and she remembered hearing your stutter. If she reiterates that to a jury, it isn't going to sound convincing. Alternatively, if she changes her story, her credibility is shot."

Brett smiles wide and pats me on the back. I feel like this should make me happier than it does. Yeah, I'm ecstatic that this is good news for me, but… "W-what do the police do now to f-find out who did it?"

"Depends." Mr. Mason shrugs. "If the detectives had their way, they'd just close the case. But if Callie's family wants to keep pushing or if they get the media involved, then the police can press charges anyway—I don't think they'll get anywhere with that—or they'll find someone else they can pin this on just to put everyone's mind at ease. They have the other guys from the party that they're questioning, but again, no evidence, no easy suspects. There isn't a lot they can do to *really* find who did it, shy of someone stepping forward with a new story or an admission. They've taken multiple statements from several people, ran their tests, and found nothing. They may mark the case as cold until—if and when—they find some other evidence. Cases like this aren't taken very seriously, though. They might think digging deeper is too much of a hassle."

It's just like Autumn said. Now Callie is going to be stuck not having any clue who raped her. If she's going to pass him by on the street. If it could happen again, because he got away with it once. If she isn't fully convinced it was me, how can she sleep at night knowing the real rapist is still out there?

Chapter Eight

Apparently evidence does not matter once a group of high school students gets wind of a juicy rumor. They grab it in their teeth and run with it like wild animals, zeroing in on the person it's about. Technically, that person would be Callie but since she isn't here…I'm next in line.

It's a subtle change. People stare at me. They whisper in class and then twist to look in my direction before someone nudges them and whispers, "Don't stare!" I am this dark shadow to point at and talk about in the halls. Suddenly everyone was Callie Wheeler's best friend just so they can say how they saw this coming, how they knew I was the sort of person to do something like this. Aaron watches me like a hungry lion, and it's all I can do to hover close to Brett's side because it's the only place I truly feel safe from being eaten alive.

It isn't just them, either. It isn't school and it isn't home. Thursday afternoon as Brett and I are walking to his car, someone whose face looks vaguely familiar approaches with a smile. I start to ask what he wants but Brett grabs my arm and begins dragging me full force to the car. The man follows right on our heels and I see he has a recording device of some kind in his hand, holding it up as he begins to say, "You're Victor Howard, right? Just a moment of your time!"

Brett pushes me into the passenger's seat before I've fully realized what just happened and he whips around, glaring. "No fucking comment," he says, before getting into the car and speeding out of the parking lot.

My heart is galloping at a steady hundred miles an hour. "W-w-what—"

"Craig something-or-other," he hisses. "He's from one of the local news stations."

I swallow hard. "I d-don't understand…"

"It's a small town, Vic. The media must have gotten wind of it and want to find out more."

No. It still isn't processing. Me, the guy who has flown under the radar all his life, the designated driver, the nobody…and now the news wants my story? This confuses me more than anything else, but I can tell Brett is livid.

"They'll turn this into a fucking sideshow," he growls. "For you and Callie both. Don't talk to them, no matter what, got it?"

"But..." If I tell my side of the story, wouldn't that be a good thing?

"*No matter what,* Vic. My dad is going to tell you the same thing." At the next stoplight, he looks over at me. "Promise?"

I slump back into my seat and close my eyes, unsure what to do with the overwhelming sense of nausea overtaking me. "I promise."

Friday morning, Craig something-or-other is back. This time with a camera in hand. He doesn't approach us, but I see him from across the parking lot snapping pictures while I stare, dumbfounded. Brett shoves me to his side and I duck my head as we hurry to the school, taking solace inside where—I'm guessing, hoping—a reporter can't follow. Mr. Mason told me the same thing Brett did: not to talk to him under any circumstance, and that he's probably been to my house and doesn't yet realize where I'm staying. That could change soon.

I am beyond exhausted. I sit numbly through classes. By the time we get to lunch, I have to quietly excuse myself and slip outside to be alone. Not that Brett listens. He follows and sits next to me on the bench and asks me what's wrong while I'm slouching forward, pressing my palms into my eyes, trying not to cry.

Brett says nothing but I feel his hand on my back, reassuring. My whole body aches from the built-up tension. I thought with the DNA test cleared, this would be over. Yet I feel like it's only the beginning.

I tried to call Mom a few nights ago to tell her about the DNA results. She didn't answer. She didn't call me back.

Indifference: lack of interest, concern, or sympathy. Unimportance.

What is it they say? *The opposite of love is not hate, it's indifference.*

I wonder if Craig Something-or-Other has shown up there. If he's snapped pictures of "the rapist's mom" while she fled from her car to the house. If he asked her questions…if she answered them.

After school, I'm not feeling up to waiting around while Brett is at tennis practice. I would walk home, except I'm worried of what might be waiting there for me. An angry mother? A prying reporter? Instead I'll head to Brett's car and do some homework or play on my phone.

I haven't even reached two steps into the parking lot when an old blue sedan pulls up alongside me and the tinted window rolls down to reveal Autumn behind the steering wheel. I remember her threat about plowing me down with her car and go still, staring at her.

She says, "Get in."

"If I s-say no, are two g-guys in suits and sunglasses going to get out and m-make me?"

Autumn actually smirks. "No, just me. Come on."

This is all sorts of a bad idea, and yet I find myself circling around to the passenger's side door, opening it, getting in, and dropping my bag to the floorboard. Autumn waits for me to buckle up before driving off.

"W-where are we going?"

She keeps her eyes glued to the road. "Shut up and you'll find out."

I run my hands over my knees, swallowing past a dry throat. "I got into the c-car with you; the least you can do is t-tell me where you're taking me."

Autumn purses her lips. "And I appreciate your cooperation, but I'm not telling you anything. So either watch and see, or jump out at the next stoplight."

"I'll h-have you know that no one will pay my ransom if this is a k-kidnapping," I try to joke. Autumn's mouth actually twitches a little at the corners, like she's trying not to smile, but she doesn't reply.

You know, if she wanted to tie rocks to my ankles and throw me in the river, no one would even notice I was gone for at least twenty-four hours. More than enough time for her to drive to Mexico.

But Autumn doesn't take me to the river. She drives to a little town house complex where she parks in a spot assigned number forty-two and twists in her seat to look at me. "You tell anyone about this and you're dead. You got it?"

"Uh…o-okay. Where are we?"

"My house." Autumn gets out of the car and I follow suit, leaving my backpack behind. She lets us inside where we walk through a modestly furnished living room and upstairs to what has to be her bedroom. Autumn insists I go in first. I have no problem being invited into Autumn Dixon's room, but this isn't under the conditions I would have hoped for.

When I step inside, the first thing I see is Callie Wheeler sitting on the bed.

Immediately I freeze and try to back up. Autumn shuts the door and leans against it, effectively cornering me, preventing me from fleeing shy of throwing her aside or something. My heart leaps into my throat and I look from Callie to Autumn and back again. "W-w-what—"

Callie rises from the bed, holding out her hands. "Calm down, I promise this isn't anything bad."

"Well, my dad does have a chain saw in the patio storage," Autumn drawls. When neither of us laughs, she rolls her eyes. "Oh-kay, well, I'll be downstairs. You sure you're all right?"

She clearly isn't talking to me. Callie smiles a little and nods. Autumn slips out of the room and I find my feet itching to chase after her and demand to be taken home. "If th-they find out I'm here and there's still a temporary restraining order…"

Callie silences me with a raised hand again. "I'm really sorry we had to trick you here, Vic. I knew you wouldn't show up if she told you what was going on."

Got that right. I stare at her, wordless. Is this some kind of plot? Is Autumn downstairs calling the cops and telling them I'm here?

She wrings her hands together. "I just…I had to see you. I needed to apologize."

"A-apologize?"

"Things…moved really fast." She won't meet my eyes. "Autumn convinced me to tell my parents, and…the police were here and asking me questions, and they kept pushing. They wanted a name, any name. I was afraid if I didn't think of something to say, they wouldn't investigate at all and so—"

"So I was the scapegoat," I finish drily.

Callie lifts her eyes a little, shoulders slouched. "You were the only thing I remembered."

I want to be angry with her, and I can't manage it. I'm not Callie. I don't know what she went through those first few days, or what she's still going through. Not for a second do I think she named me out of malice, but because she felt it was the only choice she had. This is going to scar me until they find who really did it, yes.

But it's scarred Callie Wheeler for life.

"The lab results d-don't fully clear me," I point out, leaning back against the door. I feel like distance between us is good, so I refuse to move farther into the room. "S-so what makes you sure now that I, you know, didn't do it?"

Callie sits back down on the edge of the bed and hugs her knees to her chest. "I remember throwing up and you taking me upstairs. Then it gets kind of fuzzy...but the more I think about it, the more I remembered you leaving. Like, I remember opening my eyes and seeing you walk out the door. The next time I woke up..." She trails off and it's then that I notice how pale her face is, how accented the dark circles under her eyes are, and it's not because she isn't wearing makeup. She looks...haunted. "I couldn't see him..."

She leaves it at that and I don't push. Honestly, I'm not sure I want to know all the details. "I'm s-sorry, Callie."

She shakes her head. "I don't know why you're apologizing."

"B-because…I should have stayed. All of this could have been avoided." If I'd found another girl at the party to look after her or something, anything. This is just as much my fault as it is anyone's. Callie doesn't correct me, either. She just looks at me with sympathy and regret because undoubtedly she wishes I had stayed, too.

"Everyone involved has regrets," she says quietly. "I regret drinking. You regret leaving. Autumn regrets not going. She was supposed to come with me, you know, and when she found out what happened…she hasn't stopped blaming herself. In reality, it's no one's fault but the person who did it."

"A-and you're certain now that person wasn't me?" I have to ask, because this—her answer—could determine a lot in the coming weeks or months or even years.

Callie admits, "Completely? No. But it's a feeling, and I'm tentatively trying to go with it for now. Sorry, I'm afraid that's the best I can offer at this point. I'm looking at you and I just don't feel like you were capable of it."

Not the best response, but… "I'll take what I can get."

She brushes the long blond hair from her face and turns away, a haunted look passing over her eyes. "I think that's all any of us can do right now."

Autumn drives me home without saying a word. I can't think of anything to say to her, either, so I don't bother trying to make small talk beyond giving her directions. She pulls up to the curb—where there are no reporters waiting for me, thank God—outside my house and stares straight ahead. "I guess I owe you an apology, too."

The sullenness of her tone almost makes me smile. "No, you don't. Y-you didn't know."

She presses her lips together thoughtfully and then turns off the engine. When I get out of the car, she does, too, and begins to follow. I don't ask what she's doing because it's obvious: she plans on coming in with me. Holy shit. I've never brought a girl home. Mom will still be at work so it'll just be us, but still…

I let us inside, heart thudding loudly against my ribs. The living room seems like as safe a bet as any, so I gesture for her to make herself comfortable. "S-something to drink?"

"I'm fine." She toes off her shoes and sinks down into the couch, one leg tucked up beneath her. Still nothing as to why she followed me inside. Brett has been my only houseguest, and he's easy; he'll help himself to whatever he wants. Autumn, though, looks around the living room in mild curiosity and I'm stuck standing there awkwardly, unsure of how to proceed. "Jesus," she finally says. "Stop hovering. You're making me nervous."

Muttering an apology, I quickly sit on the other side of the couch. "Um…"

Autumn doesn't look at me. "I'm going to find him, you

know. I'm going to find whoever did this to Callie and I'm going to ruin him. I don't care if it was you or someone else, I'll find out."

Some of the rigidity slips out of my shoulders. If this is what Autumn wants to talk about, I can listen. She always appears to be ready to burst at the seams, and I can't help but wonder if she has anyone else to talk to about it. Certainly what she says to Callie will be more on the supportive side and less angry, and besides that…I can't shake what Callie said to me about Autumn blaming herself for this. "I want to find him, too. I want to help. If the cops can't do anything else, th-then maybe you and I can."

She scoffs. "Working with the rapist suspect to find the real rapist, huh? There's an idea."

"C-can I ask you something?"

"I guess."

"You're taking this whole thing really personally. I m-mean, she's your friend, but—"

"She's my best friend," Autumn corrects. "When she first moved here, she could have easily fallen in with the popular crowd. And she started to, initially. Then she saw some girl being a bitch to me in the halls every day for no reason, and she ditched them, just like that, and took my side. She's the sweetest, most loyal girl you could imagine… but she's also really gullible. I wanted to keep her safe, and I guess I'm just pissed at myself for failing." Autumn shifts to pull her other leg up and turns to face me fully. A frown twitches at her brow. "If this is question time, it's my turn. Why aren't you, like, pissed off? I'd be pissed if someone accused me of rape."

I smooth my hands over the tops of my thighs. "I-I don't know? 'Cause I g-guess it'd be worse to be Callie, so I don't feel like I should complain."

"Just because one person is going through something painful doesn't mean what you're experiencing is somehow less relevant." Autumn twirls a strand of hair around her finger. Her nails are painted gray and filed to short, slightly dulled points. Somehow it suits her. All claws and fangs but not as sharp as she first appears. I smile a little.

"I'm n-not mad. Not to say I'm thrilled, either, but I'm trying my best to get through it."

Autumn draws one knee up and rests her chin on top of it. "Tell me about it. Like, tell me what you've been going through."

"I d-don't think you want to hear it."

"Yes, I do. I want to know what it's been like for you."

I can't begin to understand why she's curious about my situation. Because she feels somehow responsible for me being in this position? I really hope that isn't the case. But if she wants to know… "My mom doesn't believe I'm innocent," I murmur.

Her eyebrows shoot up. "Why?"

"N-no idea. Just doesn't."

"That's seriously fucked up. What else?"

Honestly, I don't know where to start. I feel like complaining is the last thing I should be doing. But Autumn is waiting for an explanation and so I give her one, maybe minus some of the details, but I tell her about the night the detectives came and took me to the clinic. I tell her about staying at Brett's because Mom can't stand to look at me, about Aaron and his friends cornering me in the bathroom…and I tell her about Craig Something-or-Other because I feel that part is important. If he's coming to talk to me, he might be going after Callie, too.

"Oh," Autumn says after a moment. "Craig Roberts. Yeah. I know who that is. Skinny guy, dark hair, kinda hot?"

"Uh, I guess so."

"Definitely a reporter. Callie hasn't said anything about him showing up at her house, but she's had a few smaller journalists from the newspaper trying to get her to sit down and 'share her story' or whatever." She makes a face. "Which is kind of dumb considering, you know, she was just raped and we don't even know who did it. They probably want to make an example out of her for why people shouldn't drink at parties or something."

"Maybe," I agree, almost amused at the way she can keep a conversation going without my having to say much. It's kind of nice. I prefer listening to her over talking.

"Well, your friend Brett is probably right about not talking to him. Newspeople never report things as they get them. They'll twist your words around and edit the hell out of them to make you out to be some terrible person." She shrugs.

"And th-that would bother you?"

"If it's not true, then yeah, it would bother me."

I asked Callie earlier, and for some reason Autumn's opinion matters to me, too, so I feel compelled to repeat the question: "Are you positive now it wasn't me?"

Autumn examines her nails. I find she does that a lot when she doesn't want to make eye contact. "Honestly? No. I'm still half-and-half. But Callie is starting to think you're innocent, and if you're going to help me try to find who did it..."

I open my mouth to say something when my phone rings. Autumn is silent while I pull it out of my pocket and look at it. Amjad. I've never turned down a call from him, so I hold up a finger to let Autumn know I'll be a sec and answer, "H-hello?"

"Vic," Amjad greets. He sounds...weird. Stuffy, maybe. "Can you work tonight, maybe?"

I glance at the time. It's five now, and the shop stays open until eleven. It's a longer shift than I'm used to working and I've never done it all by myself, but my desperate need to never let Amjad down rears its head. "Y-yeah, of course."

"You are wonderful. Thank you." He apologizes a few times before I get him to hang up, and then I rise to my feet with a sigh.

"Um...I g-got called in to work. I should go."

Autumn blinks and stands up. "I didn't know you had a job. Where at?"

"J-just a few blocks away. Rick's Convenience Store?"

"Oh, I know where that is." She pulls the keys from her pocket and inclines her chin. I hesitate, unsure if this means she's offering me a ride or if I need to retrieve my bike, but she isn't saying good-bye, so...

We pile back into her car and she drives me up to Rick's,

pulling to a stop just outside the door. I offer to run inside and grab her a slushie, but Autumn insists she needs to get back home and she'll take me up on the offer some other time. I get out of the car and watch her drive away, feeling oddly alone without her presence.

With a sigh, I open the door and step inside. Amjad is behind the counter and I don't have to look twice to realize he isn't feeling well. "W-what's wrong?"

"Ebola," he laments. "Maybe scarlet fever. Something deadly."

I raise an eyebrow. He beckons me behind the counter to begin showing me the details I'm unfamiliar with: how to lock up the store, how to close down the register and put the money in the safe, how to set the alarm on the building. I already have my own key, but this will be the first time I use it, and I'm already panicking a little and trying to write the details down so I don't forget. What if I mess something up or set off the alarm or something?

But Amjad seems to have the utmost faith in me. I think that makes me feel worse. He says the stock is all done so all I have to do is man the register and handle customers. When he leaves me alone, the silence of the small store is enough to almost send me into an anxiety attack. What do I do if someone I know walks in? Can Amjad see me through the cameras to tell if I'm screwing something up?

I sit behind the counter, stomach in knots. For the first thirty minutes, the only customers I see are those who pull up to the gas pumps outside and pay with their cards directly at the kiosks. Gotta love modern technology.

By six, the evening crowd has begun to descend from downtown Sacramento as a majority of offices close for the weekend. Most of the people who come into the store are there for sodas, beer, energy drinks, and the occasional lottery ticket, and thus far, no one I recognize has wandered in.

I text Brett to let him know I'm at work and not at home, since by now he'll be leaving tennis practice and wondering where the hell I am. ***I'll walk to your place after work or I can go home***, I tell him, not wanting him to feel obligated to come get me. But he texts back, ***Going out with some of the guys then I'll be there around eight***, and I have to smile a little.

And at exactly eight o'clock, I hear the door chime and look up from the game on my phone, expecting to see Brett there and—

"Evening, Vic," Craig Roberts says.

My spine goes rigid and I cram my phone into my pocket like I'm doing something I shouldn't be, even though I'm not, and do my best to keep a straight face. "W-welcome to Rick's. Can I help you?"

"Man, it was hard to find out you even worked here." He glances around and approaches the counter. "No one I talked to even knew you had a job."

One corner of my mouth twitches. "Sir, if you're not going to buy anything, I'll have to ask you to l-leave."

Craig arches one of his perfectly shaped brows—I bet he gets them waxed—and turns around. He surveys the area briefly and grabs a package of powdered doughnuts from a nearby rack. "Guess I can screw the diet for one night. So, tell me about the party, Vic."

He tosses the doughnuts onto the counter and my eyes don't leave him. What do I do? I'm not in a position where I can run away, and maybe he was counting on that. I also don't have Amjad to hide behind. I'm pretty sure Amjad could take this guy in a fight easily. "I'm n-not interested in discussing anything about my personal life with you, Mr. Roberts."

He holds up his hands defensively. "Hey, I'm with you, kid. I thought you'd be glad to tell your side of the story, especially since several people are getting Callie Wheeler's."

My heart stops for a beat. He's lying. He's probably lying. Callie wouldn't talk to any reporters; I'm sure her parents wouldn't allow it. Autumn would have told me earlier, right? "I don't want to talk to you."

"Is it true she picked you out of a lineup by the sound of your voice?" he presses. "What about when she returns to school, what happens then? Any idea?"

My blood is slowly starting to boil. Sometimes, I wish I were the violent sort just to get people like him to shut the hell up. "G-get out, please."

"I'm still a customer, you know." He points at the doughnuts.

"And I have the right to refuse service to assholes," I say icily. "P-please leave."

This time, Craig's smile fades, darkens to something that makes my stomach roll. "I'm trying to help you out here. Getting on my bad side isn't the best idea."

I've got nothing left to say so I simply stare at him,

halfway contemplating hitting the alarm under the counter that's meant to alert police of a robbery. Too bad I'd probably be the one they threw into the back of their car.

Craig takes the hint, at least. He pulls a business card out of his wallet and deposits it on the counter along with a couple of dollars, says, "Keep the change," grabs his donuts, and leaves.

I slouch back in my chair, hands clammy and trembling. Visible effort is required to pull myself away from the edge of having an anxiety attack. Craig's card stares up at me from the counter and I almost throw it away. Almost. Something tells me I should save it, just in case, so I slip it into my back pocket just as Brett wanders into the store.

"Sorry I'm late. Stopped to grab a bite to eat with Mitch and Connor and we lost track of time." He doesn't look at me immediately, but rather heads to the slushie machine and grabs the biggest cup we have. Cherry slushies are his Kryptonite, I swear. When he returns to the counter, he takes one glance at me and frowns. "You look like you saw a ghost."

"Craig Roberts dropped by," I say, and watch the color drain from Brett's face.

"Goddammit. What'd he say?"

"Said it w-wasn't a good idea for me to make an enemy of him." I slouch forward and rest my elbows on the counter with a sigh. "He's probably right, but I d-don't think telling him my side is going to help."

"It won't. He'll spin it to suit whatever angle he's trying to get at." Brett pushes a hand through his hair with a sigh.

"Sorry. I should've gotten here earlier."

I shake my head. Can't exactly expect someone to be with me every second of every day. I have to be capable of dealing with things myself. "I th-think I handled it. He said that Callie had given him her s-side of the story. Do you think she did?"

A frown pulls at Brett's face as he sips his slushie. "I don't know. I mean, if she wanted to still press charges despite the whole no-evidence thing, then going to the media would be a good way to get exposure for the case and pressure the police into doing something."

I desperately want to tell him about my earlier conversation with Callie and why I don't think she actually talked to Craig. And I would, if my lawyer were anyone other than Brett's dad.

I can't even talk to my own best friend. Remaining silent on so much is starting to make my heart hurt.

Chapter Nine

I don't pretend to understand the point of going to the restraining order hearing the following Monday, but Mr. Mason insists it'll look better on me if I do. He has me dress in the nicest outfit I own, which is left over from a wedding I went to with Mom a year ago. The black slacks and button-up shirt's sleeves are just on the short side. The sleeves, at least, I can roll up to my elbows and still look nice. There isn't much I can do about the pants except wear some of Brett's black socks and hope no one notices. I tried to slick my hair back and tame the curls a little, but there's really no helping that.

I'm a little surprised—pleasantly so—that Mr. Mason lets Brett come along. I have no clue where to go or what to do when we reach the courthouse, but this is familiar territory to both of them. We get through security without incident and Mr. Mason leads us to department thirty-three, where we sit outside the courtroom among other groups of people. Only then does the anxiety start to gnaw at me and I find myself sinking into my chair.

Brett leans over and asks, "You okay?"

"I-It's a lot of people," I point out quietly, like someone will take offense if they overhear me. "I d-don't see Callie."

"She probably won't be here." He pats my arm. "More than likely, it'll be one of her parents or something. Or they could not show up at all."

Which makes this seem like a waste to me, but okay. At exactly 8:30 a.m., the courtroom doors open and we're allowed inside, crowding into the minimal seating of the room and waiting some more. Mr. Mason tries to explain how this process works, but the words seem to echo in my ears. The entire morning goes by in a blur, from one case called to the next. Eventually the sound of my name snaps me out of the fog. "Theresa and James Wheeler versus Victor Howard."

I stand up abruptly, unsure if I'm supposed to, and I see two people in the row in front of us do the same. They both turn to look at me, gazes lingering, and turn back only when the judge asks, "It looks like no further paperwork has been filed to proceed with this protective order?"

"No, Your Honor," Mrs. Wheeler says. "We'd like to hold off for now, at our daughter's insistence." Frankly, she doesn't sound happy about that. I wonder what Callie had to say to convince them.

The judge looks over the top of his glasses, eyebrows raised. "You're sure? If you decide to drop it now, you'll have to start over from scratch if you change your minds. Unless Mr. Howard is convicted, of course, in which case a criminal protective order will be established."

My ears have started to ring again. My hands are fisted so tightly that when Mr. Mason prompts me that we're good to leave the court, my fingers have gone numb. I heard what happened, and yet I still have to ask, "Is that good?"

"It's good," he assures me. We pass by the Wheelers as they're leaving, too, and I have to stop and look at them, desperate to just…go up and apologize. To tell them how sorry I am for what they're going through, and hoping that if maybe I let them put a face to my name, they won't see me as the enemy anymore. But Mr. Mason and Brett flank me on either side and Brett quietly says, "Don't," as they usher me down the hall. I look over my shoulder and as we round the corner, I see both the Wheelers watching me go.

I wonder if they see me as Vic, or as the monster who hurt their little girl.

The rest of Monday, Brett and I are allowed to stay home and sit in front of the TV with video games. Or rather—I sit in front of the TV with video games while Brett stresses himself sick over a college essay for Harvard and a report for English, which he insists matters even this late in the game because he refuses to graduate with anything less than a 4.0 average. I heard a saying in a TV show once: first you're a child prodigy, then you're a teenage genius…but by the time you're twenty, you're ordinary. Brett spent so long being labeled as gifted for his intelligence that I think people assumed it would always come easy for him. The older he gets, the less easy it is for him to stay on top.

Come Tuesday, we're right back at school and whatever sense of relief and calm I was experiencing after the hearing has long since faded. Maybe it was just the exhaustion talking that had me so out of it. Mrs. Mason suggested taking me to the doctor to see if they could give me anything, but that would require me to talk it over with Mom and I'm not sure if it's worth it.

When I get to school Tuesday morning, Autumn falls into step alongside me. Really, she came out of nowhere the moment Brett was out of sight. Was she following me or something? "Hey."

"Uh…hi." I stop to look at her. "W-what's up?"

She inclines her chin to look up at me as though that's the dumbest question I could have asked. "Nothing. I was just saying hi. How are you?"

It might just be me, but she seems awkward. "Fine, I g-guess. Everything okay?" Did something happen? Is Callie all right? Is Autumn all right?

She nudges my arm with her elbow to prompt me into walking again. Given the direction she's taking, I assume I'm accompanying her to class. How many tardies have I racked up in the last few weeks? I don't ask why she's making me late but I'm finding it hard to believe she wanted to come find me just…because. No one except Brett hangs out with me *just because.*

"Here's my class." Autumn stops outside her first period room and turns to face me. Her hair is tied up today, but there's so much of it that a few wavy auburn strands have escaped the confines of her hair band and are dangling around her face and shoulders.

She's so pretty.

"Okay. I guess I'll see you around." I take a step back, trying to look at this odd situation from an unbiased perspective. Not coming up with anything.

Autumn says, "Sure," and watches me start to leave. I see her mouth open as though to call for me, but it's too late. I've already turned around and bumped right into someone. Someone who isn't taller than me, but definitely more muscular.

"S-sorry," I manage.

The guy shoves me back a little, scowling. "Watch it." Then he looks me over as Autumn comes up to my side. I'm vaguely aware of the warmth of her hand on my arm, like an almost protective gesture.

"I s-said sorry," I mutter.

He narrows his eyes. "Hey, aren't you that guy?"

"Leave it alone, Marco," Autumn warns.

"This is him, isn't it?" His dark eyes flicker from me to Autumn and back again. "You bothering her, asshole?"

My height is about the only thing I've got on my side. I straighten up as best as I can, trying not to shrink in on myself or inch behind Autumn. I've never been in a fight and I don't ever want to be. "N-no, I w-was just—"

"J-j-just wh-what, genius?" Marco sneers. "You've got a lot of nerve even coming to school after what you did."

Autumn's grip on my arm tightens. "He didn't do anything. They cleared him." Which is only a partial truth, but that's okay. No one needs to know the details.

Marco's attention is momentarily diverted. "Oh, you're on his side now? Did you get drunk and spread your legs, too?"

Impulse: a sudden strong and unreflective urge or desire to act. Also: what drives me to punch Marco.

I've never hit anyone before in my life. This time the action follows before I even know what I'm doing and my fist is connecting with his face and…it's nothing like the movies. There is no slow motion and he doesn't stagger back and hit the floor with the force of my swing. If anything, it snaps his head to one side while sending a surge of pain where my knuckles connected with his jawbone straight up my arm and into my shoulder.

Autumn says, "Fuck," and I'd say that about sums it up accurately.

Marco knows how to throw a punch better than I do. He hits me square in the mouth and I slam into the wall before going down. Before I can even see straight again, there are already people beginning to crowd around us to see what's going on. No one makes a move to help.

No one except Autumn. She puts herself between Marco and me, shoulders squared. Marco wipes at his mouth. Did

I make him bleed, at least? I hope I did. How embarrassing.

"Move," he snaps.

"You touch him again and I'll kick your Gucci-wearing ass into being held back another year," she snarls in a tone not unlike the one she first used when flooring me on the concrete. That tone makes me nervous and a little quivery all at the same time...as long as it's not directed at me.

Whether it's because he knows she'll do it or because he has issues with hitting a girl in front of everyone, Marco just scowls and pushes past her to head into class. Though not before stopping to look down at me, still dazed on the ground. "Guess what they say is true. Like father, like son."

Huh? What does that even mean?

He disappears into class and the crowd disperses with disappointed grumbles while Autumn turns to help me up. "What an asshole. Oh, you're bleeding." She frowns, reaching up to touch her fingers to my cheek. Yeah, and bleeding bad enough that the taste is flooding my mouth and I don't dare say anything. Instead I duck my head and move away, jogging down the hall for the boys' bathroom.

The last bell has already rung, so I'm alone. Thank God. I hit the nearest sink and spit blood into it. No teeth lost? Awesome, I'll consider that a win. Closer inspection shows the blood coming from my lower lip, which must've been sliced open on my teeth.

I watch my reflection in the water-spotted mirror; my sharp features look gaunt and hollow in this lighting. Blood wells in my mouth again, dripping from my lip partway down my chin to the porcelain. My first fight. If you can call it that. Whether it was him talking about Autumn like that, or somehow implying it was Callie's own fault that she was raped, or just an accumulation of everything that's happened finally sending me into attack mode, I have no idea.

"Vic?"

Autumn's face appears in the mirror as she leans into the bathroom. I don't turn around. "I'm f-fine."

The door creaks open and then closed. Autumn glances around to make sure we're alone. "You totally dripped blood on the way here. Let me see. Are you gonna need stitches?"

I don't have much choice but to turn around and let her look at my face. She heaves a sigh and grabs a few paper towels, wetting them under the faucet before pressing them gently to my lip. The chill burns but in a pleasant way. I close my eyes.

"Don't let him get to you," Autumn murmurs. "I mean, I know I was a bitch at first, too, and I'm sorry for that. People like to lash out without knowing all the details."

I can't say much with the paper towels half in my mouth, so I don't try.

She continues, "What did he mean, anyway? Does he know your dad?"

Deep breath. This time, I want to answer so I pull back, taking the towels from her to hold them myself so I can speak. "No. I don't even k-know him. He was, like, a one-night stand or s-something." As far as I know, anyway. Mom never wanted to talk about him. She never had photos, never had stories.

"Oh." Autumn tucks her thumbnail between her teeth and chews on it worriedly. That can't be good for her polish. "So, like, he took off when you were a baby or something?"

Something in the casual way she asks such a personal question, like she's talking about the weather, almost makes me laugh. It gets a smile out of me, at least. Gingerly and slowly I take the paper from my lip; it feels like it's stopped gushing everywhere, anyway. "My m-mom never tells me anything about him. My aunt once t-told me that I looked like him. That's all I know." Aunt Sue had only smiled when I tried inquiring further, and insisted that she'd already said too much.

Autumn sighs. "God, that'd drive me crazy."

"I'm used to it."

"My dad isn't really my dad. He's my stepdad. But he's been around as long as I can remember." She shrugs. "And my birth dad is probably on a street corner trying to skim money for heroin for all I know, so..."

It hurts to smile as much as I am. "Interesting."

"Is it? Why do you think that's so funny?"

"No reason." I duck my head. "You're just...weird. Good weird, not like..."

She smirks. "Heroin-addict weird?"

"P-pretty much." I tilt my head. "So why did you actually c-come find me this morning?"

It's Autumn's turn to look a little sheepish, but she plays it off by rolling her eyes and smiling and turning in a full circle while staring at the ceiling. "I don't know. I guess I wanted to see how it went at the hearing yesterday and make sure you were all right."

I lick my lip absently. The metallic taste is still present, but not as bad as before. "Still alive and kicking and not behind bars."

She laughs. "You know, you've hardly stuttered at all during this conversation."

I pause, considering that. She's right. "Maybe Marco knocked it out of me." When she shoves my arm and rolls her eyes, I laugh a little. "It's better when I'm calm. It gets w-worse when I'm anxious."

Autumn says, "Ahh," like this explains every mystery in the universe. "And what makes you so calm around me, Vic?"

I don't know how to answer that. At all. My face grows hot and I press the paper towels back to my mouth for no reason other than it keeps me from having to fumble for words. I shrug. She smiles. For once, there is no sadness or anger or anything extreme. Just the softness of her lips curved up so that it makes her eyes squinch at the corners. I could get used to a smile like that.

"Come on." Autumn reaches for my free hand to tug me toward the door. "Your backpack is in the hall. I'll walk you to class this time."

"She walked you to class?" Brett laughs on our way home. "Woo, that's like, a fifth of the way to first base. Congrats."

"Th-that's not the point of the story." I recount to him what happened with Marco, glossing over the details of my miserable defeat. I mainly want to tell him about what Marco said about my dad to see what he thinks. The puzzled frown that crosses his face says he's just as perplexed as I am.

"Your mom never talks about your old man, does she?"

"Not at all," I agree. "It's always been a touchy subject."

"Then maybe there's something she isn't telling you. Why don't you ask her?"

"Right. 'Cause that always goes over well."

"Never know if you don't try, Vic."

He doesn't attempt to take me home, but later that evening after he's helped me struggle through homework, he tosses me my phone and says, "Call her."

I stare at the cell like I'm worried it'll grow fangs. This is not a conversation I want to have with my mother, but my curiosity is going to get the best of me, and maybe doing it on the phone is better than dealing with her possibly having a breakdown in person. My thumb traces over the screen slowly. Brett sighs, plucks the phone from my grasp, dials Mom's number, and hands it back.

Before I can really process this, Mom's voice on the other line says, "Hello?" My mouth immediately refuses to cooperate. Mom sighs. "Victor, hello? What is it?"

Brett jabs me in the ribs and I jerk, straightening my spine. "H-hey, uh, sorry. I wanted to l-let you know the hearing went well yesterday."

"That's good," she says distantly.

"And…I j-just wanted to ask you something."

Mom is silent.

"Um, about my dad…?"

This time Mom inhales slowly and exhales a sigh right into the mouthpiece of the phone. "You know I don't like talking about your father."

"Y-yeah. I know. It's just…" I glance at Brett, who gestures for me to keep going. If I tell Mom it has something to do with everything that's going on, she'll never tell me anything. "We're doing this p-project at school about our parents. Like, ancestry stuff, so…"

Mom sighs again, more irritated than wary this time. "I have some of my family tree stuff in the garage. I'll dig it out and we can go over it."

"And—"

"I don't know anything about your father's side of the family." Her voice is short, clipped, signaling the end of the conversation. "I have some things in the oven. I need to go."

I've barely said "Okay" before she hangs up, and I look to Brett helplessly.

"I'm guessing that didn't go well?" he asks.

"The usual. She said she doesn't know anything about him and then hung up on me."

"Ouch." He runs a hand over his hair. "What about your aunt? Can you ask her? Do you have her number?"

"No. B-but I can get it." It'll be in Mom's phone, so all I have to do is go through it while she's preoccupied. Which shouldn't be difficult. My mother is a creature of habit. I know that when she gets home from work in the evenings, she'll make herself dinner and maybe put something in the oven to bake. Then she'll go upstairs and take a shower for the fifteen to twenty minutes her baking takes. That would probably be the best time for me to sneak in. She isn't likely to give me Aunt Sue's number if I ask nicely, not if she knows I'm looking for info related to my dad.

Not that I tell this plan to Brett. We've always been pretty open about our home lives, but I've spent years downplaying what happens between Mom and me. Really, it's mostly out of embarrassment. Brett's parents are pretty great. To me, at least. I see them lean on Brett pretty hard to be perfect at everything and remain at the top of the class, but I'm not their kid so my grades don't matter.

Then there's my mother, who plays Friday night bingo, bakes away her anxiety and stress, has worked at the same dead-end office job processing student loans to barely make ends meet—not because she couldn't go elsewhere, but because she doesn't like change—and who one day decided her son was a hassle instead of the little boy she was proud of.

The next day, Brett tells me he'll be late at tennis practice and tosses me his car keys to go home. Awesome. I'll wait until Mom shows up at six o'clock and hide away in my room where she isn't likely to bother me. The next hour is a waiting game. I hear her in the kitchen, making something to eat and, eventually, she walks down the hall toward her room. At that point I leave my door ajar so I can hear when the shower water goes on.

I wait five more minutes to make sure she's in there

and inch down the hall, heart threatening to leap out of my throat. I should've waited until Brett was here to do this with me. At least if we got caught, he could schmooze his way out of the situation. If Mom catches me going through her phone—I don't want to think about how that would play out.

Mom's curtains are pulled shut, leaving her room dark save for the sliver of light escaping from her cracked bathroom door. I have no idea where she keeps her phone and for a moment, panic overtakes me. What if she keeps it in there with her?

Then I spot it on her nightstand next to her purse. Bingo. I glance once at the bathroom and then activate her touchscreen. She has two unread text messages from Ruthie Biggs. My stomach flip-flops. If I read them, will she know I was going through her phone? My thumb hovers over the notification. She can't prove anything, and there might be answers in there about what all Mom has shared with Ruthie that Aaron might have found out. Most parents, I'm willing to bet, aren't secretive about their phones, and if he wanted to dig up dirt about me…

Ruthie's messages were sent two minutes ago. I go ahead and open them, figuring I don't have a lot to lose anyway. Apparently Mom is the sort to clear out her texts regularly, so there isn't much for me to scroll through. But what I can see implies Ruthie does know about me being a suspect. Mom texted her the other day, in fact:

dna tests came back negative.

Nothing in response, so I'm guessing they talked directly. Following those texts are a few of little interest. Chatter about the news, the hot weather, bingo. Then—

He asked about Don today

I read over it a few times to make sure there isn't any other way I can take that. It could be irrelevant. Even my dad's name has never been common knowledge.

Ruthie's responses:

What did you say?

Maybe it's time you sat him down and told him

Told him. Told *me*. Told me what? Damn it, if I could have waited until after Mom messaged her back, I might have more information. What's worse, why does someone not even related to us know about my dad and I don't?

Don. My dad's name is Don.

As I look up Aunt Sue's number and scribble it on the back of my hand, I'm idly wondering what kind of person he is. I used to make up stories in my head. Like, what if my dad was a Secret Service agent who loved my mom but had to leave her because his work was too dangerous? What if he was a marine who died in the line of duty? I lifted my dad up on a pedestal until I was dumb enough to voice these ideas to Mom. She shot them down quickly with a disgusted look and a curt, "Your father was no hero."

Was, she said. So then I wondered if he had died some other way. A drug addict? Alcoholic? Did he just take off when he found out she was pregnant?

I try to place Mom's phone back exactly as I found it before slipping silently out of her room and heading for Brett's car. I make it back to school in record time and wait in the parking lot. Practice should be over, but Brett always lingers around and takes his time to chat with the guys, so I'd say I have another fifteen to twenty minutes. Which means I'm pulling out my phone and entering Aunt Sue's number. The line rings four times before going to voicemail. Maybe she screens her calls; I doubt she has my number.

"Um… Hey, Aunt Sue. It's V-Victor. I was j-just…calling to talk." Pause. "I had a few questions I thought…you know, maybe you could answer?" I add my number, thank her, and hang up. Part of me expects to get a call from Mom, screaming at me for messing with her phone, but no such call comes. I've done a few sneaky things over the years, namely by saying I'm staying at Brett's house when I'm actually going somewhere else with him. But I can honestly say I've never gone through my mother's things or invaded her privacy.

I'm so engrossed in the phone that I jump when Brett knocks on the driver's side window. I unlock the doors and scoot to the passenger's seat while he gets in beside me. "Sorry, spacing out."

"Clearly." He starts the car and shoves his tennis bag into the backseat. "Did you get your aunt's number?"

"Yeah, but she didn't answer."

Just as the words leave my mouth, my phone goes off. It rings so rarely that the sound startles me. Brett never calls; he always texts, so that makes the ringtone all the more alien.

"Dude, answer it," Brett says.

I quickly swipe my thumb across the screen and bring it to my ear. "H-hello?"

"Hey, it's your favorite auntie," Aunt Sue chimes on the other end. Something she's said to me before but has never made much sense. I can count on one hand the number of occasions we've spent time together or spoken without my mother around to be the focus of our attention. Not to mention she's my *only* aunt.

"Hi," I respond awkwardly, wishing Brett wasn't here to see how dumb I am at this. "S-sorry to bother you."

"You aren't bothering me, honey," she insists. I've never been able to tell if Aunt Sue is genuine in how sweetly she speaks to people or if it's an act. I hated it when I was little. The older I got, the more I kind of craved it, though, since Mom grew to be so cold. "Just making dinner for the cats. They're on an all-raw-food diet now, did your mom tell you that? Makes their coats look amazing."

"Oh." I forgot. Mom said Aunt Sue has a dozen cats. I wonder if she speaks to them the way she speaks to me.

"Enough of that, though. What did you want to ask me?"

I can't do this with Brett sitting right here, staring at me. I get out of the car, shut the door, and lean back against it. "It's sort of…p-personal. It's about my dad."

Aunt Sue is silent.

"M-Mom has never said anything about him, and I'm almost eighteen now and I j-just—"

"Victor, sweetheart," Aunt Sue gently interrupts. "I'm not so sure you really want information on your father. He wasn't a good person."

"I th-think that's for me to decide," I insist. "As soon as I-I'm eighteen, I c-can look for him on my own. Mom won't tell me anything. You k-know she won't." The words are becoming thick in my throat, ungainly on my tongue. I'm so tired of being kept in the dark.

But Aunt Sue isn't swayed. She sighs, heavy but determined. "I'm really sorry, Victor, but this is a conversation your mom needs to have with you. It's not my place."

My jaw clenches. I close my eyes. "I'll talk to you later, Aunt Sue."

"Victor…" Another sigh, but she doesn't push. "I'll talk to you soon."

I hang up and give myself some time to breathe and calm down. When I get back in the car, Brett only looks at me in sympathy. He had to have heard my half of the conversation through the window.

"Sorry, man."

Shaking my head, I sink down in the seat and fixate on my reflection in the window. Every time I look at myself anymore, I see less and less of Mom and more of a stranger no one will explain to me.

Chapter Ten

Autumn is standing by my locker Friday morning. She doesn't even wait for Brett and me to separate before approaching, which means Brett is giving me the most bizarre, confused look as she pushes away from the lockers and waves in my direction. "Vic!"

My cheeks grow warm at the thought of what ideas must be running through Brett's head right now. "Uh, hi."

"I really need to just get your number so we stop being late for class." She sighs. Only then does she pause and glance at Brett, offer him a half smile, and say, "Hey."

Brett's eyebrows lift. "Hello."

Autumn turns her attention back to me. "Anyway—so yesterday afternoon, I cornered Marco, right?"

Oh, God.

"First, I found out he was at that party...though he swears he didn't see anything. And I made him elaborate on what he said to you."

I try not to laugh at the image of broad-shouldered Marco cowering from Autumn. Not that I can blame him. "Okay."

She talks with her hands, I realize. She gestures at nothing in particular, putting expression behind her words with nothing more than a wave of her fingers. "Right, so he said he heard it from Aaron Biggs. He's the one who hosted the party, isn't he?"

My stomach sinks. "Y-yeah, he is..."

"And his mother is best friends with Vic's mom," Brett points out. "They talk a lot."

"Obviously *too* much." Autumn reaches out to fix the collar of my shirt as though it's nothing, completely oblivious to the way butterflies begin to dance in my chest. "I just thought you should know. I have to get to class. Oh—give me your hand."

Puzzled, I extend my left hand. Autumn yanks a pen out of her back jeans pocket, takes my hand, and begins to scribble digits on the back of it. I look to Brett with widened eyes. Is Autumn seriously giving me her number? Not asking for mine in the off chance she needs me for something, but legitimately *giving me* her number? When she pulls back, she nods once and smiles.

I stare at her writing, uncertain. "What's this for?"

"You mentioned wanting to help me find the person

who hurt Callie, right? So…I'll talk to you later."

Then she's scooping up her backpack and jogging down the hall to get to class just as the first bell rings. I look to Brett again, who is staring straight at me. He asks, "What the hell was that?"

I reply, "No idea. D-do I call her…?"

"Uh, *yeah*. She gave you her digits. No chick has ever done that with you."

"Now?" I ask, realizing what a dumb question it is the second it leaves my lips. Of course not *right* now, she's in class. But later. I have permission from Autumn to call her. To talk on the phone. Not just text or whatever, but talk. The idea is mind-boggling. Would Mr. Mason consider this some form of possible entrapment? Somehow I don't think Autumn would be helping me against guys like Marco if she was entirely convinced I was guilty, especially if she's saying she wants my help. Besides, there's no restraining order, so that whole no-contact thing with Callie or her family is null and void.

Brett is unnaturally quiet while we head down the hall. Quieter still during lunch. He eats but he's looking around as though searching for someone, and it isn't until I notice him staring over my shoulder that I turn and realize who it is. Aaron. The one responsible for rumors about my dad being spread around, and probably the one who began informing others that I was even a suspect in Callie's case.

I look back at Brett, whose frown has creased the middle of his brow. I know that look. It's the same look he wore in seventh grade when kids teased me about my stuttering.

The next day, those same kids found roaches in their bagged lunches. Brett was sneaky. He never let anyone bother me and get away with it, and yet his approach was always indirect, untraceable. He isn't the type to often go after people directly. This time, though, Brett slides away from the table to take his tray and dump it. I scramble to my feet to follow after him, still cramming french fries into my mouth.

Aaron doesn't look at us as we walk by and Brett says nothing. We slip out of the cafeteria and into the quad, heading for the parking lot. I ask, "What are we doing?" and receive silence in response.

Brett searches the cars one at a time and ducks down against a black four-door, making himself comfortable on the asphalt. I stare at him until he grabs my wrist to yank me down beside him. And we wait. For what, I don't know. Brett keeps his eyes glued on a white Chevy truck just barely in our line of sight. I feel like I know that car, but I can't be sure.

Eventually, we hear footsteps. I catch sight of Aaron opening the door to the truck and sliding inside. My palms are sweating. Brett smirks. "He always comes out here to sneak a cigarette after lunch. Lean against the driver's side door, would you?" is all the explanation he gives me before he's on his feet and heading for the truck.

I should ask questions, but Brett isn't giving me much of a chance. Aaron's window is cracked slightly and a subtle plume of smoke drifts from the opening. We're approaching from behind so by the time he spots us in the rearview mirrors and starts to open his door, I've thrown myself against it and Brett is getting in on the passenger's side.

"What the hell?" Aaron starts. I lean my weight into the door until it snaps fully shut, and then twist around to look as Brett grabs a fistful of Aaron's hair and shoves him face-first against the steering wheel.

"Brett—"

Brett silences me with a look. He leans in to peer at Aaron, expression dark. "Hey, buddy. So, we've been hearing some unsettling rumors that seem to have originated from you. Want to explain that to me?"

Aaron tries to twist free, but Brett is crowding him in the driver's side seat and Aaron is trying not to drop his lit cigarette on himself or the floor. "Screw you, man, let go!"

Brett takes a deep breath and for a second, I think he might let Aaron go. And he does. Sort of. His grip relaxes just enough that Aaron starts to lean back…and then Brett slams his head back to the steering wheel, making it honk abruptly. "Try again."

"Fuck!" He tries to clamp a hand over his face. His nose is bleeding. Oh, God, please tell me Brett didn't break his nose. I grasp the door handle, preparing myself to wrench it open and put a stop to this before it spirals out of control, except Aaron is already blurting out, "My mom, okay?! Her room is right by mine. I hear her talking to Vic's mom all the time!"

Although Brett's expression doesn't soften, he does let go and slump back in the passenger's seat with his hands in his lap. "And what have you overheard, exactly?"

Aaron sags against his seat. Blood trickles down between

his fingers. He tips his head back with a groan and I fumble in my backpack until I find a package of mini tissues that I slide in through the window. He grunts at me in appreciation and promptly shoves a Kleenex up his nostril. "Jesus, did you break my nose? Does it look broken?"

"No," Brett replies calmly, "but I'll make sure I do next time if you don't start talking."

He sighs heavily and stares up at the roof. "She told Mom about Vic getting taken in for testing by the doctors, and that he was a suspect."

"And you thought that information was appropriate to spread around?" Brett asks coldly.

"What the hell do I care?" He slides his gaze over to me, scowling. "I'm not here to protect a rapist. They should've thrown his ass in jail already. Serves him right; my brother's in deep shit because he supplied minors with alcohol but yet the rapist is running free."

I frown. Some thanks for giving him my tissues.

Brett says, "The evidence cleared Vic because he didn't do anything wrong. Though you're so bent on getting him in trouble that I almost wonder if *you* have something to hide."

At the accusation, Aaron's face blanches. "What—? I didn't touch her!"

"Or maybe someone you know did. You and your brother knew most of the people at that party." Brett crosses his arms.

We're getting off-topic. I don't care about who Aaron wants to accuse. I pull open his door so I can ask, "Wh-what did you overhear about my d-dad?"

Aaron's gaze slants in my direction, distaste written across his face. "I don't know. I only heard Mom's side of the conversation."

"And what was that?"

"Something about your old man being in prison for something." He rolls his shoulders into a shrug. "Which is where you'll be headed once they pin this on you."

"He's a minor," Brett says mildly. "He probably wouldn't go to a standard prison."

Aaron rolls his eyes. "Whatever."

I don't care about that. I don't care about what Aaron thinks or says, or the semantics of where I'll go if I'm convicted. Over the last few days, I've thought as much about my father. Especially after what Aunt Sue said: he wasn't a good person. Wasn't? Isn't? Is he still alive, still in a prison somewhere nearby? I spent my whole life thinking my dad was just some one-night fling of Mom's, that maybe he doesn't even know I exist. Because I didn't want to think that he *does* know about me and has chosen to stay away, or that Mom has kept me from him. The gravity of that threatens to drop me to my ass on the ground.

I pull away from Aaron's truck and shoulder my backpack, walking away without a word—ignoring Brett's concerned call—to head back to school. Not because I want to deal with classes and being whispered about, but because I need to clear my head. A few hours to think.

By the time the final bell rings for the day, I couldn't repeat a single word of what my teachers have said or what, if any, my homework is. Not that it matters. There's no way I'll be able to focus on it anyway. I text Brett to let him know I'm going home. Without my bike the walk takes a bit, but the silence is appreciated.

At home, I go to my room and sit on the edge of my bed. All things considered, I think I've missed my room. I've missed my dictionary Brett gave me, which is the only thing I've ever been smart at. I used to think if I was going to sound stupid with my stutter, I could at least fully understand every word that came out of my mouth. I've missed my video games and music that I would play from my computer at night to help me sleep. It would drown out the sound of Mom watching TV or the absent murmur of her voice on the phone. Mom rarely came into my room, for that matter, so this was a place I felt alone and safe and unbothered.

Maybe I'm more tired than I thought I was, because the next thing I know, the sound of the front door slamming jars me awake and the light that had been coming in through the window has dimmed to a warm orange glow as the sun goes down. I run my hands over my face, breathing in deep, and sit up.

Time for answers.

I head straight to the kitchen. This scenario is becoming all too familiar, facing off like this over the same linoleum floor where we used to bake cookies and pies together every Sunday. Mom has barely turned around before I've asked, "Who is my dad?"

She looks at me only briefly and sighs as though this

conversation is already draining her. "We aren't discussing this."

"Yeah," I say, "we are."

Mom puts her purse on the countertop and turns to the fridge. "I don't hide things from you to be mean, Victor. It's my business and I choose to keep it that way."

Without thinking, I close the distance between us, planting a hand against the fridge door and pushing it shut as she tries to open it. "It was your b-business until you told Ruthie, whose son told the whole damn school. Everyone seems to know but *me*."

Mom pulls back as though struck. Not by my words so much as the meaning behind them...that *people know*. Whatever her secret is, people know and it's all her fault. "What?"

"Aaron already admitted he heard it from Ruthie." My eyes narrow. "My dad went to jail for s-something, didn't he?"

She takes a half step away from me. The tension slides through her jaw as she clenches her teeth. "Yes...he did, around the time you were born. For fifteen years."

Fifteen years... "So he's out now?"

"Unless he's been arrested again and I haven't heard about it." The moment I lean away from the fridge, she yanks the door open and grabs the carton of eggs. She places them on the counter and turns her back to me to dig through a cupboard. I doubt she knows what she's making; she probably just wants something to do with her hands so she doesn't have to put all her attention on me.

If cooking will help her relax enough to talk to me, then whatever. "What was he imprisoned for?"

She removes other ingredients. Chocolate chips, flour, baking powder. Her voice has become strained. "I don't want to get into it."

"His name is Don, right?" I stand my ground despite the wobble in her tone that suggests I'm about to reduce her to tears. "I c-can look it up. Mr. Mason could probably find him if he has a p-police record. So why don't you spare us that and just *tell me*?"

Mom goes still. I see the rise and fall of her shoulders as she breathes in deep, once, twice, and then she turns with an egg in her hand and tears beginning to slide down her face. I will not feel guilty. I will not regret my decision to get answers that everyone but me seems to have.

"He raped me. Is that what you wanted to hear, Victor? We were dating and he raped me and I had you."

She throws the egg at my feet. It cracks to pieces of white and yellow mush and splatters my shoes and I stare at it while the words resonate in my head.

Like father, like son. That's what they said. That's what they meant.

Some part of me had to have suspected it. That simple sentence gave it away and I purposely chose to ignore it, to turn my head and pretend it was anything but the truth. I brace a hand against the counter and force myself to look at her.

I quietly ask, "Why didn't you tell me?"

Her cheeks are flushed and her eyes are red, the tears

gleaming on her face. She does not look at me like I'm her son. She stares at me as someone she is afraid of, someone she can't stomach seeing. "Because you look just like him."

There it is.

The one thing that brings every other question into sharp focus. For a long while, Mom and I stare at each other, into the raw, open wounds we've inflicted on each other. Her with the secrets she's kept, and me for wrenching them away from her and making her unwrap an injury that has clearly never fully healed.

I must be utterly useless because I can't think of anything to say. No comfort to offer. Nothing at all. The only thing I can think to do to ease her pain is to turn around and walk away so she doesn't have to see my face.

Chapter Eleven

My default reaction in any kind of stressful situation is to call Brett, and yet as I stare at his name on my phone, I can't bring myself to do it this time. Perhaps because there's too much history there. Perhaps because I know he'll squeeze my shoulder and promise me everything will be okay.

Sympathy: feeling pity and sorrow for another's misfortunate.

Empathy: the ability to understand and share the feelings of another.

Brett can sympathize with me, but he cannot empathize. This is the nature of our friendship. He cares and he's fiercely protective and his life has not been without problems, but the nature of his problems has been different from mine.

While Brett worried about what kind of car to get, scoring in the highest percentile in all the standardized testing, who he was going to take to prom, and high-profile cases his dad worked on, I was silently dealing with Mom's alienation of me, of the entire school barely noticing I existed, of wondering if we'd have the money to swing Christmas, and living in Brett's shadow while he shone.

I lean back against the park bench with a sigh. Staying at home seemed like a bad idea and so I came here. Mom used to bring me to this playground when I was little. Then, when we got older, Brett and I came on our own, riding our bikes. It's dark out and the last kid went home thirty minutes ago. Anyone who shows up now will likely be someone I don't want to associate with, but I don't know where to go if I don't want to see my only friend right now.

Well…maybe that isn't entirely true. I look at the number written on my hand. One of the digits is smeared beyond recognition, but I stared at it so much today that I remember what it is by heart. I start a new contact entry to save her digits before I lose them entirely and have to look like a moron asking her for them again.

Autumn said I could call her. Did she mean it? Did she mean I could call her about Callie or the case? My stomach rolls anxiously as I push the green phone symbol on the screen and it dials.

One, two, three rings, and Autumn answers, "Hello?"

I'm so excited I almost forget to answer. "Uh, hi."

She pauses. "Vic? That you?"

"Y-yeah. It's me." Funny how the sound of her voice

instantly puts me both at ease and on edge. It calms me and yet I suddenly can't sit still.

"Oh, hey. What's up?"

"N-not much. Just…you know. Hanging out." God, how lame am I? I should've thought out what I would say before I called. I could've made something up. "You?"

"Ehh, homework. My parents are gone, though, so I might crash on the couch and watch a movie and stay up way too late."

A smile tugs at my mouth. "You rebel, you."

"Oh yeah, that's me." She chuckles. "If you're not busy, you should come by."

Busy, me? I look around at the empty park. The darker it gets, the more unsettling this place is. I've never been here when the sun goes down. "It m-might take me a while to get there." I didn't bring my bike. The park was only a few blocks away and so I walked. Going to Autumn's would require me to head back and get it.

"Shit, that's right. Are you at home? I'll come get you." Already I can tell she's getting up and rustling around. For her shoes or her keys, maybe.

"You d-don't have to do that," I say, but the idea that Autumn wants to spend time with me and is even willing to pick me up? At least for a few seconds, it blocks out the memory of what just happened at home.

"Where are you?" she asks patiently.

I pull my legs up, wondering if I should go home so she doesn't ask questions, but… "At Manzanita Park. Up the street from my house."

"Give me ten and I'll be there."

She hangs up before I have a chance to respond. While I wait, Brett texts to ask me if I'm staying at home tonight or what and I just respond, ***Yeah I'm good for now***.

It's Friday. He hates being home Friday nights; it's the one night of the week he escapes the weight of homework, studying, and college applications, and I don't feel like going out to a movie or a party with him and his friends. Especially not now. I don't want my "rapist" label to affect his social life.

As promised, Autumn pulls into the parking lot about ten minutes later. The headlights almost blind me as I trot over to her car with my hands pocketed and slide into the passenger's seat. In the dim lighting of the dashboard buttons, I see Autumn is already in her pajamas. Black sweats and flip-flops and a tank top with her long hair up in a messy, weird sort of twist only girls know how to make sense of. Some kind of female hair magic or something. And she looks so beautiful.

She grins. "Where ya headed, babe?"

"Vegas," I say playfully.

"Mm, Vegas. I'm a'headed that way. S'pose I could take you, for a price." She makes it a point to look me over and give an exaggerated eyebrow wiggle.

I laugh quietly and Autumn pulls out of the parking lot to head for her place. At least this time when we come inside, I don't think there are any surprises—like Callie—ready to ambush me. Autumn ditches her shoes by the front door, and I'm suddenly feeling the weight of how awkward this is. Here with Autumn. At night. Alone. This is not the best situation to put myself in given the charges against me, and then I have to think about how sad it is that I have to even stop and consider such a thing.

"Make yourself at home," Autumn says, disappearing into what I assume is the kitchen. I glance around and toe off my shoes, self-conscious of the hole in my sock. I shuffle to the couch and slowly sit down. It's obvious this is where she was when I called her. There's a blanket on the opposite end, a water bottle, a half-eaten bowl of popcorn. It's that exact spot Autumn takes back up residence in when she returns with a soda for each of us.

I take the offered can, grateful for the excuse to stare at my hands for a while. There's an open notebook lying faceup on the coffee table with names I recognize. When I lean over to look, I realize just what those names are. "These are…"

"People who were at the party," Autumn confirms, cracking open her can and taking a long drink. "I told you, I'm going to find out who did this. You said you were gonna help me, right?"

She draws the notebook over so it's open on both our legs, and offers me a pen. I can think of a few names—Patrick, Devon—she doesn't have on here yet, so I add them at the end of the list.

"Anything you remember about any of these guys?" she asks.

I skim the list, thinking hard. It's easier for me to scribble the thoughts that come to me on the page: Aaron, hanging with Brett and a group of guys, last I saw. Chris Christopher,

Robbie, sharing a joint when I came back down from leaving Callie. They probably saw me. For that matter… "Patrick was heading upstairs as I was coming down," I recall quietly.

Autumn squints. "Patrick. Which one is he?"

"Patrick Maloney. Aaron Biggs's best friend. Tall, big. Shaved head."

"Oh, kind of scary-looking? Okay." She takes the pen from my hand and puts a question mark next to Patrick's name. "I wonder if the cops already talked to him. If he went upstairs after you left, maybe he saw something."

Or did something, I think. Though it's hard to picture anyone I know—even if they're assholes—raping someone. It's such an inhuman thing to do.

I think of another name and add it to the book. "So, um, where are your p-parents?"

"Tahoe." She drags a blanket across herself. It's hot outside but the air-conditioning must be on high because it's actually a little chilly in here. "Once a month or so, they take 'date weekends.'"

"Date weekends?"

"Yup. Weekends where they go out of town, just the two of them. Keeping their romance fresh and exciting or something equally nauseating." She shrugs. "It means I get the place to myself a few days a month, so I'm not going to complain."

I can't help but marvel at that. "My m-mom would never leave me home alone for the w-weekend."

A smirk graces her pretty face, but she doesn't look at me as she flips channels. "Why not? Aren't you almost eighteen?"

"Yeah," I agree. "B-but she's kind of…"

"Overprotective?"

Hardly. "More like she doesn't trust me. I guess."

I don't mean for the words to leave my tongue sounding so melancholy. Maybe the scalding news she dropped on me earlier has sapped me of any energy I might normally put into making it sound like not a big deal.

Autumn looks over. I can't read her expression and so I ask, "W-what?"

She says, "You strike me as a very lonely person, Vic."

I relocate my gaze to the television where a muted sitcom plays. You can always tell by the pause of the actors where the canned laughter comes into play. "I d-don't know what makes you say that."

"Because I know what lonely people sound like." Her eyes don't waver from me. "You've got one friend at school, you walk around with your head down…I was a lot like that before I met Callie. People thought because I didn't talk to anyone it meant I was some goth bitch or something." Before I can comment on that, she continues. "And your mom. I mean, no offense, but what kind of mom believes her son—who's never really gotten into trouble before—raped a girl?"

"You believed it," I murmur.

"I'm not your mother. I didn't push you out of my vagina—"

"Gross."

"—or change your diapers, or bathe you, or teach you

right from wrong well enough that I would know without a doubt you wouldn't do something like that." She sets her soda on the coffee table and twists around to face me better. "I mean, jeez, I've known you only a few weeks and I'd say I'm convinced you aren't capable of that."

"Oh, so now you think I'm innocent?"

She looks away, shrugging. "Callie and I have been talking about it."

That could be a really good thing or a really bad thing. "Oh."

"It's just hard for her, you know? Like, she remembers things, but she doesn't know if what she's remembering is accurate or just her brain trying to fill in the blanks. But what she's remembering makes her know that it wasn't you."

Her words make my chest ache as they shine light on all the things I've thought about. Lonely? Yeah, I guess I am. It's why I've resigned myself to being Brett's shadow all these years...because if I didn't, who would I be? Who is Vic without Brett? I'm barely anything with him; I would be nothing without him.

Mom...of course I've asked myself again and again why she didn't believe me. Now I know the answer.

"My dad's a rapist," I blurt out.

Autumn's spine stiffens visibly with surprise. "Say what?"

"Mom told me earlier tonight. She got pregnant with me after my dad raped her." Funny how that one piece of information set so many things into place. It was a traumatic event she never got past. She's never trusted men, never dated, never seemed to think much of them. Even her friends' husbands were cheats and slobs and liars as far as she was concerned. I guess it was a matter of time before she began to think the same of me. She named me after her—Victor and Victoria—so I would be hers, right? To associate me as her child and not his. I was her whole world, until I started to get older and looked less and less like her sweet little boy, and more and more like the man who hurt her.

Autumn's posture softens a little and she scoots closer. "That's what Marco was talking about, huh? Oh, Vic… You're not your dad."

I can't say to her that it doesn't matter what sort of person I really am, because as far as my mother is concerned, I'm already guilty of everything. Maybe I'm not a good person. Maybe I'm destined to be like him when I get older. Maybe Mom sees something in me that I don't.

The words catch in my teeth and force tears to my eyes and—fuck. No. I'm not crying in front of Autumn. I won't. I can't. If this new friendship is going to head anywhere, I don't want to screw it up. I'm clinging to fibers of sanity enough as it is and she already has so much to deal with trying to be there for Callie and…

"You're a good person, Vic," Autumn whispers against my ear. I don't remember her putting her arms around me but there they are, loosely hung on my shoulders with her palm cradling my head against her shoulder and the notebook discarded on the floor. Her fingers slide through my hair. And it's not like I'm openly sobbing or anything, but I feel the tears stinging my eyes and threatening to fall free. I squeeze my eyes shut and turn my face into her neck, breathing in deep.

She smells like mint and soap, and her skin is warm and soft, her touch gentle, and I think that maybe this is all I've really wanted. Not Brett's sympathetic hand on my shoulder, not Mom's accusing stares or Mr. Mason's lectures. All I wanted was someone to tell me that they believe me, *in* me, a pair of arms around me that promise a better tomorrow. A little faith in who I am as a person… that's all I had secretly hoped for. Even as guilty as I feel for taking comfort in anything right now, I find myself leaning into Autumn, slipping my arms around her middle.

Neither of us says anything else. Eventually I find myself sliding down until my head is in her lap, my gaze focused blurrily on the TV. Autumn has managed to twist the blanket around weirdly to cover us both. Now and again her hand strokes my hair, the side of my face. We watch Friday night sitcoms and let the live audience do the laughing for us. When I fall asleep, it's to the sound of her breathing in and out. Maybe I don't feel entirely better, but this? This is definitely a start.

Chapter Twelve

An unfamiliar ringtone jars me awake in the morning. It takes me a minute to place it—Oasis's "Wonderwall"—and that it's coming from Autumn's phone on the table. She grunts awake, and I turn my head enough to look up at her. She fell asleep sitting up, and her hair is mostly fallen down from its hair tie and she just might be the best thing in the world to wake up to even as she's scowling in her attempt to become coherent. I reach for her phone and offer it up to her. Callie's name flashes across the screen. She answers it groggily. "Oh my God, it's too early."

The voice on the line says, "It's like nine o'clock. That's not early."

"It's early for a Saturday." She stretches her legs out,

arches her spine, tilts her head from side to side to work the kinks out of her neck. All while holding the phone with one hand and sliding her fingers over my hair with the other. The affectionate gesture makes a pleasant little tingle work its way down my spine, and I close my eyes to enjoy it as long as I can.

"Well, get up anyway. I'm coming over," Callie says.

At this, I sense Autumn pausing. But only for a half second. "Sure. Vic's here." Like fair warning.

"Oh." It's Callie's turn to pause. "Oh, he's…oh. Um, okay. Should I come by later or something?"

Autumn's reply is a dry one. "No. I'm sure we can have one last quickie before you get here."

Heat floods to my cheeks and I abruptly sit up, running my hands over my face before Autumn can see how badly I'm blushing. She says to Callie, "Bring breakfast," before hanging up. "Are you going to stick around? She'll probably get bagels."

I notice her smiling a little as her gaze flickers up to my hair and I immediately smooth my fingers through it to try to flatten it down. I know what my hair looks like in the morning. I'm just grateful I didn't drool on her in the night. "Um… I d-don't know if I should."

Autumn pushes the blanket aside and flops down across my lap, stretching like some big, lazy cat. "The restraining order was dropped or whatever, right? I don't see why you couldn't stay."

On one hand, I think this could go poorly. On the other hand, I'd really like to be around Autumn a little longer and avoid going home, or back to Brett's. Because the moment I see him, he's going to have questions about my dad; he'll pry because he cares, but I'm not feeling up for it. Just the thought of it makes me want to crawl back under the blankets and return to last night.

So I reluctantly say okay to her offer, watching her fully remove her hair tie and resisting the urge to reach out and catch one of the soft-looking strands between my fingers.

"Good boy. Let me go get cleaned up a little." She hops off the couch then, trotting upstairs and out of sight. I'm almost grateful for the break, just because so much of Autumn leaves me feeling stupidly flustered and unsure of myself. Her signals are almost like…maybe…? But no. That wouldn't be possible, and I'm not dumb enough to get my hopes up. I've gotten the wrong impression from girls before. Wishful thinking or something, maybe. Last night was just her being a good person, trying to make someone—a friend?—feel better. That's all.

While Autumn is upstairs, I occupy myself by picking up the living room. Throwing the cans in the recycling, folding her blanket, putting dishes in the sink. Nervous habit, I guess. Brett's family is big on cleanliness and Mom is always quick to nag if something is out of place.

There's a knock on the door and Autumn hasn't come down yet. I'm pretty sure I heard the shower turning on, and I've tried not to think too much about it. I hesitate in the middle of the living room, not sure whether I should answer it or not just in case it isn't Callie, but—Callie opens the door to let herself in a moment later, trying to balance two big bags of food and a cardboard drink carrier.

My eyes widen. I hurry to her side to help her balance the drinks while opening the door more. "S-sorry, I didn't know if it was you."

"No worries." She hands over the drinks to me, nudging the door shut with her hip and taking the food into the kitchen. I follow. Noting, too, that she looks…better. Her hair is done; she's wearing a bit of makeup. Not that she needs it, but it's a sign to me that she might be feeling a little more like herself.

"You l-look nice," I offer lamely.

Callie actually gives me a smile, depositing the bags from Noah's Bagels onto the dining table. "Yeah? Thanks. You look…ruffled."

I take a seat while desperately fighting back my body's instant reaction of blushing. "Uh, y-yeah. Just woke up."

"Clearly. Long night?" Her eyebrows lift.

"It's not like that," I mutter.

"Are you giving my guest a hard time?" Autumn asks, wandering into the kitchen in denim shorts and a tank top. Her wet hair hangs loose around her shoulders, already crimping as it air-dries.

Callie rolls her eyes and sits. "Bagels."

"I figured." Autumn grabs one of the bagels from a bag before sitting in the chair between Callie's and mine. I'm sneaking glances at her that, if Callie catches them, aren't going to help my case any about how nothing happened last night. "What's up? I thought you had things to do today."

"In a few hours." Callie takes her coffee from the cup

holder and leans back in her seat, studying the steam rising from the plastic lid's opening. "I sort of wanted to tell you in person…"

That gets both of our attention. We glance at each other and then to Callie.

She says, "I'm going back to school on Monday."

"S-seriously?"

"What? Why?"

"Well, I *am* a senior and I've kept my grades pretty good. I don't want to screw it up because I was too afraid."

"I'm sure your teachers will cut you a break," Autumn insists. "I mean, they haven't caught the guy yet…"

Callie doesn't look up and her voice doesn't quite match her expression. "I know that, and they might never catch him. You know? Besides, most of the people at the party were from the college Aaron's brother goes to."

"S-so?"

"So…it's like a twenty percent chance I'm going to run into him in the hall. Those odds aren't that bad."

"You're bullshitting yourself with that." Autumn tears a bite out of her bagel with more force than is necessary. She's not angry, not annoyed…anxious, I think. Her leg is bouncing. She chews and swallows before adding, "Some people at school will be assholes about the whole thing."

"Maybe. But I can't hide forever." Callie looks up finally with a meager smile. "Look, I'm not saying that I won't have crappy days or that someone won't say something that'll upset me, but I have to try. Honestly, Vic has kind of been an inspiration."

I straighten up slightly. "I h-haven't done anything."

Callie drags one of the bags over to retrieve a sesame seed bagel from within its depths. "Autumn was telling me the kind of crap you've been dealing with because of my accusations."

"I-It isn't your fault," I quickly say. She gives me a pointed look.

"Maybe, maybe not. Doesn't matter. The point being, you've had to deal with a lot, too. If you can do it, I should be able to."

"I wasn't raped," I point out. The words are harsh and make the girls fall silent for a moment, and I cringe inwardly. "I'm s-s—"

"Don't be." Callie opens her bagel and reaches for the cream cheese. She takes a deep breath like it somehow gives her strength. "If I can't even hear someone say the word, then I'm in for a lot of trouble."

This Callie is so different from the Callie I saw at the party, and especially the one I met here at Autumn's a few weeks ago. It's easier to see now how these two are good friends. Autumn is smiling a little despite her anxiousness, and I think I know how she must be feeling: proud of Callie's strength but worried for her. I am, too.

"I'll d-do whatever I can to help," I offer.

"You're sweet, Vic, but you've been dragged through the mud enough." Callie shakes her head.

"It has to do with me now." I glance at Autumn, who is cramming another piece of bagel into her mouth. "People aren't going to let me off the hook completely until the r-real guy is caught."

Autumn adds, "He has a point. But are you positive about this whole coming back to school thing? I mean, you've been keeping up with classwork at home."

"I'm positive." Callie takes a deep breath and sips her coffee. "And I already had to talk my parents into it, so please don't make me do the same with you."

"Hey, I support whatever you want to do." Autumn lifts her coffee cup as though in a toast. "So long as you're doing it for all the right reasons."

Her friend smiles. It's a nervous sort of smile, but sincere. "Oh, God, I hope I am."

Callie stays long enough for all of us to fill up on coffee and bagels. While Autumn walks her outside, I clean up our mess in the kitchen, idly hoping her parents don't come back and question the presence of multiple peoples' cups in the trash. Maybe they won't care. Other than what little she told me last night, I don't know much about her family, which makes me feel a little guilty, seeing as I spewed so many of my own problems at her. Maybe I need to try to remedy that.

Autumn returns just as I've wiped off the kitchen table, and she rolls her eyes. "You're a guest. You aren't supposed to clean."

"Habit." I toss the sponge back into the sink where I found it and give her a tiny smile. "Plans t-today?"

She presses her fists against her hips, head cocked. "Yeah, hanging out with you. Detective work, maybe. Unless you have somewhere to be?"

Well, that takes the pressure off of having to ask if she wants to do something. "No. I'd like that."

"Cool." Autumn grabs her shoes, keys, and phone, and we pile into her car. She remembers the way back to my house. Given that it's Saturday and Mom doesn't work, it's a relief to see her car not in the driveway. It's one thing if she thinks I'm hanging out with Brett. It'd be another if she found out I spent the night at a girl's house.

We park on the street. I get out, not saying a word when Autumn follows. I let us in, gesturing absently. "M-make yourself at home. Do we have time for me to get a shower?"

"Yeah, sure." She waves me off, distracted by photos of little-me hanging in the hall that she hadn't paid any attention to the last time we were here. They go up to seventh grade or so, every one of my school photos, and then stop abruptly. I try not to think about it and hope if she notices, she won't point it out.

I tell Autumn there are drinks in the fridge if she wants one and then make my way to the bathroom. As awkward as it was sitting in her living room knowing she was upstairs in the shower, it's twice as awkward knowing she's wandering around my house while I'm standing naked in a shower stall with little more than a bathroom door between us. After our closeness last night, I'm self-conscious about wanting to scrub down really well and wash my hair. Extra clean. Girls like that, right?

I keep it quick, heading into my room afterward and dropping the towel as I slide open the closet door.

Autumn clears her throat.

At the same time I'm yanking the towel back up around my waist, I'm pivoting around to see her lying on my bed with my dictionary, peering at me.

My cheeks are on fire. "I'm s-sorry, I d-didn't know you were..."

She raises her eyebrows. "It's cool. You have a cute butt."

I open my mouth, unable to find the words. If there were ever a girl in all the world who could humiliate you and charm you in a single sentence, it would be Autumn Dixon. Never have I thought about whether or not my butt was *cute*. "Uh..."

"I won't peek." She rolls onto her side, putting her back to me.

Good enough, I guess. Not that I really care if she does look, just that...well, I'm skinny and tall and not really anything special to look at, so she'd probably be reminded of one of the many reasons why I'm so not a dateable kind of guy...

On second thought, maybe I don't want her to look.

I make quick work of getting on clean boxers and jeans, and then take a seat beside her on the bed while I towel my messy brown hair dry before I bother to find a shirt so the collar of it doesn't end up soaked. "What are you doing?"

She rolls onto her back again, holding up my pocket dictionary. "What's all this highlighted stuff?"

The attempt I make at trying to reach for the book to

take it from her is a halfhearted one. She pulls it out of my reach. I sigh. "Um…j-just, you know. Words that I've memorized."

"So all the highlighted words are ones you know by heart?"

"Yeah."

She flips a few pages to find one, lips pursed. "*Holocaust.*"

Easy. I just did that one last month. "Any mass slaughter or reckless destruction of life, especially by fire."

"Cool." Another page. "*Perigee.*"

That one is trickier. I close my eyes, trying to recall the page to the forefront of my brain. "The point of s-something closest to the Earth when it's in orbit. Like a satellite. Or the moon. I think."

"You are correct, sir. Man, they have words for everything." She doesn't look up. "*Salacious*."

I pause, feeling mildly like she had to have picked that on purpose. Just to see me squirm. "Lustful. Lecherous. Indecent."

She grins. "Very good. Can you use it in a sentence?"

The expression I give her in return is flat. "Waiting in my room knowing I would be coming in naked was very salacious of you."

Autumn laughs, closing the book. "Subpar, but I'll let you slide."

"Gosh, thanks."

She crawls past me to get off the bed and goes to the closet, picking out one of my T-shirts and holding it at arm's length. It's a band shirt from some local show Brett sneaked us into last year and their logo is of a Viking riding a unicorn. She nods appraisingly and tosses it in my direction. "What makes you do that? The whole word thing."

I catch the shirt and pull it over my head. "Just something I do."

"Yeah, but *why*?"

All the reasons sound so silly when I think about how to word them. I try to compress them into their simplest form, which is basically, "So I'm smart at one thing in my life."

The curiosity on Autumn's face softens. "I'm sure you're smart at plenty of stuff."

"Uh…no. Not really." History? English? Aside from word meanings… Science? Math? I'm pretty much a failure at everything that will get me a career in any line of work that doesn't involve flipping burgers and asking, "Would you like fries with that?"

"Maybe not bookish stuff, but there are other things to be smart about in life." She turns to my dresser, pulling open the top drawer. Thankfully she got my socks on the first try because I don't think I really want her digging around in my underwear. She chucks a clean pair at my face. "Like, being a nice guy. Being forgiving and kind and loyal and all that."

I put on the socks. "Not so sure that r-requires smarts."

"I don't know about that. It requires a certain knowledge of people and how to relate to them. Empathy, you know? It's like…emotional intelligence."

"So I'm emotionally intelligent?"

"Sure."

I would laugh, but this is obviously very serious to

Autumn, so I smile instead and rise to my feet. She's paying me a compliment, so instead I say, "Thank you."

Her shoulders relax and she smiles back at me. "Come on. We've got things to do."

Chapter Thirteen

Autumn and I spend the day driving around town. We go to a bookstore she frequents across from the mall, where we can order coffee from the adjoining café and sit and read on couches for as long as we want. We stop by a pet store so she can get food for her cat, and where she corners me into holding some of their baby rabbits—despite the fact that I'm terrified I'm going to either crush them to death or drop them or both. She seems to take great joy in watching me do this. Something about it being funny and cute to see a creature so tiny in my large hands.

Lunch is fast food at the park. Or rather, the parking lot of the park. With the windows down and the seats leaned back some, the radio on, eating burgers and fries, I mention,

"I'll be making these burgers someday."

"Oh, shut up. You will not."

"Will, too. With all of my emotional intellect, I m-may be flipping burgers, but those burgers will *understand* people."

She laughs so hard she nearly chokes on her food, smacking my leg. When she can talk again she says, "You'll never be a comedian."

I couldn't care less so long as my dumb jokes make her laugh.

Then my phone going off ruins the moment. The fourth time in the last hour. And for the fourth time, it's Brett, trying to find out where I am and what I'm doing. I hadn't responded because I wasn't sure if I should. Would he tell Mr. Mason that I'm out with Autumn? Would Mr. Mason flip out?

Autumn is peering at me curiously. I type a quick message to Brett: ***out with Autumn will call later*** and pocket my phone. "S-sorry. It's Brett."

"Ahh." She finishes off her fries. "If I'm keeping you from something…"

"No," I say quickly. "No. You're not."

"Good." She opens her door and gets out. I blink once, puzzled, and get out to follow Autumn into the park, where she immediately scales the empty jungle gym and stops at the top to look down at me.

She's so cute. Cute enough that I can't resist the urge to hold up my phone to take a picture, for which she poses with her hands on the railings and smiles wide.

"What are you doing?" I ask.

"Having fun. Forgetting about life for a while. Don't you ever do that?"

I tilt my head but say nothing. I certainly don't point out that we were supposed to be "playing detective" today.

Autumn shrugs. "You've been through a lot. It might be nice for you to pretend you're a kid again, back when the most important thing that mattered was when those two snot-nosed toddlers who've been monopolizing the swings are going to leave."

Makes sense, I guess, though I suppose Brett's idea of making me "forget" about things is going to another party or hanging out with his family. Don't get me wrong, we have fun when we're together, but…it's different. *This* is different. "W-why does it matter so much to you?" With Callie, I get it. It's her best friend, like Brett is to me, and she was alone before Callie came along. But me…I'm just the guy she threatened to run over with her car a few weeks ago.

"Really?" She sounds offended by the question, leaning over the railing and squinting down at me. "I thought we were friends. Why wouldn't it matter to me?"

Friends. Yeah, of course. That's all we are. I look down at the photo of her on my phone, embarrassed. "Sorry."

Autumn rocks forward onto her tiptoes, head bowing, long hair spilling forward over the rail and dangling a foot or so above my head. I could reach up and touch it if I wanted. "So I've been thinking. We should go down that list and start talking to people."

I blink up at her, squinting against the sunlight peering through the trees and glinting off the metal of the jungle gym. "And say what? *Hi, I'm Vic and they think I raped Callie Wheeler, but was it actually you*?"

She lets out a short laugh. "I was thinking more like asking them if they saw anything. Maybe the police haven't talked to them all. Or maybe there are details they didn't want to go to the cops with because they were worried about getting in trouble. Callie told me some of the people there wouldn't admit to having gone at all because they didn't want to get busted by their parents for being at a party with alcohol; there's no way the cops have the complete list of everyone who was there."

I guess I hadn't thought about that. "Y-you think they'll talk to me, being the prime suspect?"

Her mouth purses together. "Do you want to help or not?"

"Of course I do."

"Then it's worth a try, isn't it? Nothing is going to get accomplished sitting on our asses, and we need to start somewhere."

She has a point. Maybe I'm just scared of the idea of being judged more than I already am. At least when people are whispering behind my back, I can turn away and try to block it out…but facing it head-on like when Aaron and his pack cornered me in the bathroom, or when Marco hit me, that's a little different. Harder to handle.

"Okay," I relent. "M-Monday, then?"

"Monday," she agrees with a grin. "It's a date."

It's five in the evening before I talk to Brett. He's been texting me all day with questions, confused by the one lone message I sent him. While Autumn is inside cooking us dinner, I step out onto the back porch to call him. He dislikes talking on the phone, but he answers on the second ring anyway.

"Are you dead?"

I roll my eyes. "N-no, I'm not dead."

"Good, because I was beginning to wonder if she locked you in her trunk and drove her car into the lake."

"Alive and kicking."

"Okay. So what's going on?"

I didn't plan out what I was going to tell him, but the question sparks a silly grin to plaster itself to my face. "Um, I've been hanging out with Autumn."

Brett pauses. "Seriously?"

"Yeah."

Another pause. I can tell he's trying to gauge what he's supposed to say, what this means. "Okay. Why?"

"We were j-just hanging out. We're friends, that's what friends do, isn't it?" This time, Brett is sighing and I get the feeling it's one of those sighs that suggests he wants to say something I won't like. "What?"

"I don't know, Vic. I mean, it just seems like…" He hesitates. "Are you sure she's not like…playing you?"

"Why would she?"

"Because just the other week, she thought you raped her best friend and now she's wanting to hang out with you? Sounds suspicious to me."

I try not to let the comment sting or take away the slight cloud I've been floating on all day. No one is going to ruin this for me or make me question it. He sounds genuinely worried, and that only bothers me more. "She's not like that."

"Considering she put you flat on your back and treated you like shit the first few times she met you, how do you know?"

"B-because that was different. She thought—"

"And what makes her positive that you didn't do it?"

The question rubs me in all the wrong ways. As my best friend, I thought Brett would laugh and congratulate me. Never did I think he'd act like he can't believe I'd have someone to spend time with other than him.

"Y-you know what, I have to go. She's making us dinner."

"Vic—"

I hang up without saying good-bye. There's never been a moment when I haven't supported Brett and encouraged him. He's had a total of three actual girlfriends in the last few years—not counting casual hookups—and every time he's been with them, I got nudged to the background while he was busy taking them out on dates and buying them lavish gifts. I went along quietly with it because he was happy, because he still tried to include me even though I always felt left out, and he still found time for me if I needed him.

So maybe I expected more support than this. Maybe he really is concerned given how Autumn and I met, I don't know. But I refuse to dwell on it. Especially when I turn around and see Autumn standing at the stove, balanced on one foot while she scratches her calf with the other foot. She's intently studying the recipe in one of her mother's cookbooks. This last twenty-four hours has been a godsend. I didn't realize how much I needed it. How much I needed her. Yet I still can't help but feel like I don't deserve it.

Autumn twists around to glance over her shoulder and smile at me through the sliding glass door. I pocket my phone and slip back inside, wandering up behind her to peer over her shoulder.

"Rice noodles and chicken stir-fry," she explains. "I hope it tastes all right."

"Smells good." I'm so close to her and the temptation to just lean down and rest my cheek against her shoulder is obnoxiously strong. Do friends do that? Pretty sure that would be crossing a line I'm not sure I'm invited to cross yet.

We eat dinner—which is pretty tasty; better than anything I could conjure up—and relocate to the couch to watch a movie, which feels very date night-ish considering Autumn curls up at my side and I put my arm around her shoulders and play with her hair the entire time.

When it comes time to either decide to go to bed or take me home, she turns off the TV, debates for a moment, then turns to me.

"If you know how to be a gentleman, you can sleep upstairs with me."

I blink once, not quite comprehending. Is there a guest room? I don't remember seeing one. I just remember a bathroom, her room, and one other door that I assumed to be her parents' room. So that means—

Oh.

"Okay," I say dumbly, because I'm not sure I would know how *not* to be a gentleman. But I'll admit the thought of curling up with her in bed is appealing to me in more ways than one. I do have hormones. I'm attracted to her. I can't help that much. All I can help is that I'd never do anything to Autumn she didn't ask me to do.

She locks up downstairs and takes my hand to lead me to her room. I was only here that one time and hadn't looked around much, too distracted by Callie's presence, but now I take in the details of her black lace curtains and the Japanese cherry blossom tree paintings on her walls. She vanishes long enough to get changed in the bathroom, and when she returns it's in a pair of shorts and a T-shirt.

"These are pretty," I comment, nodding to the paintings.

Autumn actually looks down shyly, smiling to herself. "You think so?"

"Well...y-yeah. Did you paint them?"

"Yep, last summer. I've always liked to paint, but last year I really got into the whole *sumi-e* style."

"You'll have to add that word to my vocabulary."

She laughs, gesturing to her desk in the corner where some odd stones, bottles of various colors, and some brushes are neatly organized. "Let's see... *Sumi-e*, the Japanese term for ink on paper. I guess. Something like that. Basically, painting with ink and water."

I commit that to memory. Probably not a definition I'll find in my dictionary. I'm trying to imagine painting with something like ink and thinking I'd probably make a mess everywhere. These paintings are intricate and beautiful. "Is th-this what you want to do after high school?" I find myself asking. "Art?"

She comes to stand right beside me, looking up at one of the canvases on her wall. "I don't know. I've thought about it, but the term 'starving artist' exists for a reason. I'd like to get into a field I can at least support myself on while doing art on the side, you know?"

At least she has that much figured out. My after-high-school goals include trying to survive. It's a time period I haven't put much thought into because Brett will be leaving the state to attend Harvard, Yale, whatever those big schools are that he's been busting his ass to get into the last several years. That'll leave me here alone.

"What about you?" Autumn asks. "You're not actually aspiring to flip burgers, I'm sure."

Looking at Autumn's paintings, I really wish there were something I was good at other than remembering words out of a dictionary. I've never been much of an artist, singer, actor, anything. Nothing in the creative arts. "I wish I knew. I d-don't know what I'm good at."

"Well, what interests do you have? Music, sports, books, movies?"

"I like music," I admit. "Brett had a guitar a few years ago I liked to mess around on."

"Were you any good?"

"I c-could play a mean 'Mary Had a Little Lamb.'"

Autumn laughs. "Okay, well…we'll figure it out. Everyone has something they're interested in." She gestures to the bed. "Sorry, I looked through my dad's stuff but he's short and kind of chunky, so I don't think any of his sweats would fit you. Besides, who knows if he wears underwear with them and that'd be kind of gross."

A smile ticks at the corners of my mouth. "That's okay."

"Just sleep in your boxers if you want." She flicks off the overhead light and crawls into bed. There's just enough light coming in through the curtains that I don't fall all over the place while stripping out of my clothes and, crawling beneath the covers beside her, I almost feel more exposed than I did this morning getting changed in the same room as her.

There's a three-inch gap between our bodies, an invisible barrier that I'm afraid to breach. After a minute of lying silently in the dark, Autumn does it for me. She nudges me into position so that she can fit her body up against me, one of her legs between my thighs, arms around each other, and her face tucked against my throat so her lips are resting on my pulse point. This is where things get tricky, because I'm closing my eyes and willing my body not to react to the feel of so much of her skin against my skin.

It's almost funny, though, how as Autumn falls asleep in my arms, the sensation of feeling turned on fades to utter calm and peace. Her breathing evens out, her fingers curled against my back slowly going slack, and when I whisper her name, she doesn't respond. I almost want to pull away to stare at her while she sleeps, but moving would probably wake her.

I marvel at this. All of this. At her. At the fact that someone as sharp-tongued, fierce, loyal, and beautiful as Autumn Dixon would ever have been lonely like me, would ever have any interest in someone as under-the-radar as I am, and how something so horrific could possibly bring something so incredible into my life.

Chapter Fourteen

Autumn shoos me out early in the morning so she can get the house clean for her parents' return. I text Brett to see if I can come over, feeling slightly sheepish given that I hung up on him last night. He responds simply ***Sure***, so I ask Autumn to drive me to his place. I get out and watch her drive away before trotting up to Brett's door and letting myself in with the key Mrs. Mason gave me my second night here.

Brett is sprawled on the couch filling out college applications on his laptop, a bowl of cereal in his hands. He glances over as I come in and begin trying to make a spot for myself amid the papers on the other side of the couch. He doesn't say hello, simply fixes his gaze back onto the television playing a marathon of *The Walking Dead.* When a few minutes pass and he more or less ignores my existence, I say, "Good morning?"

He frowns a little, chews the cereal in his mouth, swallows. "Does Dad know you were hanging out with her?"

I cast him a sidelong glance. "No. P-probably not. Don't see why it matters."

After setting his bowl on the table, Brett slowly turns to stare at me. "Because she's the best friend of the girl who's accusing you of raping her. That's sort of a big deal."

"She isn't accusing me anymore."

"Even if Callie isn't pushing it, her parents could be."

The panic bubbling up in my chest is promptly shoved back down. "They're looking for someone else now. Callie's c-coming back to school tomorrow."

That sufficiently distracts him and he straightens up, blinking. "Seriously? Autumn said that?"

I scratch a nervous hand through my hair. "No…Callie did."

"You saw Callie."

"B-briefly."

He runs a hand over his face and sinks back against the couch with a heavy sigh. "You sure know how to put yourself in the line of fire. If you say anything that could incriminate yourself…"

"How can I incriminate m-myself when I'm innocent?"

Brett takes a long, deep breath, and his voice is gentler this time. "Dad and I are just trying to look out for you, Vic. If you get too wrapped up in a pretty girl, you're going to end up arrested, and that's not a problem I can fix for you."

Guilt envelops me like a cold blanket. It's true that Brett has had to step in a lot during my life. To help salvage my grades, to protect me from teasing and beatings, and when I desperately needed to get away from home. He and his parents are the ones responsible for teaching me independence and caring, what it is to be a normal family.

"Sorry," I mumble.

Brett sighs again. "Don't apologize. As long as you're careful. Did you sleep with her?"

I contemplate crawling between the cushions to disappear. "No."

"Then what did you guys do for two days?"

More like thirty-six hours, but whatever. "S-stuff. We talked. Ate. Went shopping, watched some movies…"

"That's a long date." He smiles a little, trying to turn the topic into something lighter. "I'm happy for you."

That was all I'd wanted to hear to begin with, but even if it's belated, it takes some of the tension off my shoulders. "Th-thanks. What's all this stuff?"

He begins picking up his assortment of forms and organizing them. "Applications and instructions for essays I need to write. Whoever said senior year is a breeze obviously has never tried to get into a decent college at the last minute."

I'm both envious and pitying of him. I wouldn't know what to do with all this stuff, let alone the pressure, but at the same time…it'd be nice to be smart enough to get into any of the colleges he has a chance of getting into. Originally I thought Brett would've been content skipping the big-name schools—he applied for local colleges ages ago, until

Mr. Mason insisted he was too smart to waste his time at someplace mediocre. I think it hurt his chances, since he got a late start at applying for the Ivy League. "You'll do fine," I offer. "You got this far. This should be cake."

"Hopefully." He stacks papers into neat piles on the coffee table. "So Callie's coming back but they still have no idea who their next suspect is?"

"N-not that I know of. I mean, I doubt she could tell me even if they had a lead." I consider telling him about the list Autumn and I made and decide now really isn't the time to drag him into my issues when he obviously has enough on his plate.

Papers organized, he slouches forward, elbows on his knees and fingers steepled before him. "Is it bad I feel like Aaron knows more than he's letting on?"

I frown. "What makes you think that?"

"I don't know, man. Just...his reaction to everything. You know how he and I met, right? Because we shared a class with Callie last year. That was how they met and started dating."

My full attention snaps to him. "Th-they *dated*?"

"They kept it quiet," Brett admits. "Only a handful of people knew because her family doesn't believe in dating until you're eighteen. Didn't Autumn tell you this? She had to have known."

Saying she didn't tell me feels like admitting defeat. "Sh-she probably thought I already knew." I look down at my hands.

Brett doesn't push it. "Well, yeah. Anyway. She dumped him after two months, so it's not like they were this forever thing, but…”

“But makes it look kind of suspicious on his part that she comes to his party and ends up attacked.”

“Exactly.”

Does Callie suspect him, I wonder? “D-did you tell the police this?”

He snorts. “Of course I did. I’m not going to get in trouble for withholding information.”

No wonder Aaron was so pissed off at me. I don’t know whether he had anything to do with it or not, but even if he didn’t, it’s probably that he still cares about Callie and the idea that someone hurt her… “I don’t think he did it. Why come after me if he’s guilty?”

“Don’t know. To throw people off? To put more pressure on you?” He shrugs. “Besides, I didn’t say he did it. I said I think he knows more than he’s saying. Maybe he’s covering up for one of his or his brother’s friends.”

That seems more likely. “So w-what do we do about it? Ask him?”

“He’s not going to admit to anything. We’d have to find proof.”

We both sit back and stare straight ahead, frowning at the television while we think. Brett’s mind is undoubtedly racing while mine is more like a hamster scrambling along on a rusty wheel, but I’m trying my best. What evidence would there be that the police wouldn’t have found? I think of the names on Autumn’s list, of the friends of Aaron’s who were present, of Patrick, who was on the stairs right next to me…

Brett says, “What about the cameras?”

"The what?"

"The cameras. Didn't you see them? Aaron had disposable cameras lying around that everyone was using to take pictures at the party."

I remember them. Or rather, I remember seeing people posing for pictures, but hadn't realized it was with actual cameras rather than digital ones. "I'm s-sure the police confiscated all of those."

"Oh, I'm sure they did. But what about everyone's phones? Aaron's brother just put out the cameras because he thought it'd be cool to develop them afterward and see people acting like idiots, but plenty of people were snapping pics with their cells. There were, like, seventy people at that party. There's no way the police could've confiscated *everyone's* phones, right?"

"They went through mine," I point out.

"You were a primary suspect. They didn't check mine; I'm willing to bet they didn't check Aaron's or his brother's."

Good point. I worry at my lower lip. Aaron wouldn't be dumb enough to have taken any incriminating photos and kept them on his phone, would he?

Brett sighs. "Not that I have any idea how to go through his stuff without him noticing, and it's not like the cops are just going to issue a search warrant based off of something we say."

Very slowly, the rust is falling off the hamster wheel and it's moving a little faster as I begin to formulate the first solid plan since Autumn and I decided to solve this. "Leave it to me. I think I got this."

Chapter Fifteen

I say nothing more about Aaron or his phone. While I'm not expecting to find anything like pictures on it, I think if he *is* covering for someone or if he did it himself, he might have something that he keeps with him. A text message, a note, a letter—anything that might point us in the right direction.

This is information I keep to myself when we arrive at school Monday morning and run into Callie and Autumn. Callie's normal skirts and tank tops are absent and instead she's in jeans and a flannel over a T-shirt, like she wants to protect herself. She holds herself straight-backed and chin up, but I can tell by the way she keeps flickering her gaze to the ground that she's aware people are watching her and murmuring. *That's the girl who was raped at that party.*

"Welcome back, Callie," Brett says.

She turns her smile to him. "Thanks."

Autumn links her arm with mine despite that I'm trying to walk to my locker and she's shuffling backward as I shuffle forward. "It was boring without you last night. Maybe I should sneak you into my house and have you live in my closet."

"There are so many jokes I could make about coming out of the closet," Brett teases, but his attention is still worriedly on Callie. "Do you want me to walk you to class?"

Callie glances at Autumn and me and says, "Sure, that'd be nice." She doesn't sound like she thinks it'd be nice, but she's trying to be casual, like this is no big deal.

When she and Brett are out of earshot, I ask, "How is sh-she doing?"

"Better than I thought she would, actually." Autumn releases me so I can get into my locker. "A little nervous, but I think she'll be okay."

I nod. "D-did you know she and Aaron Biggs used to date?"

"Of course." Her head tips. "You didn't? It was only for a few months. It never got serious."

"So you don't think he…?"

"Do I think Aaron raped her?" Autumn sighs. "I'd be lying if I said the thought hadn't crossed my mind, but ultimately…no. I don't think so. He's a bad actor and an even worse liar."

"But do you think he could know something about who d-did?"

That makes her pause. She leans into the lockers, worrying at her lower lip. "I don't know. It's possible. He might cover for one of his friends, maybe."

"That's what I was thinking." Or rather, what Brett was thinking, and I'm inclined to agree the more I dwell on it. "C-come on, I'll walk you to class."

Even as we fall into step down the hall, her eyes are glued to my face. "What're you planning, Vic?"

Simple enough: "To go through his stuff and s-see what I can find. If I can figure out how."

Autumn quiets until we round the corner, and then keeps her voice down so no one overhears. "He has gym right after lunch."

Gym. That's right; during gym, it'll be the one time he's without his phone and backpack because they'll be in his gym locker. But— "How do I get past his lock?"

"I don't know about you guys, but hardly any of the girls in my gym class bother with locks in gym. It could be worth a shot."

That's true. Brett always used his lock, but I didn't because I could never remember the combination or which way to spin the dial. There's also the issue of not knowing which locker is Aaron's. We aren't assigned gym lockers because no one leaves their things there all the time. You go into the locker room, pick one to use for the day, and make sure not to leave anything in it for the next class to find.

"Okay," I say slowly, stopping outside of Autumn's classroom. She peers at me.

"Please don't get yourself into trouble."

The sincerity in which she says this is both warming and amusing. "Hey, I'm only in t-trouble if I get caught."

Autumn and Callie join me for lunch. Which is nice, because I would've been eating alone otherwise. I had assured Brett he should go eat with some of his other friends because I wasn't feeling particularly social.

Callie looks tired but digs into her food. If anyone is picking lethargically at their meal, it's me. Mainly because the butterflies in my stomach have stolen my appetite. For as confident as I'm trying to play it off, there are about two hundred ways my plan could backfire in my face.

I don't say anything about it in front of Callie. I don't want her involved. If we find something, I'm not sure I want her there to see it immediately. If we don't...well, I don't want her discouraged. So I just glance at Autumn a few times and return the smiles she gives me while Callie chats aimlessly about her top picks for college, and when I've had enough of pretending to eat, I dump the rest of my food and tell the table I have to get to class early to talk to my teacher.

No sooner have I stepped into the empty hall, though, than Autumn follows me right out. "I'm coming with you."

I glance back. "What about Callie?"

"She promised me she'd be okay getting to her next class."

I don't have time to stop and talk this out with her. I'm

on a timeline that requires me to do this carefully because if I don't, I'm ten times more likely to do something stupid and ruin it. "It's t-too dangerous. I've got it."

She latches hold of my hand and draws me to a halt, determined annoyance on her face. "Uh, excuse me? I'm not going to let you risk yourself for *my* best friend while I sit back and twiddle my thumbs. Besides, we can search through things faster if there are two of us."

There really isn't time to argue. I need to be at the boys' locker room before the end of lunch bell rings, so— "Okay, okay."

For some reason that I'm not going to question, Autumn doesn't let go of my hand. I quickly tug her along and we slip outside, across the quad and past the library to the gym. Mr. Mackey is the boys' gym teacher and we make it a point to duck down and inch beneath his office window so we aren't seen. When we get to the door, I whisper for Autumn to wait while I make sure no one is inside.

Thank God junior year was the last time I had to take gym. I did not miss the musty, stale smell of a sweaty locker room or feeling obligated to shower in front of a bunch of other guys. Either that, or risk being made fun of for putting clothes on while still sweaty from running laps.

I take a quick walk around, peering between all the rows of lockers and checking the bathroom stalls. Then I poke my head back into the hall to say, "All clear," and Autumn slips inside with me.

"Ugh, it smells like something died in here," she whispers.

We crowd into one of two enclosed bathroom stalls and

shut the door. Autumn makes a face, but without complaint sits on the back of the toilet with her feet on the seat while I stand. Here, I can get a bit of a view of the locker room. Maybe I won't be able to tell exactly what locker Aaron uses, but I can at least see which aisle he's in and that should narrow it down.

Assuming we don't get caught first.

The final lunch bell rings, which means it's only a few seconds longer before the locker room door bursts open and guys start pouring in. The sudden influx of voices and laughter puts me right on edge. This is a horrible idea. What's worse is that I dragged Autumn into this mess with me.

She nudges me in the back with her foot and I glance at her. She just smiles in a way that simply says, *Too late to back out now.*

I twist back around and peer between the small gap where the wall of the stall meets the door, and squint in my search for Aaron, praying no one calls me out for being a pervert or something.

He's a bit late, but I spot Aaron coming through the door and making his way toward the back of the locker room with Patrick. I catch only a sliver of a glimpse of the general area of their lockers and decide that'll have to be good enough. I pull back and look to Autumn with a thumbs-up.

Now it's a waiting game. Again. Waiting for everyone to get dressed. Waiting for them to file back out of the room and into the gym. Even then I give it another extra minute to ensure there aren't any stragglers before slowly, cautiously, opening the door and peering out. Quiet and empty, I think.

"See if the door locks," I whisper. Autumn darts to the door and begins messing with the push bar. I know there's a way to latch it, but hell if I know how.

Meanwhile, I make my way toward the last row of lockers and scan them. Three with locks. Three without. I start at the end and make my way down, opening each of the unlocked ones long enough to see if I recognize Aaron's neon-orange backpack. When I reach the last door and still haven't found Aaron's, I swear under my breath.

Autumn comes up behind me. "What is it?"

"It's one of these, but they're locked."

She narrows her eyes, goes to the first lock, and begins spinning the combination dial.

"W-what are you doing?"

No answer. She inputs a combination that, of course, doesn't work, and moves to the last locker. No point in bothering with the second one since it's a key lock. This time when she puts in the combo, it clicks open with ease.

I stare. "How…?"

Autumn smiles sheepishly at me. "He's in first-period computers with me. He carries his lock in the outside mesh pocket of his backpack, and it looks just like mine, so I figured if he did use it, we'd know the combination to get in."

I examine the lock she hands me. It is, in fact, a generic silver-and-black combo lock. Probably 75 percent of the student body uses them. I could kiss her for being so smart and sneaky.

She opens the door and drags out the orange backpack.

I reach back in to check the pockets of his jeans, making a slight face. When was the last time he washed these?

"Here's his phone." Autumn tosses the cell to me and, thankfully, it doesn't require a password to get in. I take a seat and start swiping through his text messages, skimming over pointless conversations in search of something meaningful. When that yields nothing, I switch to his pictures, scrolling through dozens he's taken in the last few weeks. He's definitely not someone who skimps on taking photos, which could be a very good thing for us. They're all organized by folder: *bb game, lake, school, kev's bday, lakehouse…*

"Ugh, he hoards candy wrappers like they're going out of style," Autumn mutters, pulling out his binder to flip through it. "Anything?"

"Not yet." But as I open the folder titled *parties* and see the collection of pictures Aaron took the night of the party, my stomach starts to turn.

Most of the photos are slightly blurry, thanks to crappy indoor lighting and shaky, drunk hands. Some of them are screenshots with captions that I'm guessing he received from other people and saved, images of screen grabs of Snapchats. There's a picture of Brett holding the phone and taking a selfie of Aaron, himself, and two guys I don't recognize. Probably college kids.

The only picture that gives me pause is of a crowd near the stairs, and in the background, barely visible, is me. Scaling the steps with Callie sagging against me. It's blurry enough that it could be called into question who the two people are, but come on. I recognize the shirt I was wearing, and how many other guys helped drunk girls to a room that night?

Discouraged, I'm about to give up until I get to the end of the photo reel and my heart stops in my chest. I nearly drop the phone.

Autumn jerks her head up, quickly leaning over to see. "What is it?"

Her hand immediately goes to her mouth.

We're staring at a dark photo, but it's very evident that the set of long legs we're looking at belongs to Callie Wheeler.

Callie, lying on the bed where I left her.

The picture doesn't show her face, but there's no mistaking that it's her. You can even see the wastebasket I left at her bedside in the corner of the photo.

"Oh my God," Autumn whispers.

I can't even manage that much. Thankfully, Autumn's brain is still functioning. She whips out her own phone and takes a picture of Aaron's, showing his cell with the picture of Callie on it. Her hands are trembling and it takes three tries before she gets one that isn't out of focus.

"What d-do we do?" I ask.

Autumn opens her mouth to try to say something and the words won't come. She shakes her head, turns, and runs out of the locker room.

I make quick work of shoving everything back into Aaron's bag and locker, phone included. We have the evidence we need to do...whatever it is we're going to do, but that isn't on my mind just yet. Autumn looked three seconds away from crying or screaming and I need to make sure she's okay.

It doesn't dawn on me until I'm jogging outside onto the empty basketball courts after her that I still have her lock in my hand. Aaron is going to notice that. Of course, he'd also notice if he went to unlock it and his combination wasn't working on Autumn's lock, so this seems like the lesser of two evils.

Autumn is seated out on the bleachers facing the football field, head bowed, hands clasped behind her neck. I approach slowly, cautiously taking a seat on the bench below where her feet are rested so that I can look up into her face.

"Autumn?"

"Sorry," she murmurs, not opening her eyes. "It just… caught me off guard, I guess. I mean, I was prepared for it but I wasn't, you know?"

"To b-be fair, neither of us was anticipating *that*." We had figured that if we found anything, it would be incriminating texts or something. Not a picture of Callie taken likely moments before she was raped.

When worded that way, it makes my stomach heave. No wonder Autumn needed to sit down.

"I don't know what to tell Callie." She sits up straight and draws in a ragged breath. She isn't all-out crying, but there are tears in her lashes and it makes my chest tighten.

"I'm n-not sure. The truth?"

Autumn groans. "That her ex-boyfriend is guilty? It's going to break her heart."

I sit back a little and turn on my phone to look at the picture again, holding the screen at an angle so she doesn't have to see it. "M-maybe someone else took it?"

"Are you saying that because you believe it or because you're trying to make me feel better?"

"Anything is possible." I try to smile but it comes out weak. There's nothing about the picture that would indicate it isn't one Aaron took. Why would anyone else have his phone? Why would anyone else send this to him if they took it? Or rather—why would he *keep* it if someone had sent it?

Autumn props her face in her hands, gazing out over the football field. "Maybe we should confront him directly first."

"What?"

"Just to see what he says. If he's called out on it, he could confess, and we can talk him into going to the police."

I shake my head. "Seems like a bad idea."

"Maybe." She shrugs. "But I think if we take this to Callie, she'll try to talk to him directly. I know her. Rather than subject her to that, I think we should take the step for her. Can we ask Brett? He's dealt with Aaron before."

"I d-don't want to drag him into it." I avert my gaze. Brett would help in a heartbeat, I know he would. Just like he cornered Aaron that day in the parking lot. That's part of the problem; his loyalty to me has gotten him in trouble before, and this close to graduation, this close to him getting accepted into a great college…I can't pull him down into something that might ruin his chances.

No, the person with nothing to lose is me, so— "I'll do it."

Autumn frowns and nudges me with her foot. "We'll do

it together. Stop leaving me out of things. I'm tougher than I look, and you're...well..."

I frown. "I'm *what*?"

Her eyebrows lift and I can tell she's trying to choose her words carefully. "You're... Oh, hell, Vic. You're not a violent guy, let's face it. I've seen you try."

On some base level, that statement irritates me. But I can't say she isn't right, either. I'm not a fighter, nor do I handle confrontation well. Brett was always the one who charged headfirst into things while I trailed along like a silent shadow. So maybe between Autumn and me, we can handle Aaron as a pair.

"A-all right. We'll talk to him together. But where? How?"

"I don't know," she admits. "I mean, he's always with his friends at school. Maybe we need to go to his house? If we can get his address."

"I c-can get it." When she looks at me curiously I explain, "Office assistant. I can sneak onto the computer to look him up."

"Nice." Her gaze flickers to her phone on the bench beside her and it seems to be a solemn reminder of what she has on there, and how difficult this is going to be to keep from Callie. How do you look someone in the eye, knowing the person who hurt her is someone she cared about and trusted?

Chapter Sixteen

Sometime during fourth period, Mom texts to tell me to come home after school. The request leaves me feeling slightly nauseous the rest of the day, even after I have Brett drop me off. Mom never tells me to come straight home unless she has bad news or she's pissed at me for something. Given that we haven't spoken since I found out about my dad three nights ago, my sensation of dread is only multiplied.

There's an unfamiliar car parked in the driveway with Nevada plates, and Brett casts me a curious look, which I can only return with a shrug as I thank him and get out. I watch him roll away down the street and have to fight the urge to chase after him so I'm not trapped here with whatever is waiting for me.

Inside even smells strange. Like floor cleaner and vinegar or something. For that matter, as I step into the living room I notice everything is surprisingly clean. I mean, Mom and I are clean people, but I wouldn't say we're spotless. This level of clean doesn't reflect either of us.

I head for the kitchen where I hear the water going and dishes clinking as they're being washed. At the sink, Aunt Sue stands with her hair tied back and yellow dish gloves on, hunched over a cake pan and scrubbing it with steel wool. I linger awkwardly in the door. What is she doing here? She hardly ever visits.

Eventually she turns off the water and swipes her arm across her forehead before turning around. Her gaze brightens immediately when she sees me, and she plucks off her wet gloves and discards them on the island countertop. It dawns on me now more than ever how much she looks like Mom. The same slightly frizzy hair texture, the same almond-shaped eyes. Aunt Sue is a little plumper, a little shorter, and she's never looked as hollow as my mother has.

"Oh, Victor! Look how tall you've gotten, you handsome boy." She crosses the distance between us, cupping my face in her soap-scented damp hands and drawing me down a few inches so that she can plant a kiss on my cheek.

"Hi, Aunt Sue," I say politely, aware that I wasn't exactly the nicest to her on the phone when we spoke. "Uh… W-what are you doing here?"

"Can't I come visit my sister and nephew?" She releases me, still smiling, and ushers me over to take a seat at the dining table. I stare at her because I don't know how to answer that, and she pulls up a chair beside mine, which says a lot about Aunt Sue because most people would sit across from you to have a conversation, but she likes to be as close as possible, like she has to make sure she hears every word you say. She's the exact opposite of Mom, who always subconsciously puts anything she can between herself and other people. I wonder if I do that without realizing it.

"It's just…um, unexp-pected."

"It was a bit last-minute." She wipes her hands on the bottom of her summery dress. "But I've been trying to talk to your mother and even if she wouldn't admit it, I thought she could use someone here. For support. For both of you."

My gaze latches onto my hands folded on the table. "I d-don't know why. There's n-nothing to be supportive of now. I was cleared." More or less. For now.

"I know. She called me when she found out." Aunt Sue sighs a little and places one of her hands atop both of mine. "That doesn't mean there isn't more going on here, dear heart. You finding out about your dad…I'm so sorry. Maybe I should have told you myself instead of you finding out the way you did."

I study her hand instead. Each neatly filed nail painted a pale pink. Mom paints her nails, too, but then she bites at them when she's anxious. "I d-don't know what you mean."

"She told me you two got into an argument and it just came out. Not the way I'd hoped she would approach it."

"I s-sort of pushed it until she blurted it out," I admit guiltily.

"But that's the thing, you shouldn't have had to push."

She gives my hands a squeeze. "You're old enough, and in light of what you've been going through it would've been helpful information for you to have to understand why this was difficult for her, too."

She puts into words exactly what I wish I could have articulated to Mom. It wasn't that I cared about tracking down my dad or whatever, just that I wanted to understand why she hated *me*. Why she didn't believe I was innocent.

I don't have a chance to find words for these thoughts. The front door opens and shuts, and a moment later Mom is entering the kitchen with a paper bag in her arms. She treats the sight of Aunt Sue and me casually, as though this is what she comes home to every day.

"I bought stuff to make omelets for dinner," she announces, placing the groceries on the counter.

Omelets are my favorite. I can't remember the last time Mom made them for me. As Aunt Sue gets up to help Mom put things away, I stay at the table, fingers wrung together and staring at them anxiously. They didn't just call me home to have dinner with them. Unless this is Aunt Sue's attempt at making Mom and me play nice with each other and get over this wall of tension that has built between us.

Yet while they cook and I set the table, Aunt Sue chats to us—at us, really—about her cats and work and other casual things that don't really matter in the grand scheme of what's going on, but Mom asks the occasional question and makes commentary. I'm too nervous to manage any kind of conversation.

We eat in silence, Mom and me across from each other

and Aunt Sue to my left. As I take the first few bites, the flavors of peppers and egg and bacon lure me back to a memory of a birthday years ago.

My tenth, maybe. Or eleventh. I can't recall. But I do remember Mrs. Mason picking Brett and me up from school and dropping us off at my house. I remember coming inside to find a birthday cake on the dining table and Mom at the stove, flipping omelets and melting cheese over the top. There were a few presents—from Mom, from Aunt Sue, from Brett and his family—stacked beside my cake and I stood there in the doorway, smiling because it felt a little surreal to me. Like…these people cared about me enough to celebrate the day I was born. That my mother loved me enough that she took time off work to come home and bake something just for me, with my name written across it in blue icing.

"Delicious, Victoria," Sue says appraisingly.

For the sake of trying to get along, of perhaps reaching out to Mom, I smile across the table at her. "It's really good, Mom. Thanks."

Mom doesn't give either of us a response beyond an acknowledging noise, so I don't attempt to converse anymore. I'll keep quiet and we'll eat and afterward I'll get up to clear the dishes from the table. On the rare occasion Mom and I have dinner together, that's sort of the deal. Whoever doesn't cook, does dishes. It had a lot more weight when I was younger and we ate together almost every night.

"Now that we have full stomachs," Aunt Sue begins, rising to her feet and patting her belly, "why don't we go talk in the living room?"

I glance at Mom, who stands and walks wordlessly out of the dining room. Talk about what? What is going on? My mouth is dry. Aunt Sue beckons for me to follow with a smile. She and Mom sit on the couch and I pull up the old recliner to avoid sitting right between them. No one makes a move to turn on the television, which means...we really are here to talk about something.

Aunt Sue looks from me to Mom and back again like she's expecting one of us to say something. When we don't, she takes a deep breath and kicks things off for us. "All right. Well, Victor, we're here to talk about your father."

I glance at Mom, who has her hands in her lap and is staring at them intently. "I th-thought we already had."

"Not in the best of ways. And I—we—thought you deserved a little more information."

Somehow I don't think this was really Mom's idea at all. She still hasn't said anything. Though with Sue and me staring at her, she meets my gaze briefly and then nods to a shoe box I hadn't noticed sitting on the coffee table. I lean forward to pick it up and draw it into my lap. Slowly, like I'm worried she'll change her mind and lash out at me.

Inside the box is a collection of things: police reports, greeting cards, newspaper clippings, photographs. I scan over them so quickly that for half a second, I think I'm looking at photos of myself, except—

I pick up one of the pictures. It's faded and a little worn around the corners, but not in bad shape. I'm staring at my mother seventeen years younger, smiling brightly at the camera with a man standing beside her. A man who looks exactly like me. I'm staring into my own thin mouth and eyes and jawline, sharp features, thick lashes...the same thin, lanky build and curly dark hair. Nondescript but not bad-looking. The only thing different is the color of his eyes. His are dark but mine are bright blue, like Mom's.

All at once, I want to throw the box aside and run away. How am I supposed to feel? In awe of finally getting a glimpse at my father? Horror that my mother has effectively spent years having to look at my face every day and seeing the person who raped her and left her with a child?

I feel like I'm going to throw up.

Mom says quietly, "We met at a bar after a friend's wedding rehearsal dinner. All the other girls were prettier, and yet your father only seemed interested in me. He was a truck driver, so he was gone a lot, but he would call me from the road every single day just to let me know he was thinking about me."

I have to put the picture back. It feels too heavy in my hand. I look at Mom to let her know I'm listening, but I don't say anything.

"We dated for about four months, but we didn't see each other much because of his work. He could be...incredibly thoughtful and sweet, but he was also a very overbearing man." Mom plucks fuzz from her shirt, lost in the memories. "We weren't intimate. I had been raised to think I needed to wait until marriage, and Don was all right with that...for a while."

Aunt Sue takes Mom's hand to give it a reassuring

squeeze. I have to wonder how much Mom has talked about this over the years, if at all. She's never gone to therapy as far as I know, and I would think after going through something so traumatic, it would be needed. Sue lets Mom stay quiet this time, and I don't really need her to say anything more; I can guess where the story goes from here.

"Your mother called me after the fact," Aunt Sue says. "I drove out and picked her up, brought her home. We filed a police report right away and they arrested him right before he left on his next route."

Some of the words from the newspaper clippings jump out at me. *Local Trucker Arrested for Rape. Other Crimes Begin to Surface.* "Th-there were others?"

"Two exes of his stepped forward," Mom says. "They didn't have any proof because they waited so long, of course, but their stories did back mine up and help get him a longer sentence."

"Fifteen years." If he went to jail around the time I was born, then I was fifteen years old when Don Whitmore was let out of prison. I wonder where he went after that, if he's still in town, if he's even alive, if I could find him. And if I could, what the hell would I say to him? "Does he know about me?"

"He was notified during the course of the trial, yes. He tried to write for the first few years, but I never responded."

I blink back the sudden onslaught of tears filling my eyes. Everything I'm feeling, every wave of emotion that sweeps over me is different. I want to sob and throw something at the same time. "I l-look like him. That's why you hate me."

Mom's head snaps up, her eyes wide and round in shock. "What? Victor, I don't hate you."

"She's your mother, Vic. How could she do anything but love you?"

"That's a good question." I toss the box back to the coffee table and stand up, running a hand over my face. "I love you, Mom, and th-there are no words for how sorry I am you went through what you did. But you've spent the l-last few years treating me like I'm the one who did s-something wrong, and I don't forgive you for that."

Her jaw tenses, lower lip quivering briefly. "Victor—"

"I don't want excuses. I just...just don't." The tears are coming freely now and I feel like the world's biggest baby because of it. Everyone else is going through so much and here I am, crying because oh, boo-hoo, Mommy doesn't love me. And yet the words are pouring out of me with no filter before I can stop them. "I've gone through all of this alone. I didn't hurt Callie. I never would have, but you labeled me guilty without even listening to my side of the story. B-because, why? Because I look like my dad? B-because you were so unconfident in your ability to raise a good person that you would question whether or not I was capable of something like that?"

"Vic—"

"I'm your son and I *needed you* and *you didn't care!*"

My shouting leaves the room in silence. My chest aches and it's taking everything I have not to sob openly, to blink back the tears enough that I can storm out of the living room to my own bedroom because, now? I don't care. I don't care about her excuses. I don't care how she might point out that she's made sure I've had what I need and kept a roof over my head—because in retrospect, all these years everything I've needed that Mom hasn't given me has been emotional. The one thing I wanted was a hug, a smile, an "I love you" from my mother. Apparently that was too much to ask.

Chapter Seventeen

No one tries to follow me. Mom and Aunt Sue talk quietly among themselves for the next few hours while I hide in my room, not wanting to leave even to use the bathroom. I'd rather suffer in silence than risk running into either of them in the hall.

It isn't until I've started getting ready for bed—and texted Brett to let him know not to bother picking me up tonight; I'm not in the mood for company—that someone knocks on my door. I'm expecting it to be Aunt Sue, trying to smooth things over with Mom and me, and while I'm not really in the mood to hear it, I feel like it would be cruel to ignore her. She didn't have to come here to help us with our issues. She wanted to, because she cares.

But it isn't Aunt Sue who opens my door when I say, "Come in." It's Mom. She steps inside with the shoe box of Dad memorabilia and I stare at her from over the top of my phone, wary. I might feel like I should be nice to Aunt Sue, but I'm still not in the mood to talk to my mother.

She stops at the foot of my bed and gingerly places the box down. "You were right."

Those are words I don't think I have ever heard come out of my mother's mouth. They do the trick of getting me to slowly lower my cell to give her my attention, but I still don't say anything. I'm just giving her a chance to elaborate on that thought.

Mom folds her arms, taking a deep breath. "When I found out I was pregnant, everyone told me not to keep it. Not to keep you. They didn't think I could handle it emotionally, and maybe they were right. Sue was the one person who coaxed me into making my own decision, and…I chose to have you and to raise you, even without a father."

I draw my legs up a little and sit straighter, giving Mom room to slowly sit down on the bed at my feet. This is the first time in years she's come into my room to sit and talk with me, and the scenario feels both surreal and achingly familiar. "Is that why you d-don't talk to anyone else in the family?"

"More or less. It drove a wedge between us that never really healed itself." She stares at her hands resting on the tops of her thighs. "Part of it was my fault, I suppose. I distanced myself from everyone. I refused to talk about what was really happening. It was hard enough to talk about being raped, but to discuss that I was carrying that rapist's child inside me…I couldn't do it. The words wouldn't come out."

Abnegation: the act of renouncing or rejecting something; self-denial.

Funny, I learned that one from my dictionary the night before Aaron's party.

Mom continues. "I threw myself completely into raising you and shoved everything else aside. But the older you got, the more and more I saw him…" She lifts her head to stare at my face, a haunted expression drifting across her eyes. "You look just like him."

I avert my gaze, wanting to curl into myself as small as I can, or to hide under the bed until she goes away.

"When the police showed up here, I just…I panicked. I don't know." She takes a deep breath and presses the heels of her hands against her eyes. This is taking a lot out of her, I can tell. But I won't give her a free pass by saying *it's okay, Mom.* These are things she needs to say, and these are things I need to hear.

"I'm not him." I tuck my chin to my chest.

"You're right," Mom agrees. Two times in one night; guess we're going for the gold. "You're not him. You've always been a sweet, thoughtful boy and I…I want to try to make things better between us."

I force my gaze to lift. Are these sincere words coming out of her mouth or the result of Aunt Sue's coaching? I want to believe them. Oh God, I want to. But we don't have the best track record for working things out, especially lately, so I'm reluctant to hold on to much hope for it. If I'm honest, though… "I'd l-like that."

Mom actually manages a ghost of a smile. She pushes the box in my direction. "You don't have to look at any of it if you don't want to, but it's yours now. Keep it, get rid of it, whatever you want."

Then she gets up and leaves me alone to stare at the shoe box. It's a totally nondescript box. I may have seen it a hundred times and never once stopped to realize what was really inside it. All I've been asking for is the truth about my dad, and now that I have it sitting right in front of me…do I really want it?

Can I handle it?

Slowly I draw the box closer and pull off the lid. The picture of my parents is staring straight up at me and I pluck it out to examine it again. It's a captured memory of happier times, and I wonder how it makes Mom feel when she looks at it. If it makes her reflect back and wonder what changed in him to make him do what he did. Not just with her, but with the other two women who stepped forward, too.

I set the picture on my nightstand. If I don't keep anything else in this collection, I will keep that. Maybe I'll tuck it away in a box of my own where I won't see it again for years, but I can't bring myself to throw it away.

The rest of the box is a collection of things: a few newspaper articles, a police report, some court papers of the various trial dates and details. Toward the bottom, I find some short letters that I'm almost embarrassed to read, but…I can't help it. If it's the only glimpse of who my father was I ever get, then I should take it.

Interstate 80 going over the mountains toward Reno is always an experience, especially in winter. If I weren't on such a tight schedule, I would've brought you with me so we could have gone through Tahoe. Maybe we'll take a trip when I get back? Yosemite, then Tahoe, then Vegas. You'd like Vegas.

I'm sleeping in the truck tonight to spare myself the cockroach-infested hotels in this stretch of the state. This is the reason I'd never want to bring you on a long haul; it's no place for a girl like you. I'd hate to see you so uncomfortable. But I promise, someday I'll take you all over this country and we'll see everything there is to see, in style.

The next letter goes on to talk about the dealings with one of the trucking companies, some of the men he met along the way at various stops, the number of times kids in passing cars made the motion for him to honk the truck's horn (eighteen times) and, again, how much he missed her and couldn't wait to get back home to see her again.

It's the common theme of these letters, and they aren't what I was expecting. Don Whitmore is fairly articulate, with good grammar and spelling, and seems genuinely concerned with Mom's happiness. He talks about the gifts he's bringing home for her and the places he'd like to take her someday, after they're married.

They're harder to read than the news articles are. These love notes are too personal, too much of an insight into a real person as opposed to simply *a suspect.* It's easier to feel indifferent, to hate someone you know nothing about except what they've done wrong.

Of course it crosses my mind to wonder where my dad is now. Has he been released into the world? Was he arrested again on another charge? Of course he never would have contacted Mom again; I'm sure that he didn't have a way to, or that the court told him he couldn't. But if I were to contact him…

I reach for my phone, wondering if I should call Brett or Autumn to talk to them about this. My thumb lingers over the screen. Except I know what they'll probably say: they'll say I should leave it alone, because who wants to associate with someone like Don Whitmore? Ultimately, don't I need to figure out something this important for myself?

Or do I already know the answer, and I'm just too afraid to admit it?

Chapter Eighteen

The next morning, I get to school early and sit on the steps outside, waiting for Brett or Autumn, whoever arrives first. I see Autumn's car pull into the parking lot, and when she approaches and spots me, her face lighting up immediately takes a little bit of the weight off my chest.

"Morning," she greets, ignoring the other students walking past and taking a seat on the step beside me. "What're you doing out here?"

"W-waiting for you." I hold out the photo of my parents, wordless.

Autumn takes it and peers at the faces, squinting, until her features smooth out in realization. "Is this…?"

"My mom and dad," I agree.

"Wow." She twitches her mouth into a smile and holds the picture up beside my face. "Yeah, I see it. Smoosh their faces together and there's you."

I pluck the photo from her hand with a sigh. "N-not so sure that's a good thing."

Briefly, I tell her about the conversation I had with Mom and Aunt Sue the night before. She listens intently, leaning into my side and keeping her gaze on my face. I like the way she listens, as though nothing else is as important as what I'm saying. It makes her a good friend.

When I've caught her up she says, "Have you decided what you're going to do?"

"I th-think…I think I want to meet him, if I c-can figure out how."

"He went to jail for fifteen years for a sex crime. I would think he'd be registered in the sex offender database. We could start there?"

I hadn't thought about that. Or rather, I'm not entirely familiar with how all that works, and I'm guessing Autumn's learned a lot about it in all this happening with Callie. "Yeah, we c-could— Wait, where is Callie, anyway?"

Her smile is faint this time. "Yesterday kind of took a lot out of her, so she decided to stay home today. Baby steps, right?"

"Baby steps," I agree. Maybe that's true for both of us.

I fill Brett in on everything with Mom and my dad at lunch, when my resolve for finding him has solidified enough that Brett's opinion won't sway me. To my surprise, he stares at me long and hard and finally says, "Maybe it would be good for you." It deflates any arguments I was prepared to make, but it's a good thing. I'd rather have Brett's support than be forced to argue with him on something. "Get an address," he says. "We can go this weekend if you want."

My shoulders slump in relief. Not that I've quite come to terms with the idea of seeing my rapist father face-to-face, but knowing I'll have two people with me who care brings me comfort.

Brett is silent for a few minutes as he eats before asking, "Whatever happened to you coming up with some plan to check Aaron's phone?"

"Oh." I shift in my seat, poking at my sandwich. Since I didn't stay at Brett's last night, I didn't have Mrs. Mason to slip me money for food in the morning. Should I tell Brett what we found? I wanted to keep him out of things until we knew for sure, but lying isn't my strong suit. The fewer people who know, the better. After what happened that day in Aaron's truck, I don't want to risk Brett losing his temper and causing problems for himself. "I don't know yet. We're still working on it."

"We? You and Autumn?" He frowns.

Why does he sound almost offended by that? "Y-yeah. Is that bad?"

"No, no. Just..." He's quiet a moment before smiling and

shaking his head. "It's nothing. Maybe I'm a little jealous."

I can't help but return his smile. "You're still my best friend, man."

He kicks me playfully underneath the table with a chuckle. "Yeah, yeah, I know. So if you and your mom made up, does that mean you'll be staying at home again?"

Ah. I've wondered that, too. Honestly… "I think so. J-just for now." There's no point in intruding on the Masons any longer. I've missed my room and my bed, and I've missed my solitude and time out to think, which is time I don't get when I'm at Brett's. Something is always happening at his house, between his dad's cases, Brett's studying and long conversations about his future…

"I'll drop you off at home after school then." Brett finishes the rest of his food, and he's done by the time Autumn slides into the seat beside me. She starts to say something, but pauses and glances at Brett, who raises his eyebrows at her.

"He k-knows," I assure, and Autumn relaxes.

"Oh, cool. So I looked your dad up on the sex offender registry, right?" She places her phone on the table between Brett and me so we can both see the profile she has pulled up. The mug shot isn't flattering, but it's definitely my father. "He's in Oakland. Or at least, that's the last address he reported."

My stomach flip-flops. Oakland is about two hours southwest of here. For some reason, that feels a lot closer than I thought it would. If I told Mom, she'd probably have an emotional breakdown.

Brett nudges aside his empty lunch tray. "Should we go? We could do it Friday night. I'll skip tennis."

"Friday would work," Autumn agrees.

When I don't say anything for a while, I look up to find both of their eyes on me, waiting for an answer. Yeah, this is my adventure, right? Which means I need to make the call. Friday is sooner than I thought it would be. I figured maybe it would take weeks, months to find him. Hell, that was if we ever found him at all. I had hoped all this stuff with Callie would be done and over with so I could tackle one big issue at a time.

But there isn't a reason to say no. I've waited all my life to know my father, and the fact that he isn't my favorite person right now doesn't change that.

I take a deep breath. "Let's do it."

Chapter Nineteen

Wednesday, Amjad asks me to come in to cover for him again. I was supposed to hang out with Autumn tonight, but I texted to let her know and she understood. Amjad's taking off two times in a matter of a few weeks is bizarre, but I'll do it without question.

This time when I enter Rick's Convenience Store, Amjad doesn't look or sound sick, but rather greets me with a wide smile.

"Short notice, I know. Thank you so much, Victor."

"Everything okay?" I ask, setting my backpack behind the counter. Might as well get some studying done while I'm here.

"Actually…" He smooths his dark hair back with a sheepish

grin. "I have a date."

I blink at that, surprised. "A date? R-really? With who?"

"Beautiful woman. Very smart." He nods solemnly and adjusts the collar of his button-down shirt. I've never seen him dress like this, now that I notice it. He cleans up well. "I met her through the internet."

I guess that would make sense for someone who never goes out anywhere to meet girls. I've heard Amjad speak about his wife and her death from cancer only a few times, but he keeps his wallet full of photos of her, and I've caught him on several occasions just staring at them. Trying to move on must be difficult for him, but he looks happy.

"Go on your date," I say warmly, sliding onto the stool behind the counter. "Have fun."

Amjad starts to say something when the door chimes—and in walks Autumn. My spine straightens immediately in surprise.

"Welcome," Amjad greets her, and she gives a crooked smile and points at me.

"Uh—thanks. I'm just here for him."

Well, that certainly gets me a look from my boss. Raised eyebrows and all. "Victor, is this the girl...?"

"The girl?" Autumn blinks at Amjad and then at me. "I don't know. Am I?"

My face burns. "Uh..."

Amjad offers his hand to Autumn, which she accepts, and he shakes it firmly and leans in to tell her, "Victor is a very good boy. Big heart. Hard worker." Then he gives her hand a pat and releases it. "Wish me luck."

"Good luck," Autumn and I say in unison, even though she has no idea what she's wishing him luck for.

She turns to me once the door closes, an amused sparkle to her eyes. "I'm the girl, huh? Should I be worried?"

I rub the back of my neck. "N-no. It's not like that. W-what are you doing here?"

"I thought you might like some company if you were stuck here alone all night." Her shoulders lift and fall in a shrug. "If you want company, that is."

"I like company," I agree, sliding off the stool to pull over a foldable chair. "Do you want a slushie?"

"Only if you have cherry."

I gesture to the slushie machine and Autumn helps herself to filling up one of the cups. She sits in the chair beside my stool, legs crossed and sipping her drink through the obnoxiously shaped slushie straws that I always manage to cut my mouth on. I've since pulled out one of my school books, but I doubt I'll get much studying done with her here.

She says, "You have Aaron's address, right?"

I nod.

"Then…Saturday?" She taps her nails against the side of the cup. "The longer we put this off, the more time we're giving him to find excuses."

"I know." I rest my elbow on the counter, chin in my palm. "Are you s-sure we shouldn't go to the police?"

Autumn shrugs. "Dunno. Guess I don't have a lot of faith in the police right now; they haven't exactly been on top of things. What do *you* want to do?"

What do I want to do? I sort of want to pretend none of

this ever happened. If we go to the police, would we have to explain how we got hold of that photo in the first place? We technically broke into his personal things. What if that makes the evidence inadmissible in court or something?

"We'll talk to him" is my choice. Final answer. No take-backs.

She places her slushie next to the register. "Any idea what we're going to say?"

"Don't know. The t-truth?"

"'Hey, sorry we broke into your locker but we think you raped your ex-girlfriend.' Mm. This is going to play out awesomely."

I give her a flat look. "D-do you have a better idea?"

Autumn casts me a weak smile, stretching back in her chair. "Absolutely not. At this point, we don't have much to lose, I guess."

She's right. It's been more than a month since the party already. The longer we wait, the harder it might be to talk Aaron into coming forward with any information he might have. The longer we have to keep it a secret from Brett and Callie and everyone else. For that matter, I'm not truly in the clear until the real perpetrator is caught, right?

For the next few hours, Autumn busies herself playing crossword puzzles on her phone while I stock the shelves, clean the bathroom, and ring out customers. It's been a quiet night, and even if we're mostly just enjoying each other's company without saying much, I like her nearness. I also like not being stuck here alone.

I don't think anything of it when people I recognize

from school come in to buy sodas and energy drinks, until I recognize Marco's and Patrick's faces among the four of them. Marco, who hit me in the hall, and Patrick, Aaron's friend who helped corner me in the bathroom. Beside me, Autumn shifts restlessly in her chair, a sign that she's seeing what I'm seeing.

Marco, Patrick, and their two friends approach the counter, talking about plans for the evening, and none of them really looks at me twice. I ring them up, they throw a twenty on the counter and take their change and leave...all without incident. When the door chimes with their exit, I let out a heavy breath.

"That was lucky. It would be stupid for them to say anything here." Autumn tips her head back and points to the security camera above our heads.

"It d-doesn't actually work," I admit. "Just there to h-hopefully deter people."

"Well, maybe it deterred them."

I try to push the thought aside. There's nothing to think of it, up until I've locked the store and Autumn and I have stepped outside, and I see the guys still in the parking lot by the gas pumps, lounging around their truck and turning to look right at me the moment the door is shut.

My spine goes rigid. Autumn has hold of my hand, half-empty slushie cup in the other, and she murmurs to me, "My car's right there. Come on."

Ignore them, right? Right. They're probably just loitering. I'll get into the car and that'll be that.

We've made it only halfway to Autumn's car when I hear

their footsteps approaching and every fall of shoes against the asphalt kicks my heart up into my throat.

"Hey!" Patrick calls.

Autumn tightens her hold on my hand. "Go, go, go," she hisses, and maybe it's my fault for turning back, for acknowledging them, like they're shadows in the dark that can't hurt me until I look at them and give them the power to do so. My fingers brush the passenger's side door handle when someone grabs my shoulder and spins me around and slams me against the hood of the car hard enough that it nearly knocks the wind out of me.

"Let him go!" Autumn shrieks. My vision clears enough to see her slamming her cherry slushie into the side of Marco's face, smearing red globs of sticky ice all over him. He uses his free hand to shove her aside, where Patrick and one of the nameless boys grab and hold her despite her thrashing. I only briefly spot the fourth guy off in the distance, standing in the truck bed and keeping an eye out. They had this planned.

"I d-d-didn't do anything," I rasp, still trying to get a proper breath in while prying at Marco's fingers fisted in my shirt.

"Shut the fuck up," he snaps. "You think what you did was okay? I should tie you to the back of my truck and drag you through town. Not a single person would blame me."

Callie would. "Get off me," I growl, trying to wriggle free from his iron grip. His legs are keeping mine from being able to do much good, otherwise I'd kick him square in the groin and make a run for it.

"Your face is all over the paper, Victor. Just 'cause the cops don't have the evidence to throw your ass in jail doesn't mean anyone else is going to let you get off free." He releases my shirt and grabs a fistful of my hair instead. The hood creaks and bends a little beneath the weight he's bearing down on me.

I don't see how she gets away, exactly, but I hear Patrick shouting as Autumn lunges herself at Marco, latching her arm around his neck in a chokehold. It startles him into jerking back from me and I roll away, nearly stumbling. The moment I'm free, Autumn releases him and we circle to the other side of the car, placing it between them and us.

"What paper?" she pants.

Patrick sneers. "*The Waverly Bee*. My dad reads it and showed it to me this morning when he saw there was mention of a kid from my school. And there you were."

The Waverly Bee. Craig Roberts knew where I worked, and I caught him taking pictures outside school that one day. It shouldn't surprise me if he got a snapshot or two the day he came here. We only stock the Sunday papers here. I didn't see it.

From the truck by the gas pumps, the fourth member of their group calls, "Someone's pulling in!"

Marco, Patrick, and their unnamed friend turn to look. I yank the driver's side door open and crawl across the center console to get into the passenger's side while Autumn follows, pulls the door closed, and turns the car on to quickly peel out of the parking lot. Not that I think they would have tried anything with a stranger nearby, but I don't want to risk it.

Neither of us speaks a word as we drive up the road a few blocks. Autumn pulls over to another liquor store and leaves the car running while she hops out to jog inside. When she returns, it's to drop a copy of today's *Waverly Bee* into my lap and turn on the overhead dash light so we can see.

We begin scouring the pages. Not that we need to look far. Our town is fairly small and the crime rate is low, meaning the occurrence of a local rape is enough to be plastered on the front page. So there I am, with a grainy photograph on the front, bottom right of page one, locking up at Rick's Convenience Store the night Craig Roberts came to see me.

Autumn reads the first few lines of the article out loud: "*A local high school boy is being investigated for the rape of a young classmate. Despite the overwhelming amount of evidence against him and testimony from the victim herself, many are wondering what has the police holding back from taking him into custody.*" She looks at me. "What overwhelming amount of evidence? Where is he getting his information? Can they talk about kids like this?"

"Th-they probably can as long as they d-don't say our names or something," I point out glumly. Our city has one high school. It wouldn't be difficult for someone to figure it out, considering one of the photos is of Rick's and almost everyone has driven by it at some point or another.

"Should you call the cops? Or Mr. Mason?"

"I d-don't know. Should I? W-will they do anything?"

Autumn sighs. "Maybe not. I have no idea. I mean, Marco didn't really get a chance to hurt us, so it'd be our word against his, and even then I'm not sure what punishment they could give."

Yeah, figured as much. I push the paper aside and run my hands over my face. Craig warned me about this. About making an enemy out of him. Because I wouldn't talk to him, he'll drag me through the mud instead. "I'm g-going to call him."

"What? Who?"

"Craig Roberts. He came to see me that day and I kicked him out."

Her expression falls a little. "So…you think he did this because you wouldn't give him an interview?"

"Maybe."

"I'm the one who told you not to talk to him."

I reach for her hand and squeeze it. "D-don't do that. Everyone told me not to talk to him." Besides, how do I know anything I told Craig wouldn't have been misconstrued and warped to fit his wants anyway?

Autumn takes a deep breath. She swipes briefly at her eyes and flicks off the overhead light. "I should probably get you home."

I don't wait until the next day to call Craig. His business card is still in the pocket of one of my pairs of jeans in my dirty laundry basket. I fish it out before even getting settled into bed and dial the number. It's a business number that goes straight to voicemail, and I find myself hanging up without leaving a message.

What would I say to him, in all honesty? That I think he's an asshole? That he almost got me beaten up with his lovely little article and photo? I could threaten to take it to my lawyer—being Mr. Mason—but I can't guarantee that would get me any satisfaction, either.

I toss the card on my dresser and step into the hall. Faintly, I hear the TV in the living room, and occasional commentary from Aunt Sue and Mom. As far as I'm aware, Aunt Sue will be leaving in the morning to head home. She had originally planned on staying longer, but I think she realized there was only so much she could repair between Mom and me. Not to mention, sleeping on our couch has got to be uncomfortable. I've thought about taking this situation to them, and again I decide against it. Aunt Sue wouldn't know what to do, and Mom would only get stressed out further. I don't want to bother her.

Before going to bed, I text Brett to relay what happened.

Go read today's Waverly Bee. 1st page. Bottom right. Show to your dad please.

I don't go into details about what happened at work. Brett is another person I don't want to stress out. The more of this I can handle on my own, the better.

I get showered, dressed, teeth brushed, and flop into bed with a sigh and an arm draped over my eyes. My phone beeps; it's Brett writing back to say:

Dad says not to talk to any reporters. He'll make calls tomorrow. You ok???

Great. Advice I was already following, and a response I don't think will do me any good in the long run.

Before I reply, there comes a knock at my door and I say, "Come in," without thinking about it. The door creaks open and Mom pokes her head in, glancing around like she expects I won't be alone. I blink over at her and for a moment, we just stare at each other, waiting for the other to speak first.

"Just wanted to tell you good night," she says, and the sentence is so strained and awkward that I can't help but smile.

"'Night, Mom."

She almost smiles. Almost. But it's just as uncertain as her words and she's quick to retreat. Small progress, but at this point I'll take what I can get.

Chapter Twenty

Friday night, Brett, Autumn, and I meet in the parking lot after school. As promised, Brett is skipping tennis practice for this outing, and my stomach is rolling around and threatening to make me sick all over my feet.

I have the last known address for my dad in my pocket. Although I put a lot of thought into telling Mom, I decided against it. She wouldn't understand, and it's not like I'm expecting anything amazing out of this trip. I don't expect him to welcome me with open arms, or that we're going to have any kind of father-son bonding moment.

Frankly, I have no idea what to expect.

We take Brett's car because he doesn't like not driving. Autumn sits in the back and every so often, I feel her fingertips slipping between my seat and the door to poke at my side. I eventually reach a hand back awkwardly in order to poke her knee in return, grateful for the reassurance she's trying to offer.

"You're really okay with this?" Brett asks once we get on the freeway.

I have to admit, "I d-don't know."

"What worries you about it, exactly?"

That's a good question. Sure, there are a lot of things running through my head, but to have to stop and really think of how to put it into words… "I'm afraid…he w-won't know who I am. I'm afraid he will. I'm afraid I'll hate him, or l-like him, or that he'll be a good person or a bad person." I run my hands over my face and sigh. "Sorry. I know it doesn't make sense."

"No, it does," Brett says mildly. "You don't know what to expect and you haven't had a lot of time to process any of this. On one hand, it's your dad and you want to feel some kind of connection. On the other hand, he did something terrible to your mom and you want to protect her."

"It might be strange if you *weren't* conflicted," Autumn adds.

Their words don't make me feel entirely better, but at least they put my mind at ease so I don't think I'm wrong for feeling the way I do.

They don't prod any more for the rest of the drive and I try to focus more on the music coming from the satellite radio and less on the fact that the trip goes by a lot faster than I expected it to. It's dark out by the time Brett is pulling off the freeway into a small town just outside of Oakland that I've only vaguely heard of. It's a lot of open fields between houses, and everything is so flat. No hills or the abundance of trees like we get in the valley.

My heart is hammering so loudly I can hardly hear myself think.

Autumn reads the directions from her phone and Brett follows them, until we're pulling onto a slightly more suburban-like street where small houses are crowded together and have no fences around their front lawns or backyards. It isn't run-down so much as just…old. Well-worn. I wipe my palms against my jeans and look over at Autumn and Brett, who are watching me with patient expressions. They're letting me do this at my own pace.

"W-will you come with me?"

Of course they will; they immediately start to unbuckle. They were just waiting for me to ask in case I wanted to do this by myself, and originally, I had planned on doing just that. But now, standing on the sidewalk in front of my dad's house, I think I need them at my side more than ever.

There are two older cars parked in the driveway and the windows are aglow, so I know someone is home. Will I recognize him when I see him? Will he take one look at my face and immediately know who I am?

We come to a stop at the door and it takes everything I have to lift my hand and knock. Inside, footsteps approach, and the front door swings open to reveal an older man in suspenders and sharp facial features peering at us curiously, but not unkindly. "Can I help you?"

My throat refuses to cooperate. Brett seems to sense this because he speaks up for me. “Sorry to bother you so late. Does Don Whitmore still live here?”

He blinks slowly and the lack of recognition on his face has my heart immediately sinking.

“Sorry, I don’t know any Don. We moved in about six months ago.” He looks between us, but I feel his eyes mostly on me. Maybe I look like I’m about to pass out or something, though whether it’s from relief, disappointment, or simply the sudden drop of adrenaline, I don’t know.

Thank God for Brett thinking on his feet. “I know this is a lot to ask, but we’re trying to help our friend here find his dad. I’m not sure if you rent or own this place, but maybe you have someone you could call to get information about the previous tenants?”

The man rubs the back of his neck, though his gaze seems to have softened a little. “Let me grab a pen and paper.” He disappears briefly from the doorway, returning a second later with a yellow notepad and a ballpoint pen, which he hands to me. At least I manage a “thank you” without stumbling over the words, and I scribble down my first and last name, along with my phone number, before handing it back.

“Sorry to disappoint you kids,” he says as he accepts it. “I’ll see what I can do.”

Autumn gives him a sunny smile. “Thank you. We really appreciate it.”

The door is closed and I’m vaguely aware of my hands trembling. I cram them into my pockets and turn away, jogging back to the car. Am I going to throw up? I don't know what's wrong with me beyond wanting to laugh and cry and curl into a little ball. I was stupid to think I could just show up at Dad's doorstep and expect some magical reunion.

Autumn comes up to where I've slumped against the car. Her fingers are cool and gentle as they slide through my hair, and it coaxes me into looking up at her. She takes this as incentive to wrap her arms around me in a tight hug, and I'd be lying if I said it didn't help even a little. Even more so when Brett comes up alongside us and slings an arm around my shoulders, too, and for a moment I'm simply engulfed in this warm embrace of comfort and support, and it makes things just a little bit better.

I turn down Brett's invitation to go out that night. He has plans to hit up some coffee shop art gathering, which is about as much my scene as a lake house party, and besides that…I don't really feel like being around people. He drops us off at school to get Autumn's car, and surprises me with a hearty hug and a pat on the back. "Don't let it get to you so much, yeah? We'll find your dad." I smile a little as he drives away, and then I turn to Autumn.

She tilts her head. "My parents are in town, unfortunately, otherwise I'd drag you home with me."

"Th-that's all right. You can come to my place. If you

want." As far as I know, Mom should be out at bingo with Ruthie tonight, and they usually aren't home until late.

Autumn considers. "Are you sure you're up for company? My feelings won't be hurt if you want to be alone."

"Why w-would you think I want to be alone?"

"You turned Brett down, so..."

My lips twitch into a smile. Sometimes the things she says, the small and sweet considerations she shows me, make me want to pick her up and spin her around. "You aren't Brett." That's all there is to it. There are certain things I prefer to share with my best friend. Certain moments I feel like I need Brett's guidance and presence at my side. And other things...I need Autumn. I need her gentleness and her fierce loyalty, and her honesty rather than Brett's wanting to take charge of everything and withhold information—like how Aaron found out I was a suspect—because he thinks it'll protect me.

We get back into the car and head home, where Mom's sedan is absent from the driveway. I have Autumn park across the street and we slip inside. I want to get changed and cleaned up first, but rather than wait in the living room, she follows me to my room and plops onto the edge of my bed with a sigh.

"So how are you really feeling?"

I can tell she's purposely looking elsewhere in the room to give me a bit of privacy without actually giving me privacy, and at least this time I'm a little less self-conscious as I start stripping down. To answer that, though... "I think I'm okay."

"For real?"

"I don't know. Everything is sort of…sort of a jumble." I skim down to my boxers while staring blankly at the selection of clothes in my closet. "Partly disappointed, partly r-relieved?"

She glances in my direction. "Mm-hm. Elaborate?"

"Like…" I sigh, pushing a hand through my messy hair before turning to face her. "D-disappointed because I r-really had to work up the nerve to go in the first place… but relieved because I don't know what I would have said."

Her chin is propped in her hands, elbows on her knees, cross-legged. "Are you going to keep trying to find him, then?"

"Maybe. Some part of me wants closure from it." Something, even just a glimpse of his face in person, to close the book I've always had open about the mysterious figure that is my father. If Mom had told me earlier in life about him, I wonder if things would have been easier? Of course, wondering that isn't going to make me feel any better, and I don't need anything else to be resentful of Mom over.

Autumn says, "Come here?" and I obediently move across the room to stand at the edge of the bed in front of her, almost forgetting that I'm not wearing much and there's a beautiful girl that I really, really like on my bed. She uncurls from herself a bit and brings her hands up to my waist, pressing a kiss to my stomach in a way that makes me blush while silently willing the lower regions of my body to not react and embarrass the hell out of me. "I don't really know if you should find him or not, frankly. He sounds like an asshole. But if you want to keep up the search, I'll go along with it."

I exhale. "How is this n-not weird for you? Being here with me, I mean. Doesn't it bother your parents or Callie?"

Her expression turns sheepish. She tugs me to lie down on the bed beside her. "I haven't exactly told my parents yet…"

"Oh."

"Don't 'oh' me. Have you told your mom you've been talking with me?"

She's got me there. Except I'm not so sure she'd give a damn. "No."

"I'll tell them when things die down a little." She leans into me. "I've talked in-depth with Callie about it. It doesn't bother her. She's convinced it wasn't you, after all, so why would it matter?"

"Lingering d-doubts?"

"I won't lie and say I don't think she has any. I'm sure some little part of her suspects everyone. But she trusts you as much as she's capable of trusting a guy right now."

Hearing that makes me feel a little better, at least.

Autumn's fingers touch the side of my face, tracing up my jaw and tickling along the back of my ear. She could reduce a guy to a puddle with those hands. "I believe you completely, if that helps."

"It does," I murmur. It helps a lot. Maybe her actions show me her trust more than her words, because I can't imagine she'd be lying here with me half dressed if she had any remaining suspicion that I raped her best friend. "I want you to trust me."

Her lips curve into one of those smiles I've grown to love. Her palms cup the sides of my face and she waits to speak until I manage to make eye contact, which is getting more difficult by the minute considering how her touching me is making me really want to touch her, too.

"Vic," she says.

I swallow hard. "Yeah."

She's going to kiss me. I know this a full second before she does it, but it still comes as a surprise that renders me unable to respond at first. Her mouth is as warm and soft as I imagined it would be. Thank God I don't freeze up or pull away; I lean into her almost cautiously, not entirely sure what I'm doing but like hell if I'm going to pass up the opportunity to kiss Autumn Dixon.

It's a lingering kiss, but not a deep one. Her lips part beneath mine slightly, and then she pulls back and strokes her fingers through my messy hair.

She says, "I trust you," and all the tension rushes right out of me.

I shift onto my back, and Autumn follows suit and stretches out beside me, tucked against my bare side in a way that I think friends definitely do not do unless they like each other, but I don't want to say as much in case it makes her move away. I want to ask what the kiss means, if we've stepped past the friendship line, but I don't want to ruin the moment.

"Don't fall asleep," I warn her softly. Her parents are expecting her home and although Mom doesn't make it a habit of coming into my room, there's a first time for everything.

Autumn says, "Mm-hm…"

But it's only a matter of time before we've both drifted off.

Chapter Twenty-One

I wake to the sound of muffled ringing across the room, and it takes me a few moments to place what it is. My phone rings so rarely that the sound is unfamiliar. Autumn's body is pressed neatly along mine, a leg hiked over my hip and her ponytail halfway down so that her dark hair is sticking out every which way. My phone is in the pocket of the pants I was wearing yesterday, I realize, and then it occurs to me that the sun is shining brightly through my window and…

"Shit."

Autumn makes a noise when I nudge her, but that's all it takes before her eyes are blinking open blearily and she, too, is coming to terms with the fact that we fell asleep and it's now morning.

"Shit!"

"That's what I said."

She sits up and I roll out of bed to grab my pants and phone, answering it quickly. "H-hello?"

"Vic? It's Callie. Is Autumn with you?"

Oh, I'd forgotten she had my number. "Y-yeah, she's here. Hold on." I turn and offer the cell out to Autumn and she snatches it.

"Hey? Yeah. I totally fell asleep and I think my phone is in my car... Thank God. You're a lifesaver. I'll go call them. Love you." She hangs up while I'm pulling on a pair of pants and a shirt, and we both begin searching for our shoes. "Mom called Callie and she told them I was in the shower."

Good save, Callie. "D-do you need to go home?" We had planned on going to Aaron's today, but I don't want her in trouble and grounded from seeing me altogether.

"I don't know. We'll see how it goes when I call home." She opens my bedroom door and we make the mistake of stepping into the hall without thinking.

Which has us running right into my mom, who is still in her pajamas and is on her way to her room with a cup of coffee in hand. I freeze. Autumn freezes. Mom stares, looking shocked and confused. Guess it's a good thing I thought to get dressed. "H-hey, Mom." Do I introduce Autumn? As a friend, as a girlfriend...?

Autumn recovers first, although her voice is a little higher than usual with her nervousness. "Hi! You must be Ms. Howard. I'm Autumn." She extends her hand, which Mom slowly takes out of pure reflex. "I was just coming to pick Vic up so we could go on a study date. Um, I hope I didn't wake you."

Mom blinks slowly and withdraws her hand. "No, you didn't…"

"We're s-sort of in a hurry," I apologize, ushering Autumn for the front door.

"It was nice meeting you!" Autumn calls, and we leave Mom behind, looking after us in stunned silence.

We hurry across the street and dive into the car. I can barely suppress a laugh. Autumn slumps into her seat with cell in hand. She grimaces at the sight of several missed calls on the screen, and dials home. Whoever it is answers on the first ring. "Daddy? Hey, I'm *so*, so sorry. I crashed last night and my phone was in the car…"

I can hear the vague outlines of a lecture from the other line, but no yelling. That's a good sign. Autumn seems to be relaxing.

"Yeah, I understand. I know. I'm really sorry. I promise I'll be home tonight." She endures a few more minutes of talking to him before hanging up, then slouches down and sighs.

"Good?" I ask.

"Good," she agrees. "One of the benefits of not being a troublemaker, I guess. When I do screw up, they aren't as hard on me. Sorry if I got you in trouble with your mom."

"Honestly, sh-she tends to not say anything when she feels awkward, and I'm pretty sure we made her feel awkward."

"Not as awkward as it would've been if you'd still

been mostly undressed. She would've thought I was taking advantage of you."

That gets a snort out of me. "Somehow, I don't think so."

She grins a little and starts the car. "So, I've got a little cash on me. I say breakfast before we go tackle this whole Aaron thing."

I haven't had a second to ask Autumn about last night and what it meant. But I guess our plan is still on.

I've been to Aaron's a handful of times, always with Mom, and never for very long. I remember the first time I was there, and Aaron and his brother made themselves scarce and I was stuck talking to their mostly senile grandmother for twenty minutes while Mom chatted with Ruthie. Approaching his door, then, with just Autumn feels incredibly off. His car is out front, so we know he's home. And it's the only car, so I take that to mean at least his brother and Ruthie are gone for the moment.

We exchange glances before I ring the doorbell. My heart is already starting to pound. Maybe this is a bad idea. "W-what do we do if he denies it?"

"How can he deny it? We've got proof right here." She waves her phone. "He can either tell us the truth, or we'll go to the police. Simple as that."

For some reason, I can't wrap my head around it being that easy.

It only takes a minute for Aaron to answer the door. Any other day, I would say the startled look on his face was priceless. "What are you doing here?"

"We came to talk to you about something." Autumn inclines her chin, trying to make herself look taller than she is. She's good at looking down her nose at people even when she's smaller than they are; I know this because it's a tactic she used on me repeatedly the first few times we ran into each other. "Can we come in?"

Aaron glances between us, a wary crease forming between his brows. He seems to decide we aren't a physical threat and steps aside to let us in.

His house isn't much different than I remember it. Not that I remember a lot. Just enough that I know to head down the entryway and to the right where the living room is, and where Aaron seemed to have been in the middle of watching TV. He stays right behind us and flops onto the couch, arms flung over the back of it.

"So? What do you want?"

I hadn't noticed it before, but it's more apparent to me now that Autumn is trying hard not to lose her temper. I can sense it in the way she's standing, in the way she has to take deep breaths before speaking. "We want to know what happened the night of the party."

Aaron squints, mouth slightly parted, trying to figure out the meaning of that statement. "What?"

"The night C-Callie was raped," I say patiently. "You know m-more than you've told anyone."

He scoffs. "What makes you think that? I've told the

cops everything I know."

"No, you didn't." Autumn's voice can't hide the sharp edge forming around her words. "We have proof that you didn't, so you can spill whatever you know now or we'll take that proof to the police."

The wary scowl on Aaron's face smooths out and he looks simultaneously worried and confused. "You're both fucking crazy. I don't know what you're talking about."

The cell is still in Autumn's hand and she whips it up, turns it on, opens the photo we took of Aaron's phone with the picture of Callie, then promptly shoves it in his face. "Stop screwing around, Aaron!"

Aaron jerks back like he expects she's going to grind the phone into his face, both hands coming up as though to grab it. He comes just short of doing so as he realizes what it is he's looking at. "Abject horror" is the term that comes to mind to describe his expression, and his voice is soft, barely above a whisper. "Where did you get that?"

"Can't you tell?" Autumn hisses. "It's from *your* cell phone."

"What…?"

"I'm sure you remember a day where you came back from gym and found your lock missing, right?"

Aaron's gaze flickers to Autumn, but only briefly before it's back on the phone again. If I didn't know any better, I would say his face has become extremely ashen in the last thirty seconds or so. Still, he insists, "That isn't my picture."

As though to prove it, he pulls his cell from his pocket and turns it on with shaky hands, opening up the folder with pictures from the party to scroll through them.

"It n-not being on there isn't going to prove anything. You c-could have deleted it b-by now." In fact, if he had even the smallest inkling that someone had been in his locker, he would have been smart to delete all the pictures from the party. Maybe we should've thought that through more.

Except seconds later, Aaron has the picture of Callie up on his phone, and any remaining semblance of color has drained from his face. "It's here."

"Congratulations. Now explain *why* it's there." Autumn lowers her own cell, still seething.

"I don't... I don't know." Aaron slowly offers the cell out, helpless, eyes wide, as though giving it to us will somehow cleanse his hands of it. "I didn't take that picture. I swear to God, I didn't. It wasn't there before."

Ingenuous: innocent and unsuspecting.

If there is anything I gather from how small and helpless Aaron sounds and looks right now, it's that one word. It makes me want to believe him. No...more than that, it *does* make me believe him. I wonder if this is how Autumn felt when she realized I wasn't the rapist. Frustrated, because it puts us back at square one. "Was anyone else using your ph-phone the night of the party?"

"I don't know," he repeats. "I mean, I was drunk off my ass. I don't remember. Someone may have taken it, I guess? But I don't think that's it."

Autumn asks, "Why not?"

"Because I've looked at all these pictures since then." Aaron lowers the phone, staring at it like it might miraculously give him some answers. "I've gone over them like a thousand times, trying to find some idea of who hurt Callie."

"Have the police?"

Aaron falters. "Well—they…no. I gave them all the disposable cameras and they developed the pictures, but they never asked for my phone."

Which doesn't reflect all that well on Aaron, I have to say. If the cops had already checked out his cell, that might clear him, but… "Okay. Th-then how do *you* think it got there?"

"I don't know," he stresses, and I could swear that he's close to tears. "Maybe someone planted it there. How do I know you guys didn't?! You admitted to getting hold of my phone!"

A sharp laugh escapes Autumn's mouth. "You think *we* did it? Get real."

"No, I think *he* did it." Aaron trains his suddenly sharp gaze on me and rises to his feet. The accusing stare is enough to make me want to scoot behind Autumn and hide, but I stand my ground. "He was a suspect. Of course he would do it! He would have had every reason to!"

"The lady doth protest too much," Autumn says, not backing down or cowering away. She extends her hand to Aaron. He hesitates, but slowly places his cell in her palm so that she can look at the photo up close, studying it longer. "Look, we aren't saying you raped Callie. We're asking for you to honestly tell us if you're covering for someone."

Some of Aaron's tension seems to ease out of him, though only slightly. His hands are balled into fists at his sides, and he seems to be thinking. "I don't know anything."

"You're sure?" I press.

"I'm sure," he snaps. But it isn't convincing.

Autumn and I exchange looks, both of us knowing we aren't going to get any more information out of him. She hands him back his phone. Without saying a word, we turn to leave.

Aaron starts after us worriedly. "You guys aren't going to the cops, are you?"

"If what you say is true, then it won't matter if we do because you have nothing to hide." Autumn opens the front door and looks back at him. "Right?"

His expression is a mystery to me. Something trapped between worry and uncertainty and anger. For half a second, I think he might change his mind and suddenly decide to be honest with us; instead he says, "Right," and watches us leave.

Back in the car, we slump into our seats with synchronized sighs.

"So," I ask, "w-what now?"

"Now…I think we have to go to the police. I noticed something while looking at it."

"What?"

"The time stamp in the file info. It isn't immediately obvious, but you can look to see when the pic was originally taken and when it was last modified. I don't think that photo came from Aaron's phone." She runs a hand through her wavy hair, eyes closed. I can tell she's feeling as drained and at a loss as I am. "Maybe the police can track the source of that picture or something, if Aaron is telling the truth and someone put it on there."

I consider this. "We should ask Mr. Mason. He might have a better idea."

Autumn's lashes lift and she stares off at nothing. "Yeah. That'll work. But you didn't tell Brett we were coming here, did you?"

"No," I admit. "I d-didn't want to bother him with it." He'll undoubtedly be unhappy with me for it, but I'll have to explain to him that it was in his best interest. Even now, I don't want to drag him into things, but I can't exactly go over there to have a serious conversation with his father without him finding out about it.

There isn't a point in wasting time. I give Autumn the directions to Brett's place. Although I have a key, it feels rude to just walk in when I have company, so I knock. Mr. Mason will be home today; he does most of his work in his home office. After a moment, he just so happens to be the one who answers the door.

"Hey, Vic." He glances at Autumn curiously, but his smile doesn't waver. "Brett's still asleep. He was out late last night at a study group. Come on in."

"Actually, I c-came to talk to you," I say, stepping inside. "If you have a minute."

He blinks once, closing the door behind us. "I'm getting some things ready for court on Monday, but I can spare a bit, if it's important."

"It's important," Autumn assures him.

He glances at her again, and I figure I should probably

introduce her. "Th-this is Autumn Dixon. She's, um, Callie Wheeler's best friend."

An indescribable look passes over Mr. Mason's face, and I think he's probably worried for me, and confused, and maybe a little annoyed that I would be "fraternizing with the prosecution" or something like that. But as quickly as it was there, the look is gone and he's all polite business again as he offers a hand. "Pleased to meet you, Ms. Dixon."

She takes the offered hand and shakes it. "You, too. Just Autumn is fine."

Mr. Mason ushers us into his office, where I take a seat in the chair I've sat in way too many times over the last several weeks. Autumn sits beside me, looking around in awe. It definitely feels like we've stepped from a pristine household into a law office. It should say something for how good Mr. Mason is that although he's part of a law firm, he rarely has to go into his actual office except to meet with clients he doesn't trust to have at home. Frankly, I don't think I could work with people I was afraid of, but that's just me. Mr. Mason is a unique sort of man.

"All right," he says, removing his reading glasses and folding them neatly to one side. "What's up?"

I look at Autumn and she looks at me, and I realize we're both equally nervous because we're aware that the way we came across this photograph could potentially get us into trouble. It was my idea though, so… "If w-we were to c-come across evidence regarding Callie's rape, but did so in a not-very-moral way, would it still be usable?"

Mr. Mason squints, thoughtful. "I suppose that depends

on the evidence and how you came about it. What did you do, Vic?"

"We had a hunch and went through someone's cell phone," Autumn says.

"Without this person's knowledge?"

In unison: "Yes."

He sighs and pinches the bridge of his nose, but I would almost say he looks more tiredly amused than annoyed. "We can work around that, I'm sure. Or rather, Callie's lawyer could. I'm your defense, not the prosecution, so it doesn't mean much to me."

I start to reply when there comes a knock at the door and then it swings open. Brett pops his head inside. "Hey, Dad—" He pauses when he sees me. Or maybe it's because he sees Autumn, and that sight in his house has to be a little weird. "Oh, sorry. I didn't realize you were here, Vic."

"H-hey," I greet.

Brett lets himself inside and wanders over. There isn't another chair for him to sit on, so he leans against the desk instead, curiously eyeing us all. His hair is a mess and he's in his pajamas, meaning he was, indeed, out late last night and probably just woke up. I wonder if he's hungover or if he actually did go to a study group. "What's going on?"

"Vic and Autumn were just telling me about some new evidence they came across in the case." Mr. Mason looks to his son, as though wondering if he had anything to do with us digging through someone's personal things.

"He didn't know," I'm quick to say, wanting to defend Brett.

Brett asks, "What kind of evidence?"

"We went through Aaron Biggs's phone and found this." Autumn holds her cell out to him with the picture of Callie on the screen. Brett's perplexed expression quickly melts away, replaced by a pale-faced look of nausea. He quickly tilts his chin up.

"When did you do that?"

"A f-few days ago."

"Were you planning on telling me?"

I knew that was coming. "I'm telling you now."

Brett shoots me a scowl. "Sure, after you went and did it. What if you'd been caught? Why don't you ever tell me anything anymore?"

Mr. Mason clears his throat. "That's something the two of you can discuss later, when I don't have a court appearance Monday morning to prepare for. Vic, I'm not sure whether this information is going to be useful or not, but I'd take it to the detectives."

I'm pretty sure the numbers are saved in my phone, but… "W-wouldn't it come better from you?"

"Not necessarily." He raises his brows. "But if they need me, they have my phone number. Like I said, I'm not Callie's lawyer. I'm yours. The prosecution is going to be the one interested in it."

Fair enough, I guess. Considering that Brett is giving me dirty looks, I should probably go face the music where Mr. Mason won't see it. Honestly, I wish Autumn wouldn't see it, either, but that might be unavoidable.

We step out of the office and into the hall. Brett takes

us to the living room, smooths a hand through his hair, and sinks onto the couch. Autumn is keeping right at my side and I remain standing, shuffling my feet awkwardly.

"It isn't that I d-didn't want to tell you—"

"Really? Because that's what a lot of this feels like. You didn't tell me about Aaron dragging you into the bathroom, or about them cornering you at your work, and now this? Did I do something to piss you off?" He doesn't look at me. If anything, he seems to be trying his best not to look at me.

My spine stiffens. I really wish Autumn would wait outside, but she isn't budging. "I've been trying to protect you, all right? I didn't tell you b-because you've got all of this going on"—I sweep a hand out, gesturing to the coffee table, which is still home to college brochures I've seen him looking over the last several times I've been here—"and I wanted you to stay focused. The l-last thing I want to do is ruin your chances or g-get in the way."

It's a confession that seems to make some of the irritability seep out of Brett's posture. His expression softens at the edges, eyes finally lifting to look at me. "Whatever happened to me protecting you?"

I manage a sliver of a smile. "You d-don't always have to. That's not how a f-friendship works. Let me look out for you once in a while."

He sighs. "I think you're an asshole for keeping secrets."

"I think you're an asshole a lot of the time, so does that make us even?"

Brett manages a half grin. "Yeah, whatever… Well, now that I know what's going on, at least let me help. Let's go talk to the cops."

Maybe Autumn senses my hesitation, because she finally interjects. "It still stands, though. There are reporters poking around, and I don't think you want your face in the paper anywhere, do you?"

Brett casts his gaze to her. "But— "

"Sh-she's right, man. I still don't want you getting wrapped up in things. Let me take care of it."

I feel not unlike a child having to get permission from his parents to make his own mistakes, and maybe that isn't far from the mark. Brett has looked out for me most of our lives, has kept me from doing dumb things. Stepping back and letting me assume control must be as difficult for him as it is for me to start making my own choices without him there to constantly back me up.

But Brett smiles a sad sort of smile. And he doesn't argue any further. Autumn and I head back out to her car, and before I get in, she grabs my hand and leans up to kiss me firmly on the cheek. A goofy grin passes over my face, which I'm certain has turned a nice shade of red.

"What was that for?"

She squeezes my hand and releases it, shrugs once, and circles around to the driver's side door. "I know how hard that must have been for you, making him back off like that. I'm proud of you."

I get into the passenger's side and buckle in. "Y-you don't think I'm just…trading one decision maker for another, do you?" I'm not sure if I am. I mean, am I just replacing Brett with Autumn and letting her guide my choices instead?

"The fact that you're even asking me that tells me no," she assures me, patting my knee. "It's normal to want opinions on things, you know? Asking for help with big choices. But ultimately, as long as the final decision is yours, that's all that really matters."

I think her words put me at ease, and I wish I could formulate how grateful I am for her, for her support and the simple way she says all the things I need to hear. "Th-thanks."

She grins and turns on the car, while I pull out my phone in response to its buzzing. It's a text from Mom.

Going to be home for dinner?

Well, that's bizarre. She hasn't asked me that in…as long as I can remember. My thumb hovers over the screen.

Can be. Why?

Making spaghetti at 5 if you and your friend want to come.

My friend… She isn't referring to Brett; she would have said his name. Which means Autumn. My mother wants Autumn to come over for dinner. Oh, shoot me in the head.

"What's the plan, chief?" Autumn asks, hands on the wheel, waiting for instruction.

"Uh," I say ever so eloquently, "M-Mom wants to know if you'd like to c-come over for dinner." And then I laugh. "You don't have to. I can tell her you're b-busy or—"

"I'd love to."

"Yeah, that's… What? Really?" I twist partway in my

seat to stare at her.

Her eyebrows lift as she starts driving down the street, away from Brett's house. "Well, why not? I kind of made a bad first impression on her this morning, so maybe it's a chance to try again."

"I h-have no idea how she's going to react, Autumn."

"So? I'm a big girl. I can take it, whatever *it* is." She smiles without looking at me. "If you aren't up for it, it's fine. But don't worry about me. I can handle your mother."

Chapter Twenty-Two

The remainder of my day is spent trying not to stress out at the idea of prolonged exposure of Autumn to my mother. Don't get me wrong—Mom is a very polite woman, but she's so reserved she can come across as cold and, again, I have no idea how she'll react to the girl she must know stayed in my room last night. I can't even introduce her as my girlfriend or something. I know Mom's making an effort to patch things up between us, but I have no clue how sincere she was in that, or how far she's willing to go to do it.

But Autumn promises that my mother's actions won't reflect on me, and I have to trust her with that. We don't go to the police because Sherrigan and Carter haven't returned my call saying that I want to talk to them. In theory, we could drive to the station to see if they're around, but I'm not sure I'm prepared for that just yet. One traumatizing event at a time.

When we get home, Mom's car is in the driveway and I linger just outside the front door, gulping in deep breaths to stave off the building anxiety in my chest. Autumn cups her hands to my face and she's so close I can smell whatever perfume she wears, and it smells amazing. She smiles. "Come on. You can do it."

I can do it. Yes. I hope so.

I let us inside. The smell of Mom's homemade spaghetti wafts from the kitchen, bringing back the flash of a memory of us eating together on the couch when I was younger, watching reruns of *Seinfeld* while I scooped spaghetti sauce onto a hunk of garlic bread. It makes me close my eyes, soothing away the rest of my worries. Things used to be okay between Mom and me. They can be okay again.

Autumn follows me into the kitchen where Mom is at the stove, her hair tied up and the apron she typically uses for baking fitted around her waist.

"Hey," I say, and she turns around.

"Hi, Ms. Howard," Autumn offers.

"Hi, kids." Mom places the ladle aside on a paper towel, wipes her hands on her apron, and steps around the kitchen island toward us to take the hand Autumn is offering.

Autumn says, "I'm sorry we didn't really get a chance to meet properly this morning."

"It's fine." She glances at me, and I rub the back of my neck sheepishly.

"Um… Autumn's my friend, Mom. We go to school together." I'll leave out the part about her being Callie's best friend. Not a topic I want to stir up right now.

"It's nice to meet you," Mom offers. "Dinner's about ready if you want to take a seat." She's already set the table and everything, so there isn't anything I can offer to help with.

I motion for Autumn to sit down while I shuffle to the stove, figuring I can at least help with the plating or something. If nothing else, it gives me half a second to lean in and whisper to my mother, "W-what are we doing, exactly?"

"We're having dinner, Victor." She dumps the noodles into a serving bowl and tops it with sauce. I've always loved the spaghetti sauce she makes: onions and meatballs and paprika.

But even the scent of it isn't enough to detract me from my purpose of figuring out what's happening. "That's it?"

She looks at me, and I don't see any ulterior motives written across her face. Maybe she really is trying. Maybe she actually wants to connect, wants to meet my maybe-girlfriend, because that's what moms do. "That's it."

The serving bowl is placed into my hands. I take it to the table and set it in the center while Mom follows behind with Parmesan cheese and a gallon of milk to fill our glasses. She's always been big on dinner being accompanied by milk.

Autumn pushes her chair in a little farther and smiles. "It smells delicious, Ms. Howard."

"Victoria is fine," Mom says, sitting across from us. That's a first, I'll say; I'm sure she's told Brett to call her by her first name before, many years ago, but it isn't something she does often with other people.

"Victoria." Autumn glances at me as though to make sure this isn't some kind of test.

We each take turns scooping spaghetti onto our plates and begin to eat, settled in silence that is vaguely uncomfortable only because I don't know what to expect. I'm not sure if I should be trying to make conversation, or if our entire meal will be eaten without any of us uttering a word.

Mom finally asks, "How long have you two been dating?"

I choke on my spaghetti and have to clear my throat. Dating? Yeah, I was worried she got that impression given that she caught Autumn coming out of my bedroom, but I had hoped to avoid that sort of question by emphasizing the word "friend." Instantly I'm worried this is a trick question, but it could very well be Mom just *trying* and I don't know how to tell the difference.

But Autumn doesn't skip a beat. "A week or two. We sort of just fell into it." She wipes her mouth with a napkin.

I stare at her.

"Oh, that's nice. Where did you two meet?"

"S-school." I have no idea what Autumn is doing, but I'm not going to call her out on it in front of Mom. Well, this is sort of answering my questions about our kiss last night.

"School is a big place." Mom blinks at me. Am I being too vague? Difficult? I don't know. But I can't exactly tell her the truth, can I?

"He knows my best friend," Autumn says. "I met him through her. I mean, I've seen him around school and stuff, but he's so quiet that we hadn't talked much…"

Mom seems to relax, a tiny smile gracing her thin mouth. "That's nice to hear. Vic is a good boy."

I almost flinch at how forced the words are, like Mom wants to believe them but is having a hard time doing so. My eyes drop down to my plate, where I begin separating the pieces of my spaghetti—meatballs here, chunks of onion there, noodles to the side—out of nervousness.

"He is," Autumn chimes in with a smile, reaching out to smooth my hair affectionately in such a way that it prompts me to look up at her in surprise. "He's a gentleman, and he cares so much about other people, you know? He doesn't have that typical macho, overbearing self-assuredness most guys at school have."

It occurs to me that she could just be saying these things as a means of proving to Mom that I'm not a bad son, yet there's something in the way she says every word of it that makes me believe her. My stomach is fluttering and I can't help the silly, lopsided smile that pulls my mouth up at the corners.

The rest of dinner is eaten with very light conversation that is sometimes easy, sometimes forced. Autumn politely asks about Mom's work, Mom asks what Autumn plans to do after graduation. ("I want to work over the summer to save up some money, then I have a grant to tide me over while I go to community college for food science and some art classes.")

After we're done, I assure Mom that Autumn and I can take care of the dishes, since she went through the effort of cooking, and she excuses herself to go to her room because she needs to be in bed at a decent hour in order to get up early for Sunday overtime work in the morning. In reality, it probably has more to do with the fact that she doesn't do well socializing, and this dinner wore her out. Hell, it's worn *me* out.

Once Mom has left us alone to clear the table, Autumn comes to stand beside me at the sink where I've dumped the night's dishes, and she smiles.

"That wasn't too bad, was it? Unless you think she's going to come murder me in my sleep now."

I turn on the water, exhaling loudly through my nose. "N-no. It wasn't t-too bad. Just…weird."

"Weird how?"

"She thinks we're dating now, for instance."

Autumn shrugs. "So?"

I can't bring myself to look at her. "So…? We aren't. Are we? Because it's cool if we are and it's cool if we aren't…"

"I wouldn't have said it if I hadn't wanted it. Is that what made it weird?"

She wants it, too? I stumble over that thought while trying to process it. Mom. Right, we were technically talking about Mom. "That, and Mom's trying to act n-normal. Like, doing that was a normal parent thing."

Autumn picks up a towel to dry the dishes as I wash them. "Isn't that good? I mean, I figured that's what you wanted."

"It is, but…out of nowhere, it f-feels…" How do I explain? "It feels like she's trying to dive into 'normal' when we haven't even worked out our issues, I guess. I still feel like things are tense. B-but I don't know how to fix that."

Her head bobs into a nod. "She's probably like you in the sense that she doesn't know where to start. Fake it 'til you make it, right?"

I hand her a fistful of clean, wet silverware. "You speaking from experience?"

"A little bit. Not exactly the same." She takes them carefully, places them on the counter, and gives each fork and knife her attention to dry them one by one. "When Mom married my stepdad, he and I butted heads a lot. Their marriage was kind of sudden so I hadn't really gotten a chance to get to know him. So technically, I'd met this guy all of four times in person before he was moving into my house and I was expected to treat him like a dad."

"That doesn't sound like it would go over well with your personality type," I say with a smile.

She chuckles. "Nope. Things were rough for the first two or three years, but we both tried our best. We've grown closer than I ever was with my real dad."

Now that I think about it, Autumn has only ever mentioned her dad very briefly. "Where is he? Your real dad, I mean. Is he really a heroin dealer?"

"Eh, who knows." Her shoulders rise and fall in a shrug. "For a while, he'd pick me up every other weekend. Then he moved out of state, and he'd call instead. Then it was letters, then cards on special occasions, until it stopped altogether."

I stop what I'm doing to really look at her, frowning. "Autumn…"

"The last card I got from him was on my sixteenth birthday." She lifts her chin, and surprisingly there is no sadness or regret there, and I can't begin to fathom why. "I don't entirely blame him, though, you know? Because I realized that slowly but surely, I had started slowing down contact with him, too. The better things got with my stepdad, the less I felt like I had to keep reaching for a guy who didn't really want anything to do with me."

"Your dad must love you. How could he not?"

"Maybe he does, I don't know. But distance can really change a relationship." She smiles. Her damp hand reaches up where she thumbs a few soapsuds off my cheek. No idea how they got there. "I don't hate him, I don't miss him. I guess I feel pretty indifferent these days. I'm not lacking anything in my life."

My lashes lower. "So d-do you think something's wrong with me that I want to see my dad?"

She plucks the last plate from my hands to dry it. "I'm not sure I can answer that without sounding like an asshole. Yes and no? But, I mean, I guess it's pretty human to want to see where you come from. But how do you handle all the horrible things he's done?"

Tricky question. "He's still my dad. I can hate him and love him at the same time, I think? Emotions are dumb that way."

The last of the dishes are placed on the draining board. I let the soapy water out of the sink, watching the suds and tiny pieces of food remnants swirl down the drain. Autumn presses herself neatly against my side, arms slipping around my waist, her chin propped on my shoulder.

"Do you feel like your life is lacking somewhere, Vic?"

If I'm entirely honest—and with Autumn, I try my best to be... "Yeah." I turn my head to look at her, and when I meet her eyes, the sense of calm that settles over me is a much-needed relief. "Except sometimes, when I look at you...things feel just right."

She smiles in a way that makes my chest do funny, fluttery things. "Come on. If your mom's going to bed, we can do the dorky date thing where we watch dumb movies late into the night."

"That s-sounds a lot like a date."

"Maybe it is," she remarks, sliding away from me and casting a long look over her shoulder, making me wonder if I'm ever going to work up the courage to be the one to kiss her.

Chapter Twenty-Three

Autumn doesn't stay as late as I'd like her to. After her slipup the night before, we both figure it's best for her to get home while her parents are still awake so they don't think she "accidentally" slept over at Callie's place again. Still, when she tells me good-bye at the door, I feel like her sudden absence takes all the joy out of the room. Everything else in my life might be bizarre right now, but Autumn is the one bright thing I have to hold on to. My silver lining.

Getting to bed at a decent hour is probably a good thing anyway, considering I have to be at work bright and early. Not that it matters how early I show up, because like always, Amjad is already there, awake and alert while I'm still rubbing the sleep from my eyes and trying to remember even riding my bike from home to here.

"Good morning, Victor," he greets.

I grunt in response, dropping my backpack behind the counter with a yawn. I'm on autopilot, heading into the back to clean up and restock any empty items on the shelves. Credit to Amjad for waiting until I'm done and somewhat more coherent before he says, "A Mr. Craig Roberts came by for you."

I freeze at the end of the candy aisle, stomach dropping. "W-what did he want?"

"He said he wanted to discuss the article he wrote." He's peering at me intently and I want to sink into the linoleum and hide.

"Oh," I say uselessly.

"Is everything all right, Victor? Is he bothering you?" A frown is tugging at his heavy brows.

"N-no. I mean…I don't know. What did you t-tell him?" What am I supposed to say to that?

Amjad *hmphs* and looks down at his coffee, dumping a plastic container of creamer into the Styrofoam cup. "He writes a bad article then comes to see you. He is a very self-assured man. I told him to never come back or I would file for harassment."

All the blood seems to drain from my body to pool at my feet, because I'm positive I'm going to pass out. I stand there stupidly, staring at Amjad as he stares at his coffee. He read the article. He saw it in the paper. I'd ignored the fact that he might, despite knowing he always reads the paper with his morning coffee, but…

"Y-you knew…?"

He lifts his gaze. "Of course I knew. The police came to talk to me."

My legs are going to give out. I brace a hand against the end cap. "But you…didn't say anything to me."

"You did not want to talk about it." His head tilts.

My pulse is racing. Am I going to get fired? "W-what did the police want?"

"Your mother told them you work here sometimes. They wanted to know what kind of a boy you were." He shrugs. "I told them you were very reliable, and a good young man."

My gaze doesn't leave Amjad's face. What can I say to that? I was so afraid to let him know. Not just out of fear of losing my job, but fear of him shunning me. Of letting him down. "You k-knew it wasn't girl problems."

"It sort of was." He smiles a little. "If someone comes here to bother you, you tell me. I will take care of it."

I press the heels of my hands against my eyes and take a few deep breaths. "Thank you."

His smile widens into something warmer and friendlier. "Since we are being honest now, what about this girlfriend of yours?"

I shake my head and circle around the counter to take a seat nearby him. I almost say, *She's not my girlfriend*, but…she is, isn't she? We sort of danced around the subject, but that's the only conclusion I can come to. "What about her?"

"She is pretty. Smart?"

"V-very."

"Treat her good, then." He sips his coffee and pats me

on the back. "A good boy deserves a good girl."

I can't help but smile, though I think he's got it wrong. Maybe I'm a good guy, but Autumn is a *great* girl. And I'm still not entirely convinced I deserve her.

This is all Amjad says on the subject. He doesn't prod me for information or make me go into detail about any of it. Hindsight is twenty-twenty, so in retrospect I feel dumb for not having brought it up sooner. Maybe I could have avoided more of the headache with Craig Roberts.

Through the day, Amjad acts no different from normal. He tells me about his date and how well it went, that he's likely to go out with her again next weekend, and how he never really thought he'd be interested in another woman after his wife passed away. We each dip into the lotto tickets and take one, which results in me winning a whole five dollars and Amjad winning a free ticket.

Halfway through my shift, the door chimes with the entrance of a customer—which has happened plenty already—but this time, the face I see is a familiar one.

Aaron stares at me from the other side of the counter, mouth twisted uncomfortably. He's come in here plenty with his brother and grandma, so it isn't a surprise that he knows I work here. But we are watching each other blankly, both waiting for the other to say something, and I feel Amjad noticing something is wrong because he speaks up for me. "Can I help you?"

It breaks Aaron's focus on me and he looks away, holding out a few bills. "Twenty on three, please."

Amjad takes the cash and Aaron leaves. I watch through

the window as he pumps his gas, gets into the car, and sits there. Waiting? He could be. He doesn't seem to be playing on his phone or doing anything, and the car isn't even on. He's just…sitting.

"Friend of yours?" Amjad asks, squinting outside.

"Mom's b-best friend's son. We go to school together." I turn away, taking a deep breath. The last thing I need is a repeat of what happened the other night with Patrick and his friends.

"Should I ask him to leave?"

"No. I got it." Not that I want to, but Amjad is right here and I'm sure he'll watch out for any signs of trouble.

Taking a deep breath, I head outside and over to Aaron's truck. He glances at me through the driver's side window, then inclines his chin toward the opposite door. I hesitate, then circle around to open it and get in. I don't close the door behind me because too many horror movie scenarios of people getting locked inside a car hurtling down the freeway to imminent death are playing in my head. "What is it?"

Aaron doesn't look at me. Rather, he's staring down at his phone. At the picture of Callie from the night of the party. "I really liked her, you know."

My spine goes rigid, and a heavy knot of dread forms in my gut. I don't say anything.

"We weren't together that long, but she was just…really cool, you know? Sweet and funny and great to be around. The night of the party, I got drunk enough that I even told Brett I was thinking about trying to ask her out again."

If this is a confession, I don't know if I want to hear

it. This isn't something Aaron should be saying to me; he should be saying it to the police. "Aaron—"

"Shut up. Let me finish." He runs a hand roughly through his dark hair, exhaling. "When I found out what happened, I was just...so pissed. At first I was mad at her. Like, I thought she'd slept with some guy after she gave me this big speech when we broke up about not being ready for shit like that, you know? Then it really hit me what happened, that it wasn't her fault, and then I just...really wanted to kill whoever did it."

All the air comes whooshing out of my chest through my mouth. "So you really didn't do it?"

He casts me a scathing look. "No, I didn't fucking do it, you idiot."

"S-sorry—"

"I *care* about Callie. I wouldn't want to hurt her." Aaron looks away again, and this time I sense a hesitance in his gaze that I can't place. Like he's struggling to say something but can't.

"But?"

"But Patrick made a comment about the whole thing that hasn't been sitting right with me. He said, 'No girl comes to a party wearing lace underwear not expecting to get laid.' At first, I thought he was just being an asshole. It's the type of thing he'd say."

Even hearing the comment secondhand makes my stomach turn. I slowly draw the door closed, not wanting anyone else at the pumps to overhear us. "Then what m-made you think differently?"

Aaron twists in his seat and holds his phone out to me, the screen inches from my face so that I have to pull back to even see it clearly. He says, "Look at it."

I avert my gaze automatically. Yes, I've seen the photo, but I haven't studied it in depth. It made me feel wrong. At his prompting, I force myself to look, to really look. Yes, I noticed the long line of her legs and the mess of blankets around her, the trash can that I placed beside the bed halfway in frame... But if I look closely enough, I notice the way her skirt is hiked up over her hip, and the underwear beneath—

I push the phone away and close my eyes.

"You see it, right?" Aaron presses anxiously. "I'm not crazy? Am I thinking too much about it?"

I'd be wondering the same thing. Aaron could be making things up, and yet I don't think he'd have come here to talk to me if he were. I don't think he'd sound so distressed, so scared. Though scared of what, I have no idea. Maybe the idea that he's been hanging around the person who raped a girl at his party? That could freak anyone out.

"Should I go to the police?" he asks. "I have no idea what to do."

"I called them y-yesterday," I mumble, looking out the window, trying to think. Brett would know what to do. "They haven't returned my call yet. Do you have Patrick's address?"

He blinks. "Well, yeah. But—you're not gonna go talk to him yourself, are you?"

I shrug. Alone? No. I wouldn't have a way to get there.

Waiting for the detectives to call might be smarter, but something is gnawing at my insides, making this feel urgent. I can't wait for them. I can't sit around and beg for them to hurry up with their protocol and rules so something can be done.

"D-don't worry about me. I can handle it."

Chapter Twenty-Four

Autumn picks me up from work with a grim look on her face, which only gets grimmer as we drive the distance to Patrick's home and I explain to her what Aaron told me.

She says, "He could be lying."

"I d-don't feel like he is, though."

"If you say so. You're the people-reader."

Ha, I don't feel like I'm doing a very good job at reading into anything. More like I'm going in circles while grasping blindly for answers.

"Did you text Brett?" she asks.

"Called him. He didn't answer." Which means he's probably sleeping, or out with his family, or working on his college applications. Any number of things. But at least this time he can't be mad at me for not trying to include him.

We pull up outside an apartment complex called Villa del Rio, and I instruct Autumn that we're looking for apartment 205, according to Aaron. We find a visitor's parking spot and get out, and we don't even scale halfway up the steps to his place before Autumn is nudging me and pointing to the basketball court nearby.

"Isn't that him?"

Yeah, that would be Patrick Maloney, in shorts and a tank top, doing layups. Thankfully by himself. He isn't going to be happy to talk to us. Aaron might be loud and likes to run his mouth, but Patrick is the one who didn't think twice about cornering me in the bathroom or showing up at work prepared to kick my ass. Aaron will seem like a cakewalk compared to this.

We walk to the court and stop at the edge where grass gives way to blacktop. Patrick's water bottle and backpack are slouched on the ground near our feet. Patrick does three more layups before he glances our way, and then does a double take and turns to glare in our direction.

"What are you doing here?"

I shift from one foot to the other. "Just came to t-talk, if you have a minute."

"What could I possibly have to say to you?" he drawls, turning away and taking another shot—which he easily makes.

"It's about Callie." Of course Autumn goes straight for the point. Where this is concerned, she has no patience for not getting right to the point. "We heard about something you said and wanted to ask you a few questions."

Patrick falters in his dribbling, so briefly I almost wonder if I imagined it. But he stops, ball between his hands, and stares at the net thoughtfully. "I don't know anything about that."

"Can we see your phone?"

His gaze flickers briefly to his backpack. "Why the hell would I let you see my phone?"

"Because if you have nothing to hide, then it shouldn't be a problem." Autumn tips her chin up, arms crossed.

He turns to face us. Bounces the ball to make a profound *smack* against the blacktop. "I don't have anything to hide, and for that reason, I don't have to show you shit. It's my phone. None of your business."

We aren't going to get anywhere this way. I foresee it escalating with the two of them until Autumn is throwing him to the ground and beating his face in with the basketball. The only way to—maybe—make headway is to flat out ask him: "H-how did you know what Callie was wearing that night?"

Okay, so worded stupidly, but I tried. Patrick gives me a cockeyed look. "What?"

Autumn grips my arm tightly. If she speaks, she's going to yell. Or cry. I don't want either of those things to happen. "Her underwear," I snap. "You made a comment to your friends. You knew what she was wearing under her skirt. How?"

As the words leave my mouth, Patrick's hard glare dissipates and his mouth downturns a fraction of an inch. He isn't irritated anymore. Or at least, he looks more worried now than anything else.

"Fuck off," he says, and his voice is hoarse and the words sound forced.

"We can't help you if you w-won't talk to us," I say. Never mind that I have no interest in helping Patrick if he had anything to do with Callie's assault, but if it makes him talk…

Patrick shoves a hand over his shaved head and puts his back to us, taking a shot at the basket. The ball cracks against the rim and bounces clear off to the side, into the grass. "I don't have anything to talk about."

"Yeah?" Autumn stoops down, snatching up Patrick's backpack and beginning to go through the pockets. He whips around at the sound, snarling, and reflex has me throwing myself between him and Autumn. We're close enough in build that I'm hoping he doesn't have any idea that I can't defend myself in a one-on-one fight, but I'll die trying before I let him lay a hand on Autumn.

Autumn locates his phone in the front zipper pocket and turns away as she swipes through the photos on it, and I'm observing the color draining from Patrick's face.

She goes still. When she turns around, her eyes are pinched shut and not a word comes out of her mouth. She simply holds the phone out for me to see, and I don't need to look closely to tell that the images—*images,* plural—are all of Callie passed out at the lake house.

I turn to him slowly. Patrick looks ready to bolt. "I didn't do it. I *swear to God*, I didn't do it."

I take a few steps forward until I'm only a foot or so away. "If you d-didn't do anything wrong, then there's nothing for you to be worried about. Either you did it, or you know something about who did."

He studies me, close enough that every bead of perspiration is visible, close enough that the way his pupils have dilated is extremely obvious. His fingers curl and uncurl, fidgeting, and each deep breath is ragged through his nose.

"Patrick," I say.

Something in his expression crumbles, just a little. "I just took the pictures. That was all. I was drunk off my ass and he told me to take the pictures, and that if I told anyone, he'd make sure I was the one who went down for it. But I *swear*, I never touched her."

If I cared more about how he was feeling, I would put my hands on his shoulders or try to make him feel better. Frankly, he's lucky Autumn hasn't ripped his throat out and I haven't hit him. "Wait a second, calm d-down. *Who* told you to take the pictures?"

He opens his mouth but the words won't come out. They catch somewhere in his throat between his guilt and his fear, and I'm worried he's going to grab the phone and make a run for it. Maybe he realizes that no matter how he answers, the police are going to be at his doorstep.

Autumn says, "Patrick, *who told you* to take the pictures?"

Patrick slowly sinks down to a crouch, head bowed, hands laced behind his neck. When he looks up, his eyes are glassy.

And he says, "Brett."

Chapter Twenty-Five

I don't realize that I've hit him until Autumn is grabbing my arms and trying to pull me back. Patrick is on the ground, hand clamped over his mouth. I'm shaking. I'm shaking and I'm going to be sick and Patrick is rolling onto his side, spitting blood onto the concrete, and I don't understand what just happened.

Rage: violent, uncontrollable anger.

Wrath. Fury. Outrage.

None of these is a strong enough word.

"Take it back!" The words are hollow and seem to echo into nothingness.

"You wanted the truth," Patrick hisses. His bottom lip is bleeding. He must have cut it on his teeth when I punched him. "And I gave it to you. We were drunk. We saw you take her upstairs, and Brett wanted to go look. It just got out of hand."

Even my voice wavers. Every word is an effort to get out. "I don't believe you."

"At first I was just going to use his phone to take a picture of him sitting there with her. Something stupid. Then it got carried away and he just started to mess around with her—I swear, I never meant for it to happen."

Autumn's hands are wrapped around mine, holding me in place as much as I think I'm holding her. She whips her head toward him, her voice shy of a scream. "But it did! It did happen, you son of a bitch, and you were willing to let Vic take the fall for it! You went with your friends to go after him, knowing exactly who the real rapist was!"

"I didn't want to go to jail!" Patrick howls. "They already suspected Vic; it was easy to just play along with it. It was Brett's idea to put some of the pics on Aaron's phone as a backup just in case!"

I don't care about the whys or hows or anything else. It's all background noise set behind the blaring reality of what Patrick first said to me.

I had hoped this would all lead to a dead end, that the cops would find another suspect. Someone who fit into the role perfectly. Someone who didn't go to our school. Patrick and Aaron were bad enough when I thought about how many times Callie has passed them in the few short days she's been back at school, but Brett...

Brett.

Brett raped Callie.

Brett, who comforted me and promised me everything would be okay. Brett, whose father was ready to stand at my side and defend me.

No. I'm not grasping this concept. I can't breathe.

Patrick and Autumn are still arguing when I turn and run for the parking lot.

The car door is locked. I try the handle anyway before sliding down the side to sit on the ground, staring at my cell. Brett never texted me back after I said I was coming to Patrick's. Why didn't he text me back?

Patrick is lying. He has to be.

Brett is not that type of person. More than that, he would never have thrown me under the bus, never have let me take the fall for him.

Autumn finds me several minutes later. Her eyes are red from crying. She sinks to a crouch in front of me, hands on her knees. It's the first time I've seen her at a loss for what to say.

"Maybe we should talk to his parents first," she says quietly. "Unless you want to go to the police."

Mutely, I shake my head. How can I go to the cops and turn in my best friend? Especially when I'm not convinced he did it.

"Victor." Autumn extends a hand, touches my cheek, tries to coax me into looking up at her. "We have to do something."

I force a deep breath into my lungs and out again, despite how tight and disorganized my insides feel. "I need to t-talk to him."

"I don't think that's a good idea. We need to—"

"*No.* He's my best friend. I can't just t-take someone else's word for it without t-talking to him."

Autumn runs a hand over her face. She's as tired as I am. And while my concern has shifted involuntarily toward my closest friend, I know she's still focused on Callie. I should be, too. But I'm not sure how to balance my worry for them both. Autumn's whole social world is Callie. Mine is Brett.

Brett couldn't do this. He *wouldn't.*

There's some misunderstanding. Patrick is full of shit.

"I'll drive you, if you want," she offers.

Logically, that would be best. But my brain isn't clear enough yet to talk to Brett. I need some air. I need some silence. I need— "I can walk." If my sense of direction isn't skewed, Brett's shouldn't be more than thirty minutes away. I can use my phone if I need directions.

Autumn gets up at the same time I do, brows knit together. "Vic, you don't have to do this alone."

Looking at her face, I think I really understand why Autumn has wanted to help so much these last few weeks. It isn't just because she cares about me, or about Callie. It's because she's felt so helpless to undo what happened to her best friend, helpless to control anything about this situation. If it were anyone else but Brett, I would gladly bring her along, but this is something I have to do. This is something I need to tackle on my own.

I cup her cheeks in my hands, bowing down until our foreheads touch. She's struggling to stay composed, to keep from crying any more, and I wonder what else she said to

Patrick, what Patrick said to her.

"I *need* to do this alone," I murmur, covering her mouth with a kiss before she can protest. Autumn's fingers curl against my chest, twisting the fabric of my shirt to hold me where I am, and her mouth is soft but so insistent and desperate in the way she kisses me back, as though I can somehow fix all of this with a wave of my hand. God, I would if I could.

When I pull away, she closes her eyes, taking a deep breath and straightening up. Of all the moments in my life I could have picked to gather the courage to kiss Autumn Dixon, and this is it. Desperate and sad and raw, and tasting of tears. Still, Autumn tries to smile through it. "Call me when you need me."

That's all I need. To know she'll be there when this is over, that if somehow—some way—Brett is gone out of my life, I won't be all alone.

I underestimated the walk to Brett's. It takes me closer to fifty minutes in the heat as opposed to thirty. The only car in Brett's driveway when I get there is his, and for a second my stomach lurches at the thought that he went somewhere with his parents, and no one is home.

The key Mrs. Mason gave me is still on my key chain. I don't think twice before using it, and my throat won't even cooperate enough to call out Brett's name. He isn't in the living room or the kitchen. Further investigation leads me upstairs, where I hear the shower going in the hall. Brett's shower.

My hands have gone clammy and numb. I step into Brett's room, making a straight line for his cell phone, which is sitting ominously on his desk, near his glasses and homework. I wrap my fingers around the rubber casing and turn on the screen, stopping only when my gaze is caught by the corkboard behind Brett's desk.

I've seen it a hundred times before. It's not like the photographs I'm looking at now are any different than they were the first, second, third, hundredth time I looked at them. Now, maybe, I'm viewing them with more brevity and each image of Brett and me—from grade school to high school and every summer, holiday, birthday in between—stabs my heart a littler deeper.

"Vic?"

I turn around, his phone in hand. Brett steps into his room in sweatpants and a T-shirt, towel around his shoulders and short, wet hair plastered to his forehead.

"What're you doing?"

This is stupid. I should just tell him. I should tell him what Patrick told me so he can explain and put my worries to rest. "I j-just got here from talking to Patrick."

Brett blinks. He slides the towel off and chucks it into his laundry basket. "Why would you go see him?"

My grip tightens around the phone. I have to force it to relax. "He has pictures on his phone from the night of the party. Of Callie."

Brett pauses, straightens, turns to watch me with a serious crease to his brow. "What?"

"Patrick has pictures of Callie. He said he took them for someone." I don't stutter, but the tone of my voice wavers like I'm regretting every word that is coming out of my mouth.

"Jesus." Brett combs his fingers through his hair, but he doesn't move from his spot. If anything, his gaze has grown more intense. "We should call my dad. Let me see my phone."

Reflex almost has me handing it to him. I want to. If I could pretend I don't have a reason to mistrust Brett right now, my world would be a much brighter place. "I n-need to look at the pictures on your phone, Brett."

His mouth downturns. "No, you don't. Let's call my dad."

He extends his hand, waiting.

I lift the phone, breathe deeply, and turn on the screen again, punch in the pass code I've known since the day he got the phone, and open to Brett's photos.

"You're overreacting, Vic," he says quietly.

No response. I'm too busy skimming through Brett's phone, flipping through pictures from the night of the party, of which there are plenty. A number of them of himself and Aaron, himself and Patrick.

There are no pictures of Callie. I lower the phone. Tears prick my eyes.

"Feel better?" Brett hasn't lowered his hand. "Can I have it now, please?"

Does it prove anything? I don't know. I want it to. My eyes are burning with fighting back tears, and I step forward to hand over the phone.

It beeps once, and the still-active screen presents me with a pop-up from Patrick that reads:

> ***I told about callie. The cops know about both of us. Sorry***

The cops know.

Patrick was telling the truth.

Did Autumn leave him so racked with guilt that he had to tell? Or did he know his secret was out and didn't want to wait around for the police to show up at his door?

Either way, I can see the anger settling over Brett's features, darkening his eyes, curling his mouth. The last time I saw that look was when he cornered Aaron in the parking lot, an act that now makes my chest tight with how wrong it was. Brett snatches the phone from my hand and turns away. He drags in a shaky breath. He types something back to Patrick and chucks the phone to the bed. His hands go to his hair, gripping the short strands fiercely in frustration. "Fucking moron…"

"Brett. What did you do?"

He turns halfway to look at me, raising a finger. "This is your chance to leave it alone, Vic. They have no evidence against me, and Patrick had the pictures."

God, my throat is so dry and my eyes feel like they're going to spill over. "You did it. You raped Callie."

"I was *drunk*," he groans. "I was fucking *drunk* and she was barely conscious, she can't remember hardly any of it! *I* didn't even remember it at first!"

"Oh, please. You weren't *that* drunk. You were sober enough to drive yourself home. She remembers enough. She remembers it happened."

"So I should throw away my whole life, my whole future, for one mistake? Vic…" He closes the distance between us, his hands clasping the back of my neck to force me to look right at him, and I've never seen Brett look so crazed and frightened, so unlike himself. "I'm eighteen. She's a minor. If I were prosecuted…that's it. I'm gone. I'd be labeled as a sex offender for life even if I got a short sentence. No future for me. No Ivy League college. I'm *going places* in my life, yeah?"

I try to blink back the tears and only succeed in catching a few in my lashes. "What'd you do with the pictures?"

"What?"

"Patrick said he took pictures." And it was obvious he didn't have all of them.

Brett's mouth twitches and he says, "They're gone." But he ruins it by casting a quick glance at his laptop. He does have them. And deleting them now isn't going to keep the cops from recovering them.

"You were going to let someone else take the fall for it. You were going to let *me* take the fall."

He shakes his head quickly, like I can't possibly understand. "That was never my intention. I didn't care if it was someone else, but you—no. That's why I asked Dad to take care of your case. You, Aaron, Patrick…you're still seventeen. You might be tried as minors and your record would be sealed when you hit eighteen. Dad could've gotten you off with a light sentence."

His words make me cold all over. "So it was okay if *my* life got ruined because of jail."

The laugh Brett lets out is sharp and acidic as he pushes me back and steps away. "*What life?* Jesus Christ, Vic! You're barely graduating. If you go to college, it'll be some crappy community place. I didn't want you to get involved in this, and I had no idea Callie would pinpoint you. That's why I had Patrick snatch Aaron's phone and slip that picture on there. He's an asshole. You and I both would've been fine. Dad even said so."

I close my eyes for a moment. "Your dad knew."

Brett's fingers tighten. I can feel them against my vertebrae, begging me to look at him. "I didn't know who else to tell," he whispers. "I thought I was just…going nuts. After I found out you had gone through Aaron's phone, I had to tell him. I didn't know what to do."

And Mr. Mason wanted to protect him.

I don't know who I'm looking at, but it isn't my best friend since grade school. It isn't the Brett who stood up for me, who taught me to ride a bike, who helped me pass all of my high school finals. Because the Brett I knew would never hurt someone like this and then not take responsibility for it.

Or maybe he would have done this, and I've really never known him at all.

He presses his forehead to mine and I think he's close to tears, too. This is a look I've never wanted to see on him. Such unbridled fear and uncertainty.

"Vic. I need you to do this for me. I swear to God, it was a *mistake*. I've worked so hard to get where I am and I fucked up, I know I did…but tell them I was with you. Tell them Patrick is lying. The two of us against him, we can do it. You're my best friend. You're all I've got. Please, Vic. *Please*."

I am small.

Helpless.

"I've worked *so hard* not to be ordinary," Brett says.

Heartbreak: crushing and overwhelming grief, anguish, distress.

Everything I've lived up until this point, most of my existence, my social life, has revolved around my best friend. Trying to make him proud, trying to make him happy. Playing his secretary and puppying around while he made friends and I lurked on the sidelines.

Some small inkling of me feels like…he's almost right. He has this big, beautiful future full of endless possibilities. He could become president; he could cure Ebola or cancer. He could invent something. Go into space… There has never been anything I thought Brett couldn't do.

Me? I'm a useless waste of space who can barely manage a coherent sentence. He's right: I'll be lucky if I get into college. It'll be a miracle if I *graduate* from college. If I end up doing anything more with my life than flipping burgers.

And yet…

For any mistake I've ever made, I never would have set Brett up as my whipping boy. I never would have sacrificed him to save myself. I never would have let anyone take the fall for my mistakes. If spending time with Autumn has taught me anything about myself, it's that I don't have to be brilliant or extraordinary to be special. I'm worth something more than being a scapegoat.

An image flashes across the forefront of my brain, of Brett and Callie the day she returned to school. Callie's fear, about how she might walk right by her rapist and never even know it. In the end, her rapist walked her to class and tried to comfort her.

I don't know what the right answer is for me…

But I know what the right answer is for Callie. I have to protect her after I failed to do so the night Brett assaulted her.

I take a step away, pulling Brett's hands from my neck, my shoulder. "I love you, man, and you're my best friend. But if you're really sorry…you'll plead guilty and take your punishment."

Brett's face crumples. He stares at me like I'm a stranger to him.

That feeling is mutual.

My chest hurts. It's hard to breathe. I'm on the precipice of falling to pieces and I just want to get outside and get some fresh air.

He doesn't try to stop me.

I bolt down the stairs two at a time and dash outside. Even when my feet hit the sidewalk, I don't stop. I need to run, to get away from Brett's house and the memories there, away from the looming monster I'm going to be partially responsible for bringing down on him and Patrick.

Eventually, I stop running because I can't breathe and

my legs are wobbling. I keep walking. I walk all the way to work and every inch of me hurts, and Amjad looks up at me when I step inside like he's seen a ghost.

"Victor, what happened? What's wrong?"

I don't begin to know what to say. He flips the door sign to BE BACK LATER and ushers me into the back, pulls up a folding chair for me to sit, and I hunch over, breathing in, breathing out, trying to gather the pieces of myself back up. I'm vaguely aware of Amjad taking a bottle of beer from the freezers and placing it against the back of my neck. Surprisingly, the shock of cold helps me focus.

I have no idea how long we sit there like that. Once my breathing has evened out, Amjad takes a seat across from me. I roll the bottle of beer along the nape of my neck, then press it to my forehead. Pretty sure he can't sell this now.

"What happened?" he asks gently.

I don't want to talk. I don't want to do anything, is what I mean to say.

What I actually say is the truth.

I say everything. The story comes spitting out in fragments and stuttered pieces that I have no idea if they are making sense. I tell him about the party, about how guilty I've felt, about Autumn and Brett, about my dad, about how my best friend is going to jail and I know I've made the right decision but I don't know how to feel at peace with it. I just need to say it or my chest is going to burst.

Amjad listens to everything with patience. He leans forward, elbows on his knees, and his voice is so soft, the way I would picture a father's voice to sound. "You are making a right choice, Victor. Focus on the light you'll be shedding over that poor girl."

Is that what it will do, I wonder? If I testify against Brett, if he and Patrick go to jail, will Callie feel better? I have to think this is what she would want, because what happened to her was not okay.

Amjad has to get back to work, but he tells me to hang out in back as long as I need to. Which I do. I go behind the freezers and let the cold air wash over me, soothing the heat that's sunken into my bones from the run-slash-walk here. Only then do I text Autumn to let her know where I am, that I'm all right, that I can walk home because I don't want her to worry about me. She texts back within thirty seconds to say she's on her way.

I let Amjad know I'm okay and heading home, and go outside to wait. A phone call to Sherrigan and Carter is due, even if they haven't returned my last one. Might as well tell them what they missed, though I sum it up for them on the limited voicemail time I'm given. Patrick and Brett are the culprits—but they'll probably know that by the time they listen to this—and I can give a statement if needed. I know Autumn will, too.

She pulls up to the front of the store just as I'm finishing my message. I get into the car and her arms immediately find their way around me, holding tight, practically putting her in my lap, and I don't think I realized how much I needed that until now. I nestle my face into the warm curve of her neck and breathe in deep.

When I finally pull away, it's to give her a smile that I

hope is as reassuring as I mean for it to be. "I'm okay."

Autumn's eyes are a little glassy. She blinks a few times and smiles back, managing to get her almost-tears under control. "I'm really proud of you. I know it wasn't easy to do."

No. It wasn't. Truthfully, I wonder if I would have the ability to do it again. If I could have walked into that house if I'd been 100 percent certain of what I was going to find. I like to think I would, but who knows?

"Can we go home?" I ask. The weight of the day is pressing down on me, and for once, I'm desperate to feel the comfort of my own house around me. I'd even like to see Mom, just for a sense of normality.

Autumn says, "Of course we can," and shifts back properly into her seat.

Mom isn't home when we get there. I get changed into pajamas because I fully intend on sitting around doing *nothing* the rest of the night, and Autumn sits with me on the couch while I lay my head in her lap, and she pets my hair as I drift in and out of sleep and dreams.

Autumn is gone before Mom gets home. She said she needed to go to Callie's and find out if she heard anything from the police yet, and if not, to fill her in. I have a feeling Callie's family would be the first to know. Autumn asks if I want to go with her, but I'm not sure it's a good idea. Callie knows me, sure, but we aren't close and I don't know how her parents would feel having me there.

Instead I continue watching TV until Mom gets home. She puts her things away and I hear her in the kitchen for a while—probably putting something in to bake—but then she emerges and takes a seat on the couch beside me. At first I wait for her to say something, but I think she's just… watching television with me. Or trying to. Not sure she's getting the humor of *South Park*.

I hit the mute button and take a deep breath, which spurs her into looking at me curiously. "Am I bothering you?"

"No," I say quickly. I don't know how to get out the rest without simply blurting it. "Brett raped Callie Wheeler."

Even without directly staring at her, I can see from the corner of my gaze how Mom's mouth opens and her eyes widen in shock. "What?"

I refuse to let it sting that she sounds so surprised that *Brett* would do such a thing while she was willing to immediately believe that I had. I'm trying to let that go. "He raped her while this guy named Patrick took pictures. I th-think the cops have already taken Patrick in." By now, maybe they've gone to Brett's, too. I'm not sure how to find out.

Mom presses a hand to her chest, slowly turning her head back to the TV. She has no idea what to say. Not that I blame her. I don't know what to say, either. What can be said?

Eventually she offers, softly, "I'm so sorry, Victor."

I mean to say *it's okay*, but the words get stuck in my throat, because it isn't feeling very okay right now.

Chapter Twenty-Six

The next morning, Mom keeps me home from school. I might stress out about the missed classes this close to finals, but I got a phone call late last night from Detective Carter, asking if I could come in sometime this morning, and I wasn't exactly going to say no.

Mom drives us to the station. It's the first time I've been here, seeing as they took my initial statement at the clinic, and I almost feel more nervous now than I did then. If that's even possible. I haven't gotten a text back from Autumn yet about what happened at Callie's, and I didn't want to call and bug her in case she had other things going on. For that matter, it took a lot for me not to text Brett to find out what's happening on his end. I don't know that he'd even answer.

I wonder if I'll ever see my best friend again outside of a courtroom or prison.

Sherrigan comes into the lobby and beckons me into the back, instructing Mom to wait for us. I leave my phone with Mom in case Autumn texts or calls. Sherrigan sits me down in a small, quiet room with a tape recorder and a notepad, and asks me questions with the same unimpressed tone of voice as he did last time. How did I come to find out about Patrick? What happened during our conversation? What happened when I spoke to Brett? He focuses a lot on Brett, actually. Which makes sense, I guess. I have to struggle to keep my sentences coherent and from reducing myself to a stuttering mess.

I don't leave anything out. Everything from Autumn and me getting hold of Aaron's phone, to going to Patrick's before calling the police because we didn't want to report false information. Sherrigan listens to everything I say with patience, and I'm exhausted by the time he reaches out to turn off the recorder.

"I think that'll be all for now. If we need anything else, we'll give you a call."

The heels of my hands press into my eyes. At least this time, he was kind enough to give me a glass of water as a reward for sitting here for two hours. "H-have Patrick and Brett been arrested?"

He rises to his feet and gathers his papers, glancing at me. "I'm not really in a position to tell you that, seeing as Patrick is a minor. Though whether the court will try him as one, who knows."

That doesn't answer my question about Brett, but I leave it alone. I know contacting him won't reflect well on me, but I can find out other ways, I'm sure.

Sherrigan leads me out of the room and back to the lobby. The moment I turn the corner, I see Callie and her parents seated across from where Mom is. I wonder if they even know who the other is.

Callie lifts her head and spots me. Her eyes go wide and she leaps from her chair, startling everyone with the speed in which she rushes to throw her arms around me. My chest constricts painfully. I remember the first day at Autumn's apartment, the way Callie still seemed leery of me, and now this. How far we've come.

"I'm so sorry, Vic. I'm so, so sorry," she whimpers, voice thick with tears.

"W-what do you mean?" I put my hands on her shoulders to nudge her back a little so I can look at her face. "Why w-would you be apologizing to me?"

Her big eyes are watery, and by the fact that she's wearing eyeliner and mascara, I'm guessing she wasn't expecting to be crying today. Girls seem to think ahead about these things. I can barely remember where I put my shoes when I try to leave the house.

"For everything," she whimpers. "For accusing you, for Brett. I just found out when we got here…"

I open my mouth, waiting for her to calm herself down before trying to ask questions. "I th-thought Autumn went to tell you that it was him and Patrick yesterday."

Callie's parents step up behind her, and I can feel

Sherrigan lingering behind me, Mom still by her chair but standing, all of them puzzled as to what's going on. Callie draws her bottom lip into her mouth briefly, frowning. "Yeah, she did…and the police called me as soon as Patrick was arrested, but…"

Her mother murmurs to her, "Honey, he may not have heard."

I feel like someone has dropped a pound of lead into my stomach. "Heard what?"

Callie looks at her parents and back at me. "Oh… Oh, God. Brett's in the hospital."

Chapter Twenty-Seven

"I see. Yes, thank you very much."

Mom hangs up and lowers her phone, taking a deep breath. My eyes haven't left her face the entire phone call, but judging by her tone, I'm guessing it's not good. She leans back in the car seat and looks over at me.

"No, we can't see him."

"B-but did they say if h-he's going to be okay?" I ask, voice wavering.

"They won't tell me much. We aren't family."

We used to be, I think. Brett always felt like family. His parents felt like my parents. I look out the window and keep my silence, letting Mom drive us home without further questions.

Suicide: the action of killing oneself intentionally.

Attempted, in Brett's case.

Callie didn't know much. Or maybe I didn't hear the words coming out of her mouth because all I could do was stare at her impossibly wide, teary eyes while she explained to me what she'd been told, but her voice seemed to go in and out of range.

After I left Brett's house, he went down to his father's office, took the lockbox out of his desk, removed the gun, and shot himself. He didn't even bother trying to delete the photographs of Callie's rape from his computer. He must have known there was no point.

The vision of his face is so vivid when I close my eyes. His terrified look of horror at the idea of his entire life, of everything he's worked for, of *perfection*, going down the drain.

It's past noon when we pull into the driveway. Stepping inside, Mom asks, "Are you hungry? Do you want lunch?"

"No, thanks," I mumble, because I'm pretty sure anything I put in my stomach right now is going to come right back up.

Mom closes the door behind us. "Victor."

Deep breath. Sigh. I turn around. "Yeah."

She holds my phone out. Oh, I'd almost forgotten she had it. "You had a phone call."

I take it mechanically. "Autumn?"

"No." She studies my face. "From an elderly gentleman named Dave. He said he located your father."

Every one of my veins floods with ice. Just when I thought

the day couldn't get worse… "What?"

"He said you left your number with him when you came to his house. He should be in your call log."

The phone suddenly feels hot in my hands and I kind of want to throw it. I'm not sure what to say. "Mom, I wasn't… I m-mean, I didn't— "

She cuts me off with a raised hand. "Don't. You're old enough now. I can't stop you from reaching out to him if you want to."

I drag in a breath, feeling like I can't quite get enough air. "I d-don't know what I want. Everything's been such a mess lately." And if I'm honest— "I don't want to hurt you."

Mom steps closer until we're toe to toe. I think maybe she wants to hug me, but she hasn't done that in so long she's probably forgotten how. Her smile is thin and obviously forced, but yet again I'm stumped by the fact that she's even trying at all. "Everything is going to be all right."

It isn't really comforting. Not on a huge scale, anyway. But I'm able to give her a soft smile in return before retreating to my bedroom. All I want is to be alone. I don't even plan on calling Autumn for a bit. I just need the silence.

My room feels eerily empty for some reason, like the lack of Brett's presence is somehow palpable. I sit in the center of the floor, dragging a shoe box out from beneath the bed. Inside it are cards and photos. If I were to put them into piles of Mom, Brett, miscellaneous, Brett's pile would easily be the largest. He wasn't really the card-giving sort, but his mom always made sure I had one tucked into my birthday gifts each year. Most of the pictures are of the two of us.

I take the stack and begin placing them out. Grade school, middle school, high school. Interestingly enough, I don't think I'd ever noticed that the number of photos we took together decreased the older we got. There is only a small handful of them from after eighth grade.

Is it possible that, somewhere along the line, Brett and I really did grow apart as friends? Was there a disconnect there I didn't see?

Now I may never know.

Reminiscing isn't making me feel better. If anything, I'm starting to feel angry. I take every picture, every card that reminds me of Brett, Mr. Mason, or Mrs. Mason, and shove it into the trash can next to my bed.

I want them gone. I want everything gone.

Two hours later, I finally dare to look at my phone. I have four missed texts from Autumn, asking if I'm okay, telling me to call her. I hesitate and decide that, first, I'm going to call back the old man from Dad's place.

The number is the last one on my call log. It rings three times before a low voice answers, "Hello?"

"Hi, is this Dave? Th-this is Vic Howard, um." Pause. How awkward. "I c-came by the other day looking for my dad?"

"Yeah, yeah. How you doing? I felt real bad you came

all that way and I didn't have any information for you, so I did some digging. I might've gotten a forwarding address, if you want it."

Do I? Seems stupid to not take it in the event I want it eventually. Then again, it could be setting myself up for disappointment like last time. "Y-yes, please. That'd be great."

Dave slowly reads out the address to me, spelling the street name with care and making sure I've gotten each letter correctly. *N* as in Nancy. *C* as in cat. Alternatively, he could've just said "North Carolina Street" and I would've gotten the idea, but I don't interrupt him.

I thank Dave profusely before hanging up, stare at the address for a while, and tuck it into my pocket. Maybe I will go out for a walk.

Mom doesn't protest when I let her know I'm leaving. I shoot Autumn a text—***home. Ok. Going for a walk to park***—and she must be waiting for me, because she answers back almost immediately, ***Company y/n?*** I give this some thought before replying *yes*.

She doesn't have to ask which park. It's the same one we went to before, and I sit on the benches, facing the jungle gym, recalling the pic on my phone of Autumn with her beautiful face and smile leaning over the railing. I close my eyes and breathe in deeply. Ever since stepping foot inside Brett's house, I feel like someone is squeezing the air right out of me.

The sound of Autumn's car rumbling into the parking lot reaches my ears after a while, but I don't open my eyes just yet. Her door opens, closes, and the steady rhythm of her footsteps approaches…and then fades. I finally look up in time to see her crawling to the top of the jungle gym.

She leans over the railing as I approach, her hands braced on the metal bar and her gaze fixed at some point beyond me.

I say, "Hey."

Autumn takes a deep breath. "Callie told me what happened."

"Figured she w-would." Better her than me, because I'm not sure I could have gotten the words out.

After a moment, she tips her chin down to look at me, gaze soft and sad. "I'm sorry, Vic. I'm so, so sorry."

She sounds it. Because I know now that for as much as Autumn wanted to protect her best friend, she had wanted to protect me, too. I close my eyes and count to three to calm my nerves. "How's Callie?"

"She's…you know. Up and down. Relieved, angry, happy, crying, sad. Lots of mixed emotions."

"I c-can understand that. Why are you up there?"

Her boot taps once on the wooden platform. "Because I'm debating."

"D-debating what?"

"I'm not sure it's really appropriate to talk about it right now."

Nothing feels appropriate to talk about. Brett is half dead in a hospital room. Because of me. The fact that I'm even here and not at his side feels wrong on so many levels. I always knew the day would come when I'd be on my own, when Brett would outgrow me or go to college or move on and this is just…not how it was supposed to happen.

I don't voice any of this to Autumn. "Go ahead."

More hesitating. "At Patrick's place…you kissed me."

Heat rushes to my face. "Uh…y-yeah. I did. Sorry?" Am I supposed to apologize? Is that what this is about? She kissed me before that, after all.

"Don't be dumb." She turns away, the wind prodding at her long hair and brushing it across her soft face. "I just… wanted to know if you meant it, or if it was a heat-of-the-moment kind of thing. It's fine if it was or whatever…" She takes one look at my expression, blushes, and turns away. "Like I said, not the best time to talk about it."

Honestly, maybe it is the best time. Because it's the first time I've felt even a sliver of hope or warmth since seeing that text from Patrick, since ruining my best friend's life. "Guess we never really finished the conversation about what it meant. Did you want me to mean it?"

Autumn scoffs, looking almost offended by my question. She disappears into the enclosed tube slide, which opens right at my feet, so I turn and when she reaches the bottom, I put my hands on her knees to slow her descent so the slide doesn't drop her ass-first onto the sand.

Autumn doesn't miss a beat with this. Her fingers grab the front of my shirt and drag me in until my mouth is against hers and I have to hold on to the edge of the slide to keep from falling forward completely onto her.

It isn't some big, romantic, movie-like kiss. It's clumsy and spontaneous and wind-chapped, but I wouldn't think it anything but perfect with the way her lips part against mine, coaxing me along and warming me from head to toe. When she draws away, she stares at me like I'm stupid as she says, "What do you think, genius?"

I wet my lips. "Not entirely sure."

"Yeah? Then let's try that again."

She pulls me closer again until I have to kneel on the slide and brace my hands on the overhang of the tube. This time, it's a little more real. This time, I'm at least not caught entirely off guard, so I can lean in to kiss her back, to savor the way she doesn't just kiss with her mouth, but her whole body, with her hands on my chest and in my hair, like she wants to wrap herself around me and can't get close enough. And I need this, want this, something that can push away the pain and the guilt to make room for something that doesn't hurt so damned much.

When we break apart, her hands are cupping my face and I think I might pass out from not remembering to breathe, or because she stole my breath away. If I wanted to be so cliché. Her thumb strokes my cheek and there's so much affection in such a tiny gesture that it makes my insides flutter. "How was that? A little better?"

I smile crookedly, still with my head lost in the clouds somewhere between disbelief and awe. "Yeah. Think so."

Chapter Twenty-Eight

It's the first week Callie has been at school every day and hasn't gone home early. I'm proud of her. And while I still sometimes notice something a little off about her demeanor, and I know the whispers still going around school are reaching her ears, she holds her chin higher and refuses to let it get to her. Autumn smiles and says it's because she isn't afraid of running into some invisible monster anymore.

I'm glad for that, although the more pessimistic part of me thinks there are still others out there. Other monsters. Men and women who would take advantage of Callie or anyone else just like Brett and Patrick did.

This is not a thought I voice to Autumn or Callie. We have a couple weeks of school left for the seniors, my grades have been slipping throughout all this, and I have work to do in order to catch them up. Any of the whispers I happen to hear about Brett will need to be tucked away for later processing, because I can't afford to deal with it now.

Rumors are rampant about his botched suicide attempt. Someone said he tried to hang himself and the rope snapped but left him brain damaged. Someone else said he tried to OD. I don't correct them, mainly because I don't know the whole story, either. Aaron asks me about it in the hall on Tuesday, and others ask me throughout the week. Different stories altogether are cropping up in the local papers.

Craig Roberts even got a new story after sneaking into the hospital, making it past the nurses, and snapping a photo of Brett's room before they caught him and hauled his ass away. Not that you could make out much anyway, but it was the thought of it that left cold butterflies in my stomach.

Sometimes I wonder if I could slip into the hospital to visit, then I think about how his parents are probably by his side, how I'm not family so they'd never let me in, how Mr. Mason probably told the staff to keep me, specifically, out. So much for the family I thought I had.

Autumn helps me study after school and stays for dinner a few times. She promises once school is over and my head is on a bit straighter, I'll be going to her house to meet her parents, which is one thing I'm more than happy to put off for now. One nerve-racking thing at a time.

Because when Friday rolls around, Autumn, Callie, and I are piling into Callie's car and driving two hours south, hoping none of our parents call with an emergency that requires us home quickly.

There's a distinct sense of déjà vu in doing this. Except Callie is the one in the driver's seat and she keeps glancing in the rearview mirror at me with a bright smile that says everything is going to be great. Autumn knows better, but she slips her hand back so I can hold on to it, regardless.

The address Dave gave me is an apartment. The complex is old but not bad, and my dad's unit is number 321 near the front, so it isn't hard to find. We park in the visitor's section and get out, lingering anxiously in front of the car.

"Do you want us to go with you?" Callie asks.

Autumn squeezes my hand as though to silently reassure me that they will, under any circumstances, stick right by me if I need them. I smile a little. "A-actually, I think I got this."

They watch me approach the apartment, where the outside light is on and the living room window is dimly aglow. Let's face it, this could turn out to be another dead end. Just because Dave got this address doesn't mean anything. It could be years old, for all I know. He could have moved again.

I glance over my shoulder at the girls, who both wave and give me a thumbs-up of encouragement, then turn back around to knock on the door.

From inside, the TV volume lowers. When the door opens, it's to reveal a man who looks like me but older, grayer, with a few days' worth of growth on his face, and I don't think I've ever been so conflicted in all my life.

Don Whitmore smiles at me, perfectly friendly, with a tilt of his head. "Can I help you?"

This man is it. This is my father. There's no denying it, from the slope of his nose to his messy hair and jawline. He is me, many years from now.

He's also the man who raped my mother.

My father, the rapist.

Do I hate him or love him? Inconclusive. But it's not because I'm feeling so many things at once this time.

It's because I don't feel anything.

I say, "I'm s-sorry. I have the wrong apartment."

When I turn away, Don Whitmore steps half outside his doorstep. "Hey, wait, kid?" And I look to him questioningly for him to ask with a puzzled look, "Do I know you from somewhere?"

Glancing back at Autumn and Callie by the car, thinking of Amjad, of Mom and Aunt Sue…maybe this was stupid. Maybe I needed to come here to see how stupid it was. Because this man is my blood, but I couldn't care less if I never laid eyes on his face again. A smile comes surprisingly easily. "No. You don't know me."

This was all I think I needed. A method of severing any remaining strings I had holding on to the idea that my father was out there somewhere, this miraculous person who died a hero, or who would enter my life again and make everything better. I feel a little at a loss without those dreams to hang on to, but I think I'm getting closer to being okay without them.

Don doesn't try to stop me again as I return to the car—where Autumn is waiting with open arms—and then back home, where I go straight up to Mom and hug her tight.

Chapter Twenty-Nine

Ten weeks later

"Your parents will kill me if they find out I'm here," I say, pulling up a chair. "Sorry. You probably don't want to see me, but I wanted to see you. I m-mean, I didn't want to…but I needed to. I guess it wouldn't feel real until I did."

The monitors beep, slow and steady, unchanging day in and day out.

Brett has been in a coma for eighty-two days, and the limited brain function makes me wonder if he can even hear a word I'm saying.

Carter told me the bullet must have been guided by God's hand itself or something, because it passed through his mouth—where he'd put the barrel of the gun—and exited up and out the back of his skull while nipping just the right amount of the delicate workings of his brain to make him like…well, this, but not kill him.

"They told me it's rare, but sometimes people like you can wake up." I pause, rubbing my palms on my jeans. I thought I'd be a stuttering wreck doing this, yet my voice remains even and steady aside from the occasional stumble. *Stay calm. Think my words out before I say them.* I'm working on it.

"I don't think you want to wake up, though. You wouldn't be the s-same." If I'm entirely honest— "I'm kind of pissed off at you for that, too. Patrick's facing jail time. He doesn't have a f-fancy lawyer father like you do. So in the end, if you die, you still aren't having to pay for what you did. I won't forgive you for that."

These aren't things I had planned on saying, but they're finding their way off my tongue regardless, and that's okay. Carter said she could get me fifteen minutes before she'd have to drag me out, because I'm not supposed to be here. No one without a uniform is. Brett might be comatose, but he's still being tried for the rape of Callie Wheeler, and it is all happening while he's oblivious.

"I guess I can't forgive you f-for leaving me, either. But whatever. Y-you know, I came here to talk to you, because maybe some part of you cares and I don't want to think our friendship wasn't real. So…I wanted to tell you that I'm okay without you. Maybe I was always okay without you, I don't know. I just wanted you to hear that because in the end, I sort of think you were the one who wasn't okay without me."

I won't voice the guilt I feel over that. Over everything. The sense that I had the power to change things at some point in time, in the course of our lives as friends, to make all this turn out differently.

Amjad says I deserve better friends than Brett.

Mom hugs me because she doesn't know what to say, but hey, a hug is an improvement.

Autumn says I need a therapist…and she's probably right. Now that I've graduated (by the skin of my teeth, but still—!) I can do that. I can think about me. I'll be going to college in a few months, and I'll be something more than Brett ever thought I would be.

Carter pops her head in the room and clears her throat. That's my cue to leave. I spent most of my time sitting and staring at Brett's face, thinking that from this angle, he didn't look much different. Thinner, paler, but otherwise like the same guy I've known most of my life.

I blink back the sudden sting of tears. Nope. I told myself I was done crying over this. Over him.

Yet I can't help but murmur to him, "I'm sorry," and I rest a hand against his arm and wonder if Brett would forgive me.

If I would want his forgiveness even if he did.

As I turn to leave, the monitor blips, something irregular, nothing I've heard since I've been in here. I look at Brett, and the machines blip again. Once, twice. And then they're back to normal. A way of communicating? I could almost laugh bitterly. Knowing Brett, it could be anything from an "I forgive you" to a "go fuck yourself."

I've made progress, I think as I head out the door, because I don't think I'd care which it was anymore.

Acknowledgments

Another book finished!

Modern Monsters was one of those stories that jumped out at me years ago, probably around the time I finished *Suicide Watch*. There are amazing stories out there already that tackle the subject of rape and the aftermath on the victim, but I haven't come across any that touch on the way it affects the accused, whether or not he's guilty. I wanted Vic's story to show what he endures, as well as touching on Callie's strength in surviving what happened to her.

It was entirely coincidence that this book ended up hitting closer to home than I would like, and parts of it were difficult to write. Rape is not an easy subject to talk or write about, and others have done it far better than I. My hope for this book is to touch on the impact these things have not on just the victim, but on everyone around him or her, how the ripple effect can do such tremendous damage. I hope I've managed to come close to keeping true to the roller coaster of emotions.

This marks the second book I've gotten to do with my amazing editor—Stacy Cantor Abrams—as well as my first with Tara Quigley. Words cannot express how incredible these two are to work with, how insightful, intelligent, and hilarious they are! If I never work with another editor in my life, I'd be content so long as I get to keep them. They are to thank for making sense of the drivel I put on the page.

Thank you to everyone at Entangled for helping me realize another dream. I couldn't ask for a better set of people to work with. I view so many of them as friends after all these years, and I don't know what I would do without them.

And as always…thank *you*, my readers. I put these emotions in words as best as I'm able all for you, to get a laugh, a smile, a tear. I hope I succeeded.

Modern Monsters Reading Group Guide

1. *Modern Monsters* is a crime drama, an examination of interpersonal relationships, and a character study. Taking these three themes and stories into consideration, when do you think the climax of the book occurred?

2. Victor quoted a television show that said, "First you're a child prodigy, then you're a teenage genius...but by the time you're twenty, you're ordinary." Do you agree with this statement? What have been your experiences with "gifted and talented" students? Is there too much pressure on teens to get the best grades, participate in the right extracurricular activities, be accepted to the college of their choice?

3. When did you suspect the reason Victor's mother became distant toward him? Should she have kept this secret from him for as long as she did?

4. Victor realized his mother's behavior and attitude toward him changed during middle school. However, many young teens experience an alienation or disconnect with their parents during adolescence. Is this a normal or healthy phenomenon?

5. Throughout most of the novel, Victor was portrayed as completely dependent on Brett. What did Brett gain from the relationship? What factors, besides the fact that he was the rapist, helped Victor overcome his reliance on their friendship?

6. Was Victor a strong or a weak person? How did his feelings of guilt affect his behavior?

7. What did Autumn see in Victor? Discuss your feelings about their relationship.

8. Patrick said, "No girl comes to a party wearing lace underwear not expecting to get laid." Is this a common belief among teenage boys? Does the way a girl dresses indicate something about her?

9. At what point in the novel did you suspect Brett was the rapist? Did the author do a good job creating suspense?

10. Discuss Brett's relationship with his father. Were you surprised that Mr. Mason would risk his career to protect his son?

11. What role did Amjad play in Victor's life?

12. Should Victor have sought out his father? Were you satisfied with the way Victor handled their meeting?

13. Were you surprised that Brett tried to commit suicide? What do you think will happen to Brett?

Prepared by Nancy Cantor, Media Specialist,
University School of Nova Southeastern University

Resources for Victims of Abuse

After Silence
www.aftersilence.org

RAINN
www.rainn.org

Victim Rights Law Center
www.victimrights.org

1in6
1in6.org

Rape Victim Advocates
www.rapevictimadvocates.org

The Voices and Faces Project
www.voicesandfaces.org

Check out more of Entangled Teen's hottest reads...

Naked

by Stacey Trombley

When I was thirteen, I ran away to New York City and found a nightmare that lasted three years and left me broken. Only now I'm back home and have a chance to start over. And the first real hope I see is in the wide, brightly lit smile of Jackson, the boy next door. So I lie to him, to protect us both. The only problem is that someone in my school knows about New York. And it's just a matter of time before the real Anna is exposed...

Lola Carlyle's 12-Step Romance

by Danielle Younge-Ullman

While she knows a summer in rehab is a terrible idea (especially when her biggest addiction is decaf cappuccino),Lola Carlyle finds herself tempted by the promise of saving her lifelong crush and having him fall in love with her. Unfortunately, Sunrise Rehabilitation Center isn't quite what she expected. Her best friend has gone AWOL, she's actually expected to get treatment, and boys are completely off-limits...except for Lola's infuriating (and irritatingly hot) mentor, Adam. Like it or not, Lola will be rehabilitated, and maybe fall in love...if she can open her heart long enough to let it happen.

Paper or Plastic

by Vivi Barnes

Busted. Lexie Dubois just got caught shoplifting a cheap tube of lipstick at the SmartMart. And her punishment is spending her summer working at the weird cheap-o store, where the only thing stranger than customers are the staff. Coupon cutters, jerk customers, and learning exactly what a "Code B" really is (ew). And for added awkwardness, her new supervisor is the very cute—and least popular guy in school—Noah Grayson. And this summer, she'll learn there's a whole lot more to SmartMart than she ever imagined...

How (Not) to Fall in Love

by Lisa Brown Roberts

Seventeen-year-old Darcy Covington never worried about money...until her car is repossessed. With a failing business, her Dad not only skipped town, but bailed on his family. Fortunately, Darcy's uncle owns a pawn shop, where Darcy can hide out from the world. There's also Lucas, the supremely hot fix-it guy—even if he isn't all that interested in her. But it's here amongst the colorful characters of her uncle's world that Darcy begins to see something more in herself...if she has the courage to follow it.

Love and Other Unknown Variables

by Shannon Lee Alexander

Charlie Hanson has a clear vision of his future. A senior at Brighton School of Mathematics and Science, he knows he'll graduate, go to MIT, and inevitably discover the solutions to the universe's greatest unanswerable problems. But for Charlotte Finch, the future has never seemed very kind. Charlie's future blurs the moment he meets Charlotte, but by the time he learns Charlotte is ill, her gravitational pull on him is too great to overcome. Soon he must choose between the familiar formulas he's always relied on or the girl he's falling for.

Whatever Life Throws at You

by Julie Cross

When seventeen-year-old track star Annie Lucas's dad starts mentoring nineteen-year-old baseball rookie phenom, Jason Brody, Annie's convinced she knows his type—arrogant, bossy, and most likely not into high school girls. But as Brody and her father grow closer, Annie starts to see through his façade to the lonely boy in over his head. When opening day comes around and her dad—and Brody's—job is on the line, she's reminded why he's off-limits. But Brody needs her, and staying away isn't an option.